Copyright © 2024 by August Lindsay

All rights reserved.

Thank you for buying an authorized edition of this book. No part of this publication may be reproduced, distributed, or transmitted in any form or by any means, including photocopying, recording, or other electronic or mechanical methods, without the prior written permission of the publisher, except in the case of brief quotations embodied in critical reviews and certain other noncommercial uses permitted by copyright law.

Published by August Lindsay Publishing

First Edition 2024

This is a work of fiction. The names, characters, places, and events depicted are purely the product of the author's imagination or are used in a fictional manner. Any resemblance to real persons, living or deceased, actual businesses, companies, events, or locations is entirely coincidental.

Book cover design by Ana Arias

Library and Archives Canada Cataloguing in Publication

August Lindsay

Scotch & Shortbread/ August Lindsay.

For my adorable mom, who might be even more giddy about this book than I am. She's the only person who lets me prattle on incessantly about writing and publishing for hours and actively prods me for more!

And also for my dad, who was the most loving, heroic, and humble human I've ever known. Growing up, he would tell me I was such a romantic, his blue eyes sparkling with adoration, and he was right; I'm a romantic to my core.

Scotch & Shortbread

Scotch Series
August Lindsay

August Lindsay

Scotch & Shortbread

Scotch Series
August Lindsay

August Lindsay

1
Candy Canes and Ireland

Blue and red lights flashed in her rearview mirror and a siren whooped. "What? No!" Quinn groaned. "Crap, crap, crap." She exhaled in frustration. The entire drive she'd had it on cruise control, but running behind and dying to see her friends, she sped up a little. Fine, more than a little. "Arghh," she growled as she reluctantly pulled over to the shoulder on the quiet stretch of highway, pained knowing her friends were probably already at the inn enjoying a nice boozy eggnog.

Quinn blew out a breath as she sat in her baby blue Volkswagen bug that whirled with the scent of spiced holly berries car freshener, hoping and praying to the girls-Christmas-weekend-vacay-Gods that she would get a nice understanding cop. It was Christmas time after all. Surely cops didn't *want* to give out tickets over the holidays. She absently grabbed a candy cane from her stash of road trip snacks on the front seat, peeled it open, and began sucking with a nervous gusto.

There was no room in her well-planned budget for a speeding ticket. What had she been thinking taking it off cruise control? She was kicking herself now. As she contemplated how she was going to talk her way out of a ticket, she paused to appreciate the sweet fresh peppermint flavor of her candy cane. Savoring it, she told herself everything would be fine because as her grandmother would say, Quinn had the gift of the gab. She could talk her way to the North Pole if need be.

Her Grandmother would also say that honesty was the best policy. Quinn would simply explain the situation. She was not a speeder. It was just a momentary slip, and with the excitement of getting close to the mountains and seeing her friends, well she'd gotten ahead of herself. Next time, she'd be more attentive. Yes, it would be fine. A smile touched her lips as she looked out the windshield to the massive rocky snow-capped mountains. This weekend was going to be epic. Nothing could put a damper on her spirit. Or so she thought.

Quinn caught movement in her sideview mirror and almost regretted looking as she saw the officer get out of his truck. Yikes! Her pulse kicked up a few notches, and she crunched down on the candy cane. *Holy hell*. This cop was the kind you steered clear of. Tall, broad, and positively lethal-looking in his black uniform. *Shit*. Yeah, probably not the nice understanding type.

Was it always like this? Quinn felt a bit queasy as her heart rate ticked faster than a court reporter typing. Her confidence from a minute earlier evaporated. This was the first time she'd been pulled over, and she could say, with one hundred percent certainty, that the holy shit surprise of receiving a photo radar ticket in the mail was a far nicer option than the current anxiety-inducing experience of having to come face to face with a cop. Especially a cop who appeared as intimidating as the dude stalking towards her car right now.

Quinn felt like a kid who'd just been caught smoking in the high school washroom. She felt absurdly anxious and guilty. *Gawd Quinn, it's not like you have a dead body in the trunk*, she thought sardonically. No matter how she tried to rationalize the situation, she just felt more skittish. Her overactive imagination was in full swing. It was a speeding ticket, not a jail sentence, she tried to assure her overzealous brain. Peering in her view mirror, she saw him closing in on her car, and her heart leapt. God, he was big, and his deadly serious expression from under the shadow of his police cap sent a cold shiver down her spine.

The officer knocked on her window, jarring Quinn from her spiralling thoughts. The first thing that caught her eye was a black gun holstered in the belt around his waist.

"Jeezus." She drew in a shaky breath. Perhaps she'd lived a sheltered life, but she had never seen a real gun up close. Her overactive nervous brain immediately considered the possibility that he could shoot her if he wanted to. Cops could do things like that. *You're being ridiculous*, she scolded herself. Then another horrifying thought came to her. What if he had shot people with that very gun? He knocked again, stirring her out of her odious train of thought. Quinn anxiously pressed buttons and finally hit the right one and her window slid down.

"License and registration." His voice was deep and brusque and he didn't spare her a glance.

"Wow, not even a hello," she muttered under her breath. Irritation momentarily superseded her nervousness at his curt manner. Despite her current state of anxiety and deranged thoughts, deep down Quinn believed that police officers were inherently good people. After all, they swear an oath to serve and protect or something like that. So was civility too much to ask?

"I clocked ye at nineteen clicks over the speed limit." His deep voice dripped with disapproval. Not giving her a moment to think never mind respond, he snapped again, "I asked for yer license and registration. Tell me ye dinnae huv a problem with that."

Quinn was stunned into silence, causing him to lean down and peer at her through the open window. Her breath hitched at the piercing stormy, blue eyes that glowered at her. A fresh wave of nerves rippled over her skin.

Despite his deadly serious gaze pinned on her and even though he was completely unnerving her, the most ridiculous thought came to mind. Dark stubble shadowed his strong jaw and his lips were set in a serious line. And for some reason, Quinn wondered what it would be like to kiss those scowling lips.

"Looks like we do huv a problem then?" His voice was irritated and gruff as he looked at her expectantly.

His icy glare almost made her shiver. Right, the man was terrifying, not kissable, she decided, scolding herself for even thinking such a thing.

Her heart fluttered nervously. "Officer, I didn't mean to..." but he abruptly cut her off.

"License and Registration," he repeated, enunciating every consonant not interested in anything she had to say.

That got her back up. Terrifying or not, she didn't appreciate him being a total dick. Maybe she had been going too fast, but it was only for a moment. He should at least allow her to explain. Didn't she have a right to state her side of things?

"Yeah, I heard you the first time," she snapped without thinking. Reaching into her oversized tan leather tote, she dug around for her wallet.

"I need ye to step oot of the vehicle."

What in the heck? Quinn wondered what was with this guy commanding her about like he was some kind of eighteenth century lord of the manor. And was that an Irish accent she detected? Maybe in Ireland, his abruptness was normal, like a cultural thing. Although she always thought Irish people tended to be chipper-like. Trust her to notice something like that at a time like this. Quinn's mind tended to wander away. She was a slave to her curiosity. Occasionally, her rabid inquisitiveness could be a problem—the present perhaps being one of those occasions—but she was who she was, take it or leave it.

"Are you from Ireland?" She eyed him quizzically. Any irritation she'd felt had all but flitted away at least for the time being. In typical Quinn fashion, she didn't even think before she spoke. "My great grandparents on my mom's side were from Cork, or wait, Derry, no Dingle?" She couldn't quite recall. "I've never been myself, but I love how in pictures all the villages look like the houses are trying to snuggle up closer to each other to keep warm. Just all cozied up you know?" When he didn't answer, she added, "They must be extra cozy at Christmas time I would imagine, although I don't think it gets as cold as it does here." She looked at him expectantly as if awaiting him to join the conversation.

Quinn wouldn't call herself an extrovert. Far from it really, she loved solitude, but she also thoroughly enjoyed meeting new people especially if they were from other parts of the world. She had never travelled outside of Canada, and aside from visiting her best friends who lived in B.C., she'd never been anywhere other than the Canadian Prairies.

People and their stories fascinated her, but people from other countries were like the cherry on top of her fascination cupcake. It was probably what made her love reading and writing so much. Nothing better than intriguing characters and their stories. She was feeling skeptical about her present company though. When she looked up she found his piercing blue eyes, the churning depths of a stormy ocean, glowering at her again.

"I believe I asked ye to step oot of the vehicle," his deep voice rumbled.

As gruff as he sounded, Quinn still found herself oddly charmed by his accent, but that was immaterial. Shooting him a look from under her brow, she clarified, "You didn't ask, more of an order, but it's fine, I have my license and registration right here," she said once again ignoring his request for her to get out of her car. "Here you go," she threw him a dimpled smile as she re-inserted the half-eaten candy cane into her mouth and handed him her papers.

From what Quinn could deduce, the cop had two expressions. One was an irritated scowl, and the other—which he was throwing at her now—was a mystified scowl. The mystified scowl intrigued her, especially when his eyes locked on her candy cane. Quinn found herself slowly moving the candy cane in her teeth and between her lips as if in slow motion, as she grew self-conscious under his study. Then his stormy eyes snatched back to hers. If she were a weak woman, she'd have cowered under his domineering glare. Instead, she snapped off a bit of candy cane in some kind of weird defiance, and when he abruptly turned away, she wondered if the man was the living embodiment of the Grinch.

She snuck a glance at him as he was looking down at the clipboard that now held her papers. Hmm. Even with that accent, he was still 100 percent intimidating, but he was also rather easy on the eyes. His jaw was nothing short of a masterpiece really, topped with a sexy five o'clock shadow accentuating all that raw manliness. She hadn't determined whether he tipped more towards sexy or towards danger, or maybe he was the balance of both.

A thin scar ran diagonally down the side of his squared chin. How had he come by it? Had he been in a brawl? She almost snorted thinking how that would have gone for the other guy. Hmm, or maybe it was one of those childhood scars from playing outside with his friends. She imagined him as a child running in the emerald hills of Ireland. It made him seem much more enchanting.

It was intriguing that the scar only seemed to add to his handsomeness. Her eyes slipped to his mouth again. It was rather sensual. Scowl and all. She was curious though what those lips would look like if he smiled. At this point, she wondered if he ever did smile. The man was awfully serious as he concentrated on the clipboard.

She continued her study of him, taking in his nose. It was long and narrow with slightly flared nostrils. It was a strong-looking nose, proud. Her gaze continued upward to his piercing stormy blue eyes... Oh shit, those eyes were glowering at her with an intensity that sent electricity pinging down her spine. She flushed, feeling embarrassed. If he hadn't caught her open perusal before, he certainly had noted it this time. *Nice Quinn*, she chided herself inwardly.

"Oot of the vehicle now." His brogue was thick, and this time there was no doubt in her mind that he meant it. She felt a pang of trepidation. Lilting Irish accent or not, he was making her nervous. Why did he want her to get out of her car? So she was speeding a bit, okay maybe more than a bit, but still, what was with this guy? Such a Grinch. A giant intimidating Grinch. Well, she wasn't one to be intimidated—nervous yes, intimidated no. Despite his size and the fact he was a cop and, sure, she had been speeding, it didn't give him the right to be a total ass about it.

Quinn crunched off a big piece of her candy cane, chucked the wrapped bit down on the passenger seat, and got out of her car, slamming the creaky heavy door behind her to demonstrate her displeasure.

2
Hot Jerk

THE GRUMPY GIANT GLANCED up at her from his clipboard, disapproval was written all over his too-handsome face. Those stormy blue eyes penetrated her with their intensity.

The shiver she felt dance down her spine had nothing to do with the cool mountain air. Quinn shifted uncomfortable with her body's sudden unexpected reaction to him. Now that she stood before him, his height and breadth were so distinctly masculine it made her feel petite and...feminine. Like he was some kind of alpha god, and she was the woman his intentions were set upon. Quinn slowly crunched the piece of candy cane in her mouth as she openly stared at him, but this time, his glowering blue eyes gave way to something akin to male satisfaction. Her breath hitched at the not-so-subtle change in his countenance, and a bit of candy cane nearly choked her.

He held her gaze for only a split second, but it was long enough to leave her certain that he knew all too well the heady effect he was having on her. When he turned away from her to talk into his two-way radio, she wondered if she'd imagined that look in his eyes. The moment passed so quickly. Was it just her overzealous imagination?

Quinn had taken her coat off in the car for the drive, and the crisp mountain air that now snaked its way through her thin sweater was more than enough to cool any fires. She crossed her arms over her chest trying to keep warm.

"It's freezing," she muttered, subtly trying to indicate that he should hurry up with whatever it was he was doing.

With his broad back turned to her, he paid her no attention. He was still talking back and forth on his radio. She didn't hear what he was saying. She didn't care really. What she did care about was why the heck he had her get out of her warm car if he was just going to yak away to someone else. She just wanted to get back in her toasty car, crank her Christmas tunes, and get on her way to see her friends and start their girl's weekend.

Was the sadistic man deliberately taking his sweet time as she stood there shivering? Frustrated, her impatience got the best of her.

"Excuse me, officer, I hate to interrupt, but could we speed things up here? I have plans, and this is putting a dent into them." She hadn't meant to come across as snarky, but even she heard the sarcasm in her voice.

The cop turned back to her and looked down at her with a dark arched brow. She wasn't sure what was more annoying, his intimidating manner or the fact he was decidedly hot. He currently towered over her. He had to be well over six feet and built like a bull, but she refused to be intimidated. Standing her ground, she gave him a challenging look back.

"Have ye been drinking?" he asked, leaning in closer to her, his sheer size made her step back. A hint of cologne wafted in the crisp mountain air tickling her senses. She suddenly had an urge to reach up and pull him to her so she could breathe him in. How could someone with his demeanour smell that amazing? Such a contradiction. God, what was with her? He just asked her if she'd been drinking, and all she could focus on was his cologne. Quinn stood a little taller, despite herself.

"Not yet, but thanks for asking," she quipped matter-of-factly with a smile that didn't reach her eyes. She thought she saw a slight twitch in his lips. If he was going to crack a smile, he reigned it in quickly. Pity.

"Where are ye headed, Ms. West?" He was looking back down at his clipboard and started to scribble something.

Ooh, so formal, she thought. But she was cold and just wanted to go already. "Calen."

"Visiting?" he asked not looking up.

"Yes," she said, her teeth beginning to chatter. "Well, sort of." The sun hung low in the sky and would likely set within the hour. Out of nowhere, big, fluffy snowflakes began to float around them, and Quinn was instantly distracted, as if there wasn't a giant cop glowering at her. "Look, it's snowing," she said breathlessly, as she lifted her palms to the air like those snowy puffs held some kind of Christmas magic.

Feeling his glare, Quinn looked back and caught the cop's gaze on her. He had that mystified scowl look again, but less scowly this time. Realizing she'd gotten distracted, she carried on with what she'd been saying, "I'm going to Calen to meet up with my girlfriends. We haven't seen each other in ages." She sighed and then grinned, adding, "It's going to be an epic girl's weekend, but I'm planning..."

"Come," he cut her off, not the least bit interested in what she was saying, and the irritated scowl made a reappearance.

So rude, she thought, but she reluctantly followed the brute as he led her to the back of her car. He pointed to her broken tail light, and she cringed. She planned to get that fixed, but it wasn't in the budget this month. Damn. She was kicking herself now. She supposed she could have pulled some money from this weekend's party with the girl's budget.

"Ye have a broken tail light," he said more calmly than she'd expected.

"Mm-hmm." She nodded in quiet agreement. She couldn't very well lie and pretend she knew nothing about it. She'd come out to it about two weeks ago after picking up some groceries. No one was in sight, and she stood there looking around the parking lot wondering what in the heck happened. Frustrated, she'd gotten in her vehicle and put it out of her mind.

Quinn could feel his cool gaze penetrating her as she stared blankly at the back of her vehicle at a rare loss for words.

"Ye knowingly drove on the highway with a broken tail light?" It was more of a scolding statement than a question, and she felt well and put into her place. She didn't say anything.

"When exactly do ye plan on getting it fixed Ms. West?"

She looked up at him. Why did he have to be such a jerk about everything? Clearing her throat, she tried to keep the snark from her voice as she said as calmly as she could, "I'll find a shop in Calen, Officer."

"Sergeant," he corrected her.

She barely held back an eye roll.

"Bob's shop. It's just on the corner of Main Street and 4th Ave."

"Lovely. Bob's. I'll go there tomorrow. Now, can you just give me my ticket or whatever and let me be on my way?" She didn't even try to hide her impatience this time. This time, it was the cold that made her shiver. She was freezing, and as she pulled her arms a little tighter across her chest, she couldn't stop her teeth from chattering in the crisp mountain air.

"Ye can get back into yer vehicle." Mean Hot Cop seemed to finally take pity on her.

"Thank God," she muttered as she brushed past him to hurry back into her car.

Cranking the heat when she got back in, trying to warm up, she realized she was getting hungry. Looking at her dwindling pile of road trip snacks, she picked up another candy cane, unwrapped it, and popped it in her mouth while she awaited her fate. A moment later, the cop walked up to her driver's side window.

"Scotland. Not Ireland." His deep voice sounded proud and strong. Quinn was taken off guard as he bent to look at her. Her breath caught with his face almost eye level with hers. His piercing stormy blue eyes looked downright sexy this closeup. She felt oddly flattered that he'd told her where he was from. Like they'd finally made some headway, and he gifted her by being a real person and not just a jerk cop.

A magnanimous feeling washed over Quinn, and she smiled brightly, "I haven't been to Scotland either, but I bet it's amazing. I saw *Braveheart* years ago. Such a great movie. I don't know if it was actually filmed in Scotland, but if it was, the scenery was just beautiful and the castles..." She sighed dreamily thinking about it.

And just as she was about to ask if he'd watched *Braveheart*, it all went sideways. Quinn had thought she'd cracked his façade, but no, the moment flitted away into oblivion like steam from a mug of hot chocolate. Completely ignoring that Quinn had spoken at all, never mind complimented the man's homeland, the cop pulled a ticket from his clipboard and unceremoniously handed it to her.

"Three hundred dollars!" Quinn spat shocked. Apparently, she was wrong, and he was a cold mean jerk cop after all. How could he gouge her like that? She hadn't been going that fast, and she'd promised to get her tail light fixed. Grinch was too nice to describe him.

"Next time, slow down, Ms. West, and make sure ye get that tail light taken care of."

"Oh yes, because I'll have plenty of cash left over after having the tail light fixed to pay for this ticket too." Her voice was shrill with frustration.

"Something to think about next time you want to blow past the speed limit," he snapped sternly. He gave her one last look of disapproval before he turned and strode away.

Quinn was incensed. Any heated tingles she'd felt were thoroughly doused. *Cocky ass*.

She growled frustrated and then hollered out her window to him needing to have the last word, "Oh, don't you worry, I'll be a star driver 'cause I definitely wouldn't want to chance running into you again, *Sergeant*!"

He stopped but didn't turn, and Quinn decided not to stick around to see what he'd say or do next. Signalling to pull out, she took one last glance at him in her rearview mirror and breathed a sigh of relief to see that he'd gotten into his truck. As she drove away, she took a deep breath, relishing the Christmassy scent in her car. She wasn't going to let some grumpy jerk cop ruin her excitement. Cranking her Christmas tunes, she set her focus on getting to Calen to see her girls.

3
Bad Fucking Day

Alex was in a black mood. For the better part of a year, he'd had the plan to go back home to Scotland for Christmas. When he'd booked the flight, his focus had been on seeing his family again, but since booking, he'd considered cancelling it more times than he could count. It was one thing for him to make that decision, but without his consent or knowledge, his plans had been changed for him and *that* pissed him off.

Out of nowhere and only a couple of days before he was supposed to get on a plane, he had been informed that his vacation days were going to be cut short. Instead of two weeks off, he'd have less than a week. Six days. It annoyed the shite out of him just thinking about it. He was given some bullshit story about a clerical error, but he knew better.

Rod had been busting his balls for weeks about Alex getting time off even though Rod had seniority. He had no doubt who'd be getting time off for Christmas now. It didn't matter that Alex had put in the request last year, and it had been approved. It should have been a done deal. As much as he enjoyed his job, the politics could be infuriating. At least it was not like the politics in Scotland. Canada was a walk in the park in comparison, but the whole situation frustrated the hell out of him anyway.

As he'd sat in his cruiser his mood ever darker, the VW flew past, and he'd wondered why in the hell people thought it was okay to blast over the speed limit like it didn't apply to them. He wasn't a traffic cop, but the thought of hand-delivering a ticket to some ignorant arse was an irresistible prospect.

The moment the lass stared up at him with big innocent eyes, he wished he'd left traffic policing to the next guy. It annoyed him that he had to silently remind himself that he was immune to the lasses. Every last one of them. She was work to him, and that was it.

Alex was well aware that he looked dangerous and menacing with zero effort. But when he did try, well, he could make grown men piss their pants in fucking fear. That was never pleasant, but in his line of work, having an edge wasn't a bad thing.

At six foot four and built like his Norse ancestors, Alex was intimidating to most. Never mind the fact he was in a dark mood this afternoon, but apparently, the lass he'd pulled over was completely oblivious to the danger he knew emanated from him.

When he gave her a direct order to give him her license and registration and she blatantly ignored him, he didn't know what to think. Alex stared at the lass mystified, wondering what in the hell was happening. Was this tiny innocent thing honestly going to give him grief? With his foul mood, he'd almost relished in it, daring her in his head, *Go on little lass, give me yer best*. But then she started blethering away like they were old friends having a chinwag over tea, rambling about bloody Ireland! And the entire time, he couldn't seem to tear his eyes from her too-full lips and her red tongue occasionally darting out as she sucked on a damn candy cane!

Annoyed at his wayward thoughts, his jaw clenched tightly, and the dreamy smile vanished from her lips, leaving Alex to question the strange remorseful feeling that snaked through him. No. He wasn't here to make her smile or to play nice.

It galled him that he'd given her a very direct order and she casually dismissed him more than once and even had the nerve to chide him for not "asking." This did not happen to Alex. Ever. Christ, he wanted to command her to stop sucking on that bloody candy cane too. He had no doubt the lass wouldnae listen to that order either.

Didn't she understand that he could cause her a boatload of trouble? Alcohol could perhaps explain her overconfidence, and he asked if she'd been drinking although he knew the answer. He asked expecting her to smarten up, but instead, it seemed to make her even more feisty. She might have bravado, but she didn't show the telltale signs of alcohol consumption. He could have leaned in close to her to check for the sour smell of liquor on her breath. It would have been perfectly acceptable for him to do that, but he didn't. Instead, it was like an urge he fought, knowing damn well she'd smell like a minty candy cane and lord knows what other tempting sweetness.

Christ, and then when the snow fell—that pleasure-filled look on her upturned face. The woman acted like she'd never seen snow before. Alex found her both odd and fascinating. He was about to give her a hefty fine, and there she was, with not a care in the world, as she delighted in the damn snowflakes.

Alex shook his head, blowing out a breath and shaking off the memory, as he looked down at the clipboard in his hand. Quinn West. He refused to feel bad about giving her that ticket. It was the set amount for her infractions. In his opinion, if you choose to break the law, you pay the price. He sighed. Maybe he'd been a bit tough on her though. He wouldn't feel bad about the ticket, but he shouldn't have let her stand there shivering. He felt like a bit of an arse for that. He could hear his mam's voice now, scolding him that she'd not raised her boys to be uncouth. It was a shame he'd not be seeing his family now this Christmas.

Scraping a hand across his stubbled chin, his thoughts turned back to the lass. She hadn't shied away from eyeing him in the way lasses do. Why he cared was beyond him. He was plenty used to the lass's wandering eyes. Even his coworkers razzed him about his "effect" on the ladies.

It wasn't something he gave much thought to. He had a job to do. He wasn't on the squad to pick up women. Hell, that was the last thing he wanted. Alex preferred a solitary life. He had no intention of settling down with a lass. Relationships only brought complications. He'd learned that the hard way. The last thing he wanted was for things to go awry in his world. He'd finally found some peace and contentment. Canadian lasses were as lovely as any other, but he'd decided to steer clear, especially while living in this country. Canada was his refuge, and he didn't want anything to take away from that, not even a lass. Especially not a lass.

Alex wasn't unfriendly per se, but he didn't make a lot of small talk while he was on the job. He found it often led to more trouble than it was worth. As a cop, a healthy distance was generally wise. That and Alex wasn't an idiot. He knew he was a decent-looking guy, and he didn't want to risk any starry-eyed lass getting the wrong idea because he was "friendly."

The running joke with Alex's workmates when they teased him about the lasses fawning over him was that he was immune to women. Truth be told, it was less of a joke and more of a reality. He was a man of discipline, and he was incredibly disciplined when it came to women. He was disciplined with everything in his life, and that was how he liked it.

This lass had given him that appreciative once over, and she wasn't exactly coy about it. With the way she sucked on that damn candy cane, Alex had to admit that was a bit hard to ignore.

For such a small thing, she certainly had plenty of attitude. She barely stood as tall as his chin, but she didn't hold back when she threw daggers at him—or when she blatantly checked him out. She was bold, and God, but she could talk. If Alex were on the prowl, he knew without a shadow of a doubt, that Quinn West would not be on his radar. The woman was a handful, and he'd only been in her company for maybe twenty minutes.

Alex sighed. There was one thing that was gnawing at him though. Lasses checked him out, and Alex barely noticed for the most part. But when Quinn West checked him out, for some fucking reason unbeknownst to him, he felt his cock bloody tighten in his uniform.

What in the hell was that about? He never allowed that to happen. It was not that lasses weren't appealing to him, but it was literally the very last thing on his mind when he was on duty. For that matter, it was far from front and centre when he was off duty. Acting on any kind of attraction while in uniform would be completely unprofessional and inappropriate. Not to mention, the last thing in hell he wanted. He rubbed his jaw, staring out at the snow that was now coming down in earnest.

Alex was always cool and in complete control, and that was how he liked it. He prided himself on being disciplined with everything in his life. It was the reason he'd been in special operations back in Scotland. He didn't get distracted. Except today apparently, he frowned.

And why did she make him feel like he was sharing something intimate with her when he told her he was from Scotland? Alex ran a hand through his hair. People always asked where he was from, and he never thought twice about answering. But with her, he had to admit, he felt a distinct pride in telling her his heritage. He loved Scotland and was a proud Scotsman, but why he wanted her to know where he was from was beyond him.

She hadn't hid her irritation when he'd asked her to step out of her vehicle. He had the distinct impression that he annoyed her much like wet snow in your boots. People reacted in many different ways to cops. He was certainly used to people being pissed off at him, but something about this lass, all hot and cold, got to him.

He shook his head, fed up with thinking about it. His thoughts turned to his Christmas holidays. Now there was another cluster fuck. He'd have to cancel his trip. *Bloody pish.* At least he had cancellation insurance, but he hated that he wasn't going to see his family.

It had been two years since he'd left Scotland, and he had been looking forward to seeing his two nephews. They'd probably grown and changed so much. And God, it would be good to see his siblings and parents. They'd all been through so much with the loss of his oldest sister Helena. Drew, his youngest brother, had fallen off the rails for a few years, but he'd started to come back around again. Everyone seemed to be healing and doing well up until Alex's world got turned on its head and he'd moved to Canada.

Even though he spoke with his family fairly frequently on FaceTime, he missed them. It was a good thing he'd intended the trip as a surprise. Lachlan, his brother with the two boys, was the only one who knew of Alex's plans to come home for Christmas. At least they wouldn't all be let down.

Alex had been hesitant to book a trip home. As much as he looked forward to seeing his family, there were some things in Scotland he'd rather not revisit. Perhaps Rod had done him a favour.

Looking out the front window of his police truck, the snow blew across the highway. He hoped the lass made it to Calen safely.

Alex looked down at the copy of the ticket he'd just written her. *What the hell?* He'd left the date blank! *How in Mother fuckin' Mary's name did that happen?* In all his years as a cop, he had never forgotten to put the date. A low growl escaped him. Automatically an invalid ticket. He didn't make mistakes, especially not on something as basic as the date. He had almost started to feel a bit better, but now, a fresh wave of irritation gnawed at him.

4
The Girls

DESPITE ARMFULS OF LUGGAGE and bags, Quinn managed to get through the front doors of Calen Mountain Inn. Green pine garlands wrapped in white Christmas lights decked the rich warm wood-panelled walls, and a bushy fresh Christmas tree twinkled in all its glory in the front lobby.

"Quinn!" She turned and saw her two friends as they ran up, embracing her in a crazy, wonderful hug. Quinn almost toppled over, but her heart was bursting. The three women had been best friends since junior high, but now they lived in different parts of the country. Unfortunately, they didn't see each other as often as they'd like, but when they did get together it was always epic.

They headed down the hall to the four-person room they had booked. Megan Mitchell and Belle Chan had arrived about half an hour before Quinn and had already settled in.

"He was hot though, right?" Meg teased taking a sip of her red wine as she winged on black eyeliner on her already cat-like gold eyes. Meg and Belle had pretty uneventful journeys to the mountain town, making them all the more intrigued to hear about Quinn's experience with the cop.

"Pfft. Upon reflection, I think he was too much of an ass to be hot." Quinn puffed back still frustrated that he'd actually given her a ticket at all, never mind one for three hundred dollars. It was ridiculous, and she didn't even want to think about how she was going to pay for it.

Her friend Belle eyed her in the way that only best friends could when they detected a lie.

Quinn huffed. "Well, I'm not saying he wasn't attractive physically, but seriously, he was cold and mean which made him completely *not* hot." Her mind agreed with the sentiment even if, at the time, her body had not.

Megan laughed. "You already said he *was* hot. His piercing blue eyes, perfect jawline, accent, and all that."

"I lied. Hot is pushing it." Quinn felt irritated that she couldn't seem to make up her mind. Yes, he was good-looking, but his mean personality wrecked it. What personality, really? He'd barely said a word, just glowered at her.

Megan ignored her. "Scottish accent, tall. Even the mean part doesn't sound so bad," she quirked her brows playfully.

"Yeah, well, how about the three hundred dollar ticket! And I swear he made me get out of the car just to be a jerk. It's like he took pleasure in letting me freeze my butt off."

"Maybe he wanted to check out your frozen butt." Belle quipped giving Quinn a sly look over her shoulder from where she stood primping in front of the full-length mirror.

"Noo," Quinn half whined, denying the very possibility. Had he really even looked at her? In the way a man looks at a woman. He'd watched her but mostly with his irritated or mystified scowl. There was that one moment though when he was almost eye to eye with her at the car window. His eyes had held something more—something she didn't have time to put her finger on except to decide it was sexy. Quinn had definitely checked him out though. She could barely help herself. The man was far too good-looking.

Other than that smouldering sexy look that lasted for just the briefest, tastiest moment and was likely some figment of her imagination, there was no doubt in her mind Mean Hot Cop definitively did not notice her. Not in that way, anyhow. Nope, instead, he looked at her with almost contempt in those stormy blue eyes. So grouchy. And such an ass.

"Trust me. All he cared about was punishing me." She threw the offending ticket down on the bed.

"You say that like it's a bad thing," Megan murmured with a quirk of her golden blond brow.

Quinn glared at her.

"I mean think about it, he even has his own handcuffs." Meg bit her lip and looked ready to swoon.

"Megs!" Quinn chided, and Belle gave Megan a friendly, shush-it-up shove with her hip.

"*What?*"

Quinn rolled her eyes. Belle had grabbed the wine bottle from the oak dresser and began filling up Quinn's glass, before topping up Megan's and her own, emptying the bottle.

Quinn took a hearty sip. It was frustrating. She really couldn't afford any extra bills right now. She had worked out a budget to get her through the next couple of months, but it was tight. This stupid ticket would take its toll. Even going out tonight, she would have to choose her food and alcohol frugally.

"It does seem on the high side, especially considering it's Christmas time," Belle said picking up the ticket off the festive red and green plaid duvet to examine it.

"Exactly," Quinn huffed, crossing her arms, wine glass still in hand. She took another deep sip, then bit at her lower lip worriedly.

"Fine. He's an asshole," Megs conceded but then grinned slyly. "A hot asshole, with handcuffs, come on girls, like who doesn't like that??"

"Ugh, Megs!" Quinn shouldn't be surprised by her friend. Megan always seemed to fall for the bad boys. She openly preferred her men a little on the asshole side.

"You know I'm right." Megan laughed.

"Hey, he didn't put a date on here," Belle said.

"What? Really?" Quinn sat beside her on the bed, taking the ticket from her to examine it.

Meg leaned over them both. "Ha!" She laughed out. "No date, no crime!"

"It was hardly a crime," Quinn said, still feeling touchy about it all and completely ignoring the point.

"Quinn, you can fight that ticket. They'll throw it out. They have to," Meg said more seriously.

"Really?" Quinn didn't know about such things.

"I'm 99.9 percent sure no date equals no ticket."

"Ha! Ha!" Quinn felt a rush of triumph in her veins. It was like an odd kind of Karma. That cop had seemed to take such pleasure in fining her, and now the fine would be thrown out. Too bad for him! She felt like she'd won. Big jerk. And she also felt some relief. Now, she wouldn't have to worry about where she'd have to cut into her budget. Thank God.

"I wonder if he realized?" Belle asked curiously her black brows knit together.

"I hope he did, and I hope it ticked him off and ruined his day." Quinn huffed, polishing off her wine feeling pleased at the turnaround of events.

"Oh, Quinn, play nice," Belle scolded her for her pettiness. It was not like Quinn to be spiteful.

"Fine, I know, I know. I don't wish him ill, but I am glad that I don't have to pay. I can't help taking the slightest pleasure in knowing Mr. Hot Cop, Mean Cop, messed up!"

5
It Could Be Any Cop

As they got ready to go out for dinner, Quinn felt a peace in her heart that she hadn't in a long time. Life hadn't always been easy, but here she was, on the precipice of new beginnings. The need for change in her life was almost choking her, so she finally just decided she was going to go for it. Once the decision was made to move to the mountains, she wondered what she had been waiting for. It seemed that people were always dreaming of one day doing "something," but when was that one day? What moment in time would propel them to go after their dreams and do that "something?"

In the summer, her best friends had talked about meeting up in the mountains for a little pre-Christmas girl's trip. It was the perfect opportunity. Quinn always dreamed of living in a small town. She'd head to the mountains, meet up with the girls, and then stay for a while. Try it on for size and see if it was the right fit. Maybe it was her thirtieth birthday looming on the horizon that helped propel her to just go for it, but somehow, it seemed the perfect time for a change, the perfect time to get on with the rest of her life. The perfect time to finally write her novel.

After her girls left, Quinn intended to stay at the inn for a week or two in a smaller room until she found a place to rent. She would continue to do her freelance writing, and if she had to pick up some work in one of the local bookstores or cafes, she could do that. But at least here in Calen, she would make writing her novel a priority, and she would get a chance to live a different life.

All freshened up and makeup on, the ladies headed out for dinner. They wandered through the town, taking in all the sights and sounds. Cute boutique shops, cafes, and artisan restaurants lined the main street. Each was decked out in boughs of greenery and twinkling Christmas lights. Holiday tunes played from outdoor speakers, and even the air smelled of the season with some outdoor vendors selling spiced cider and mulled wine.

Of the many restaurants lining the main street, each looked to have its unique appeal, but Belle had researched the one in particular that the girls were headed to. It was known across the country for its hearty home-cooked flavour and cozy aesthetic. As they strolled through the town, Quinn's stomach growled. She hadn't eaten anything much aside from cereal in the morning and candy canes on the drive.

"Are we close yet?" she asked.

Belle smiled. "Right here." She nodded towards the charcoal black framed windows through which soft candlelight created a warm glow against the backdrop of richly coloured walls.

"Perfect." Quinn grinned pulling open the door to the mouth-watering scent of the food.

"Good call, Belle. This may have been the most satisfying meal I've eaten in my entire life," Meg leaned back in her chair patting her belly as if she were Santa post Christmas Eve cookies.

"Scrumptious," Quinn concurred. "Oh my God, I'm full though."

After paying their bill, they headed back out to the main street. The temperature had dropped a bit, but after all the food they'd eaten, they agreed to wander about the town before heading back to the inn.

Quinn felt on a high as she and her friends strolled the decked out town taking in all the Christmas festivities. It was so good to spend time with her girls. She always felt more herself around her best friends. They never lacked conversation, and they were always laughing about something. Quinn was sure she could be stuck in jail with her girls and still have an incredible time. But being in Calen with them felt extra special. The town had so much natural beauty, and with all the Christmas charm everywhere, it was like a dream. She was giddy to go on some hikes and discover all this mountain town had to offer. Quinn loved to write, but she equally adored being in nature. This place could be the perfect fit for her. It could be home. A wave of excitement washed through her.

As they rounded the corner of one of the town streets, Quinn spotted a parked police truck and her heart skipped a beat immediately thinking of Hot Cop. Mean Cop, she corrected in her mind.

Seeming to notice the change in her friend, Belle asked "Are you okay, Quinn?"

"What?" she asked distracted. "Oh yeah, fine." She smiled, trying to tamp down her ridiculous reaction to seeing a stupid police truck.

"Oooh, a cop truck. You think it's your cop?" Meg asked with way too much enthusiasm.

"Who cares?" Quinn sniffed. "And he's not *my* cop," she added with a scowl.

"Oh please, you're not fooling anyone missy," Meg retorted with a chuckle.

Quinn couldn't help but smile at her friend calling her out. Her girls knew her too well. She couldn't keep any secrets. As they got closer to the truck, Quinn felt her pulse quicken, and it annoyed her. Was she worried about seeing him? Well, she had told him she hoped never to run into him again.

"Aww, look there's a dog inside!" Belle said as they were approaching.

"It's definitely not the cop who pulled me over then. That guy isn't nice enough to have a dog," she scoffed. "Come on, girls. Let's just go."

Even though she doubted it was his police truck, Quinn still felt a growing anxiety about possibly crossing paths again. A perverse part of her wanted to see if he was as handsome as she recalled, but the wiser part knew better. It didn't matter. He was a jerk, and she didn't need him ruining her lovely evening with her friends.

Belle and Meg ignored Quinn and made their way to the truck window to get a closer look. The moment they did the dog began to bark ferociously.

Belle jumped back and stumbled into Meg. "Holy shit."

The door to the cafe opened and the cop, Mean Cop...Hot Cop...strode out with a coffee in hand. God help her, he was tall, dark, and stupidly handsome, and for a moment, her heart stopped before it stuttered and started again.

He glanced up, seeing the women at his truck, and his incredible blue eyes caught hers for the briefest of moments. Long enough to send a little shiver down her spine. Why'd he have to look so good?

He strode past the women to his barking dog in the truck and put his arm up in a precise well-practiced move. "Enough," he commanded, and the dog instantly calmed turning from a feral beast to a docile pup. It was like watching the transformation of a Marvel film character.

All three women stared in awe and fascination. The cop turned to them, with an apologetic look on his too-handsome face. "I hope Bear didnae scare ye. He takes his job very seriously when he is on duty," he explained in his deeply accented voice.

Much like his owner, Quinn thought.

"'Tis fine now if ye'd like to see him closer. He willna hurt ye."

To her chagrin, her friends had also transformed, but into tittering girls. They were all flirty smiles as they stared up cow-eyed at the cop. Unbelievable. Her best friends were charmed by the brute.

"He's so cute," Belle cooed, moving closer to the window again.

"Och, Lass, you'll hurt his ego with words like that. He's a trained killing machine," the cop teased with a grin that could break hearts.

Quinn's mouth almost hit the ground. Who the heck was this guy? Mean Cop actually had a sense of humour? Mean Cop could actually be nice? It was like a total 180 from what she'd experienced with him. And that smile! She'd known it would be good, but God, her legs felt boneless even as her mind was irritated by the whole scenario playing out in front of her.

This switch in him frustrated her. Why had he been such a royal ass to her earlier? It grated, and she felt the need to say something bubbling up inside her. Without thinking she blurted, "By the way, that ticket you gave me is defunct."

The words flew out of her mouth like she was a prize fighter taunting a challenger to a match. His cool gaze fell on her, and she instantly regretted saying anything at all.

Like his police dog, his demeanour changed in an instant. Suddenly, he seemed taller and broader if that was even possible. And intimidating, God, he was intimidating. Quinn stepped back, feeling a wave of tingly nerves, but as she stepped back, he stepped towards her, closing the distance between them. His hulking muscular form all dressed in black with his eyes glowering on her. Quinn's pulse beat furiously as fear infused her veins.

"Say it again, I dinnae think I quite heard ye." Mean Hot Cop looked down upon her with danger emanating off him. Their bodies were only inches apart.

Quinn swallowed feeling her body tremble. "You forgot to put a date. On the ticket. So it doesn't count," she said with more bravado than she felt.

A slow menacing smile curved his lips. "Aye, but I can easily arrange a replacement fer ye, Ms. West." His stormy blue eyes were icy cold on her as they glared at each other in a stand-off. Quinn was about to retort when she felt her best friend's arm wrap through hers and yank her away. Quinn almost stumbled as Belle practically dragged her down the cobbled street.

"What the heck Belle?" Quinn grunted.

"No need to write any more tickets, Officer. We'll keep her out of trouble. Have a nice evening," Meg called back to him as she looped her arm around Quinn's on the other side.

The two girls hauled their friend away not wanting her to get herself in any more trouble. Fortunately, Quinn had the good sense to go with her friends and not open her mouth again. But she wanted to. She wanted to turn right back around and give him a piece of her mind.

Even as her friends led her away, she glanced back over her shoulder, and he stood, watching them leave with a cool arrogance about him.

"What a total ass!" Quinn huffed as they rounded the corner. "Like, who does he think he is?" She was infuriated as adrenaline coursed through her. Obviously, he was trying to intimidate her. Well, she wasn't going to let him. If she saw him again she would tell him exactly what she thought. "Seriously, girls, just because he's a cop, doesn't give him the right to be such a jerk!" Her girls had dropped arms with her now and were suspiciously quiet.

Quinn stopped walking and looked at Meg and Belle. "Okay, what's going on?" They looked at her as if neither wanted to speak. "What?" She looked back and forth between the two.

"Honestly, Quinn, I think he was actually really nice," Belle said quietly.

"*What?*" Quinn was incredulous. "Didn't you hear him threaten me with another ticket? And all that bravado, he was trying to intimidate me!"

"If he'd wanted to give you a ticket, he totally could have. And you asked for that, Quinn. He was being completely lovely, and it was you who brought up the ticket." Meg shrugged.

"Pfft." Quinn blew out an exasperated breath. "He's not lovely." She sniffed in conclusion.

"Oh yes, he is." Belle smiled dreamily. "Did you see that smile?"

"The one that could make a nun stray?" Meg grinned, completely ignoring Quinn's exacerbation.

"Right?" Belle quipped.

"He is a beautiful, beautiful man," Meg announced as if she'd never encountered a more perfect specimen.

Belle was nodding heartily in agreement.

"Ugh! Girls, you are supposed to be on my side!" What was wrong with them? Sure, he was good-looking, but seriously, he wasn't a flipping god.

Belle laughed. "We are on your side, silly!"

"I think he likes you," Meg added with a sly smile.

Quinn scoffed. "You are insane. He can't stand me!" It grated that he didn't seem to like her at all. She got along with practically everyone, but for some reason, it was like she was a thorn in his side. Well, the feeling was mutual.

"I don't like him, and he doesn't like me. Not that it matters anyway. I doubt we will be running into him again."

"Uh-huh," Meg said appeasingly, but Quinn could sense she disagreed.

Quinn stopped walking and turned to her. "Why would you think that he likes me?" she asked, feeling completely floored at her friend's ridiculous assertion. "It's obvious I tick him off, and he definitely ticks me off." She huffed, crossing her arms.

"Sparks were flying, Quinn. There is some kind of electricity crackling between the two of you," Meg said, and Belle nodded in agreement.

"Whatever. I'm done talking about that jerk cop." Quinn huffed, choosing to ignore such a ridiculous notion.

"Hot cop," Meg corrected breathily.

Quinn rolled her eyes.

6
Christmas Introvert

Intense stormy blue eyes held hers as he backed her against the wall. "Are you arresting me?" she asked huskily. Arousal slowly drizzled through her as his strong body pressed against hers, his mouth hovering so close, so tempting. She wanted him to kiss her. But in a flash, she realized she was naked, and everything seemed all wrong.

"You should put your clothes on." His lips lifted in a cocky smirk.

Embarrassment and anger bubbled up. "Jerk," she snapped. As she tried to step around him, she realized he'd handcuffed her. "No," she moaned, "No."

"Quinn. Quinn!"

"What, what?" she snapped as she rolled over in her bed not fully awake yet. Why on earth had she dreamed that? She lay replaying the dream, feeling a groggy mixture of horniness and irritation. Cracking one eye open, she saw Belle standing over her.

"What?" she said again, hoarsely trying to clear her muddled morning thoughts.

"I can't tell if that was a good dream or a bad dream you were having," Belle quipped with a raised brow.

"Ugh," Quinn grunted not sure herself.

"That good, eh?" Belle asked still staring down at her.

"Nothing worth retelling," Quinn said with a yawn. She didn't want to think any more about that man. And it annoyed her she'd had a dream about him. He was just as infuriating as in real life!

"So, breakfast?" Belle grinned brightly down at her.

"God, it is so beautiful here," Belle said letting the sun beat down on her face from where she stopped on the mountaintop.

"Heaven on earth," Quinn agreed, catching her breath while taking in the view. After a few hours of hiking along a trail and gaining elevation, they'd come to a clearing that overlooked the town below them. Quinn was sure she'd never seen a more spectacular vista. The sun streamed through brilliant blue skies illuminating the picturesque town that lay nestled among the giant snowy mountains. The air was crisp, and everything was quiet except for the sounds of nature. The snow rustled on the trees as the warm sun melted its surface. Birds were happily singing. Quinn took a deep breath, soaking in nature's salubrious effect on her very soul.

"I didn't think I'd ever feel hungry again after that breakfast this morning, but I'm getting pretty peckish," Belle said digging through her pack for a snack. Quinn would be willing to bet that Belle could plow through a plate of cookies faster than St. Nick on Christmas Eve, but it didn't matter what she ate, her five foot two frame always stayed perfectly slim and petite. Sometimes it was hard to not be envious of Belle's incredible metabolism.

"When I saw the line up for that breakfast place, I'm not gonna lie, I wanted to bail, but dang, it was worth the wait. Have you ever seen cinnamon buns that size? Shoot, I could totally go for another one now," Megs swooned, sucking in her lower lip and pressing her eyes closed, as if she could will a sticky hot cinnamon bun to magically appear.

"Oh my god, me too. They were so good. And the eggs Benedict was chef's kiss," Belle said, pulling out a chocolate-covered granola bar from her pack.

"As much as I love this, I'm done girls," Meg said after a few minutes. "My legs are dead."

"Hiking a mountain is no joke," Belle muttered, pressing her booted toes against a rock to stretch her calf.

Quinn was ready to head back too; her muscles were trembling from the exertion of the climb. Technically, the descent was supposed to be the easier part but, her leg muscles quivered in protest as the women began their trek down.

"I heard the weather is supposed to change in a couple of days. Calen is supposed to get a record-breaking snowstorm, and the temps are set to plummet," Meg said as they began their descent.

"Really?" Quinn hadn't paid much attention to the weather forecast here, but it didn't matter to her because she intended to work on her novel over Christmas anyway.

"You sure you don't wanna come back to my place for the holidays?" Megs nudged her.

With a father she never knew and a mother who passed away when Quinn was a teen, she had spent most holidays alone—aside from some time with her grandmother. She had grown rather accustomed to it. Sometimes, her heart longed for a big family Christmas, and she wondered if she'd ever know one. But for the most part, Quinn was content with her own company, even over the holidays.

Quinn looped her arm through Megan's. "I'd love to, but honestly," she paused taking in a deep breath of fresh mountain air, "I think I need this. I need to have some time with myself. And with my book. This is a new chapter for me. A new adventure. And I'm kind of excited about being in this snowy mountain town for Christmas."

Despite having the gift of gab, Quinn preferred quiet solitude and her own company. There was something so cathartic about being alone with her thoughts. Not that she didn't also love being with her friends, but she was excited to have some time to really dig into her book. This little mountain town was already filling her with inspiration.

"But what fun will it be if you have to be stuck inside the whole time because it's too frickin' cold and snowy?" Belle asked.

Ironically, the thought appealed to Quinn. She could be a total introvert, keep her jammies on, order room service—or maybe stock up at the grocery store, she amended, keeping her budget in mind—and write. "It will give me the time I need to dig into my writing. Besides, the inn has a restaurant, and I spied a yoga studio nearby. I'll have everything I need."

"Well, you won't be getting to that yoga studio if the weather gets as bad as they say," Meg said skeptically.

"I'll do yoga in my room then. It'll be fine." Quinn wasn't worried in the least.

Belle and Megan didn't look convinced. "But it's Christmas! You shouldn't be alone for Christmas." Belle frowned as if she were a child, who just discovered a lump of coal in their stocking. "Christmas is a time to be with friends and family," she argued.

Quinn stopped on the trail and smiled adoringly at the two women. "And I'm grateful to be with you both now. Honestly, girls, I'm happy to have some time with just me and my book. I'll order Christmas room service and spend the day with my characters. You know how I am." She laughed. Being stuck in this mountain town while it snowed and having nowhere to be but in her room writing her first novel, sounded dreamy to Quinn.

Belle and Meg looked at her as if she was nuts. Quinn chuckled. "Aww, girls, it's where I want to be. Truly. But I promise we'll meet up again soon in the new year."

Neither of them looked convinced, but thankfully, they let it go. Quinn was grateful the cop hadn't come up in conversation again. Although she found her thoughts turning to him anyway. He'd crossed her mind more than a few times throughout the day. She wondered why he'd given her such a hard time with the ticket and when they saw him again last night. It galled her how he'd been so jovial and pleasant until his attention turned to her. Maybe she had started it last night, but still, he didn't have to be so cold towards her.

It was the contradiction that gnawed at her. Cold hardened cop when it came to her but warm and sweet as fresh-out-of-the-oven gingerbread cookies with her friends.

It annoyed her mostly cause that soft side she glimpsed was even more lethal than his dangerous cop side. That smile of his... Her belly fluttered at the memory. She knew it would be good, but it was far better than she imagined. Her friends were right—he was dreamy, at least when he smiled. Not that he'd directed that smile at her. The man was a puzzle, and she wished her curious mind didn't thrive on solving them.

7
The Purple Deer

"Shit," Meg moaned as she bent to slide on her black pleather pants. "My ass. God, and my quads," She struggled to wrangle her pants up her legs.

"Right?" Belle quipped as she straightened her chin length glossy black hair. "I hope we don't die tonight trying to dance at a bar."

Quinn stared down at the high heel shoes she'd just pulled from her case and contemplated whether or not she could handle the torture on her already fried leg muscles. Finally having succeeded in getting her pants on, Meg sidled up to Quinn and looked down at the strappy sexy shoes. "Do it. Once we get a couple of shots in us, we'll be golden."

"Right, good point." Quinn laughed.

"I can't believe it's our last night together already," Belle said forlornly as she put on her signature Charlotte Tilbury glossy red lipstick.

"Yeah, but we're gonna have a blast tonight, find some cute guys, have some shots, and dance... Maybe not all in that order." Meg laughed. "But it's gonna be epic. I can feel it."

Belle and Quinn gave each other a knowing look. Megs always thought a night out at the bar was "epic." In fairness, the girls did always have a great time when they went out and partied.

"There are only three bars in this town, so let's hope there is life in at least one of them," Meg said as she turned on her heel and strode back out of the first bar as fast as she'd gone in.

The next bar they went to looked like an old saloon aside from the neon sign above the door that read, The Purple Deer. Judging by the packed parking lot it appeared as if the entire town might be in it.

"This is more like it," Meg announced as they walked in. There was a live band playing and they had the dance floor filled. The place was buzzing with atmosphere.

The three women manoeuvred their way through the crowds of partygoers to the bar. Drinks were the first order of priority.

"Ladies, ladies, you're just in time!" A ruggedly cute guy in a plaid button-up shirt—who'd clearly already had a few—was standing at the bar with a pile of shots lined up in front of him. Megs, not missing a beat, sidled up beside him.

"What are we celebrating?" she asked as she helped herself to a shot glass and raised it to the guy who was offering them up.

"I'm celebrating that you finally got here." His tone was flirty, and his eyes were glittering on Meg. "I've been waiting for you all night." He grinned slyly under his scruffy blond beard, taking his shot and then boldly putting his face right in front of hers.

She grinned back and took her shot. "Guess the wait is over." She eyed him coyly, throwing the ball back in his court.

He passed her another shot looking impressed and took one for himself.

Belle and Quinn stood back, watching the exchange in rapt fascination. The two were eyeing each other as if it were some kind of flirty showdown. After watching the pair chuck back another shot, Quinn finally tore her gaze away and turned to the tall lanky bartender.

"Can I get two vodka crans please?"

"Doubles?" he asked.

Quinn glanced over at Meg, who already appeared tipsy and was clearly having a flirty, fabulous time. "Sure. Doubles." Quinn nodded, ready for her own tipsy, fabulous time and perhaps a little distraction from her achy legs. Maybe she'd find some hottie to flirt with, too.

It was quiet for a Saturday night, Alex observed as he headed to the town's hot spot for a quick patrol before the end of his shift. Striding into The Purple Deer, he noted the heavy scent that hung in the air. A well-worn potion of perfumes and colognes laced with sweat and alcohol. The place was packed. He should have known this was where the town would congregate the Saturday before Christmas.

As he wound his way through throngs of people, he automatically scanned behaviours and kept a lookout for anything suspicious or out of the norm. Nothing caught his radar tonight—not even the flirty long-eyed looks from several women as he made his way towards the back bar.

Alex was a pro at ignoring lass's advances. Some women were extremely forward trying to vie for his attention, but he was a disciplined professional. Occasionally, one would catch his eye. Some lasses were attractive to him, he'd not deny it, but women did not fit into his current life plans. It was easy to ignore their overtures especially while he was in uniform.

Some lasses downright ogled him as he passed by them, but he was used to it—immune. And it wasn't just the lasses. Occasionally, there were men too. It was part and parcel with him being a six-foot-four muscular cop at a bar with varying states of inebriated horny people.

It was a good night if he didn't get his arse pinched. He could make a fuss about that sort of thing, but it wasn't worth his time or energy. Instead, he stayed focused on his purpose, watching for anything suspicious. Seeing an intimidating cop walk through the bar was a good little reminder to behave and not do anything stupid aka illegal.

"Barnes, Hanson." He nodded, acknowledging the two constables who already stood along a back wall surveying the crowd.

"Sergeant," they greeted him with a quick nod.

"Full house," he commented.

"Tame though," Barnes responded. "We got it covered, Sergeant," he assured his superior.

"Aye, well, I'll leave you to it then." Alex smiled and turned to head out, but his eyes were drawn to the dance floor. It had thinned out when the band played a slower song, and he watched mesmerized as a lass swayed to the music. She wore a sheer lace blouse and a short black ruffled skirt that sat high on her curvy thighs. The way she moved was sensuous yet completely carefree, and she appeared utterly oblivious to anyone watching. Alex felt his jaw tick from the tension strung through it. Many eyes were watching her. Not just his. Quinn West. Again.

Calen was a small town, so it shouldn't surprise him that he seemed to keep running into her. Yesterday, he'd been feeling really good right up until he'd crossed paths with her. He'd just received his Christmas bonus which was substantially better than he'd anticipated. It was the end of his shift for the evening, and he planned to head to the grocery store to load up on food and drink for the holidays as he was no longer going to be heading home to Scotland. The idea of staying in his cottage over Christmas had begun to appeal to him more and more.

As he'd come out of Vy's cafe, he noticed Ms. West immediately. When the lasses were friendly with him, he thought he could maybe make up for being a bit of an arse the day before, but no, she'd gotten under his skin in a matter of seconds. He didn't know how she managed to do it. And now, here she was in his sights again, and God only knew why he couldn't seem to tear his gaze away from the infuriating woman.

"Lookin' a little distracted there, Sergeant Mackenzie," Barnes teased him, tilting his gaze towards the dance floor.

"I gave her a speeding ticket recently," Alex responded, bluntly dismissing Barnes's intent. He didn't need the guys razzing him about a lass, especially not this one.

"Mm-hmm." Barns grinned knowingly, and Hanson seemed to be enjoying himself too. Alex had a reputation. They all teased him for years that women drooled over him while he always stayed cool. Sergeant Mackenzie was immune to women, but the two constables seemed to think they'd discovered a chink in his armour.

"Ah boys, even if I was looking, which I'm no', that one is far too much trouble." Alex nodded in Quinn's direction.

"I thought cops are always looking for trouble?" Hanson challenged with an arched brow.

Alex grinned. "No' this cop," he said as he straightened his cap and headed towards the door. Fighting the urge to glance toward the dance floor, he called back over his shoulder, "Have a good night, lads."

Aye, Quinn West was the kind of trouble he had no wish for.

8
Drunk Girl Speak

After a few drinks, Meg was making out in the corner with the shooter dude. Belle had also found some guy who'd snagged her attention. They were slow dancing and eyeing each other suggestively. And Quinn swayed to the music by herself on the dance floor full of couples. She was feeling the effects of the vodka crans and was happily lost in her own world. The music demanded her to move with it.

Sipping her drink through her straw, she just let the melody flow through her. God, the band was really good. It was maybe a smidge disappointing that she hadn't found some hottie to dance with, but at the same time, she didn't mind. In her mind's eye, she pictured the cop. She thought about his smile. If he'd led with that, everyone would be putty in his hands. He was probably taller than every guy in this room, definitely the most muscular. She looked around as she sucked back the remainder of her drink.

Realizing her glass was empty, she turned and made her way to the bar for a refill at the end of the song. She was feeling tipsy, but one more wouldn't hurt. Her thoughts were still on the cop. She was thinking about what Meg said—that he liked her. At the time, she was far too frustrated to question Meg about it, but thinking on it now, she wondered what sparks her girls thought they saw between them. Not that it mattered really. She probably wouldn't see him again anyway. Or would she? Small-town life wasn't like the big city. Maybe she would run into him again. Butterflies danced low in her belly at the thought. Before she could push away the sensation, someone bumped into her making her spill her newly poured drink down the front of her white blouse.

"Oh sorry," some guy muttered, proceeding to paw at her chest as if to dry it.

"Hey!" she snapped pushing him away from her. He threw his hands up in a truce as he stumbled backward. Quinn scowled and made her way to the washroom. She leaned her chest awkwardly under the tap and simultaneously tried to wave her fingers in front of the tap sensor. Giving up on that, she tried to shove her chest under the hand dryer to try and dry up the worst of it. Straightening up before she fell over, she looked in the mirror and sighed.

"Ugh." Her pretty white sheer blouse was now ultra-sheer and wet with an obvious pink hue.

Two women piled into the washroom. One of them went into a stall, and one stood beside Quinn, putting down two shot glasses filled with some kind of clear alcohol and began checking her makeup in the mirror. She caught Quinn's reflection.

"Aww sweety," she said sympathetically looking over at her. "You look sad."

"I know, someone spilled my drink on me," she whined. "My new blouse is stained. My friends abandoned me. Well, sort of. They are having fun with *boys* no doubt and you know what?" She looked at the woman with curly hair who was looking back at her like she was her long-lost sister, empathy, kindness and love all floating around in her squinty hazel eyes as she listened attentively. "Not one boy even asked me to dance," Quinn said with an exaggerated pout.

Quinn's mind was feeling fuzzy from the drinks, and when the long-lost sister woman in front of her wrapped her in a big supportive hug, she had no qualms about hugging her right back. They swayed locked in their drunken embrace for what felt like ages. When they pulled apart, the curly-haired woman picked up a shot glass and handed it to Quinn, "Here, friend, you could use it more than me."

Quinn nodded, taking the glass while appreciating the woman's care for her. She shot it back. "Here have another," the woman said. "My friend and I can get more after."

"Thanks," Quinn said not even phased by the drunken exchange.

"Come on, Tanya." The woman's friend snagged her arm. "I want to go find those cops, especially the big muscled one. My God, did you see his biceps? I swear they are bigger than Miley Cyrus' hair at the Grammys."

Released from Tanya's hold, Quinn had to focus on her balance, but she needed to know. "What cops?" she blurted with her head feeling fuzzy.

"Ah girl, you didn't see them? They're in the bar. So hot."

Quinn's brain was functioning a little slower with the effects of her vodka crans and the two shots she'd just taken, but this conversation had her intrigued. "Wait, like off-duty cops?"

"Oh, hell no, like on duty, cops in uniform. As in hot as hell." The woman looked at Quinn slyly.

"Really? Here now and one with big biceps? Was he really tall and mean-looking with blue eyes?"

"I don't know what colour his eyes were!" she snapped exasperated. "But I do know I'm gonna get out there and find out!" And with that, she grabbed Tanya's arm and hauled her out the washroom door, leaving Quinn standing there.

Quinn looked back to the mirror and saw her drunk self with a giant pink stain on her blouse, she realized she'd had more than enough to drink, and it was time she headed back to the inn. There was the drunken part of her that wanted to run into Mean Hot Cop, but fortunately, she still had some sense and realized that may not be the best idea right now. Not that she liked the idea of these other women trying to find *her* cop.

She smirked at herself in the mirror and then giggled. So silly. He wasn't her cop. And good luck to those women. He was a mean ass. They had no idea what they were in for. She shook her head and walked out of the washroom.

The bar crowd had thinned out, and Quinn went in search of her friends somewhat nervous that she might run into the cop. She found Meg right away. She and shooter dude were still making out in the corner, and Quinn decided not to interrupt. As she passed the back bar looking for Belle, she noticed two cops leaning up against the wall and smiled both relieved and a little disappointed. Mean Hot Cop wasn't here after all.

Nearly doing a full circle of the bar, she eventually found Belle at a smaller sidebar. She was standing with the guy she'd been dancing with. "Hey, Belle." She sidled up beside her friend. "I'm going to head back to the inn."

"Oh, I can come with you if you want," Belle said. Quinn knew her friend would come if she wanted her to, but she could tell that Belle wasn't ready to leave yet. Quinn didn't mind in the least. She intended to get out of her clothes and high heels, chug some water, and crawl into bed.

"No, no, you stay. I'm good. Meg's is in the back with the shooter guy so just don't leave without her."

"Okay, for sure. We'll see you later then. Love you!" Belle gave Quinn a squeeze.

"Love you too. Be safe."

9
Mean Cop. Hot Cop.

Sitting in his police truck outside the Purple Deer with his trusty pup Bear sitting up front beside him, Alex was finishing up some notes for his reports in the morning. When he looked up a group of three men stumbled rowdily out the heavily carved wood door of the bar. He watched as they lit up smokes. The door opened again, and a woman came out with curvy bare legs ending in black high heels and a dark green coat hugged tightly to her. Shit, he recognized her immediately—Ms. West.

The men zeroed in on her like wolves to prey, and Alex slid on his leather gloves his fists tightening, ready to bring down thunder. One of them jeered towards her, but she didn't respond. Instead, she tightened her arms around her thin wool coat and tucked her head down as she hurried forward through the parking lot. Even from this distance, her body language was obvious. She wanted to get the heck out of there. Alex saw her glance towards them as she tried to navigate through the thickening snow. But they weren't going to let her get away so easily.

One of the men leered towards her, grabbing the tie around her waist from behind. Alex was out of his truck in an instant, and he headed towards her, anger boiling dangerously in his veins as he pulled himself up to his full breadth and width. Drunk or not, guys like these, the ones who felt privileged to prey on women for sport, disgusted him. He never understood it. Salacious fuckers.

The guy who now roughly turned Quinn to face him clocked Alex almost immediately and to Alex's satisfaction he saw his eyes widen in fear before he released her and hastily turned back towards the door and slipped inside. His buddies turned, and seeing Alex coming, they wasted no time dropping their cigarettes and high-tailing it out of there too.

As Quinn walked out of the bar, she snugged her thin wool coat tighter around her. The crisp mountain air had turned frigid, and it didn't help that her little blouse was still damp against her skin. She was focused on getting to the inn as quickly as possible without freezing to death or falling for that matter. It was slippery with the new falling snow, and she now regretted wearing her strappy high heels.

The wind was blowing around icy snow. She was vaguely aware of the group of guys she passed as she stepped out. When they started catcalling her, all she could think was that she needed to get the heck out of there and fast.

She felt the tug on the back of her coat, and suddenly, she was tangled up against some dude. They were almost both falling over, the overwhelming smell of his smoke and alcohol breath accosted her as he leered towards her face, muttering something about giving him one kiss before he'd let her go. Quinn's mind was fuzzy despite the fear that tore through her.

Trying to get her feet balanced under her, she was about to throw a knee into his groin when he abruptly let her go and practically ran inside. Quinn was momentarily dumbfounded as the other two guys followed suit. Not sure what changed their minds, but thanking her lucky stars all the same, she huddled her coat up around her ears, tucked her head, and turned to get the heck out of there.

Hurrying through the small parking lot with her head down, she suddenly slammed into a solid wall. Before knowing what had happened, she registered strong arms steadying her, and just as quickly, they released her. It all happened in a flash.

Gathering her bearings, Quinn realized she'd run right smack into the cop. Relief washed over her that it was him and not another creepy dude. At least, she knew she wasn't in danger now. The guys behind her had made her more nervous than she cared to admit.

For a hazy drunken moment, Quinn savoured being rescued in solid comfort Mean Hot Cop's ridiculously strong arms. She could have romanticized the thought to no end. But then it occurred to her how quickly he'd released her, and she'd barely caught her balance. Glancing up into his too-handsome face, she shouldn't have been surprised to find him scowling at her, as per usual. Why did he seem to dislike her so much?

"Are ye all right?" His tone was serious despite his charming Scottish brogue. That voice, so deep and rich, seemed to rumble through her. Why'd he have to sound so hot? His intense blue eyes locked on hers, and she swore she could feel the sizzle right down to her frozen toes. He towered over her like he had last night, but this time, it made her feel safe.

Swallowing, she glanced back towards the door.

"They are gone," he stated seeming to know the direction of her thoughts.

"Good." She nodded, letting the relief sink in that they were no longer a threat. "I'm fine. No harm done."

Putting two and two together, Quinn now understood why those guys took off in a hurry. They must have seen Mean Hot Cop coming. The thought made her giggle, pleased to know he'd scared the shit out of them. She grinned up at him. "Thank you for coming to my rescue."

"Ye shouldna be leavin' the bar alone." He was still scowling at her, and Quinn was reminded why he irritated her.

The only problem was that he also seemed to make her heart flutter. Like right now. He stood so close to her. She could practically feel the heat emanating off his black uniform-clad body and onto hers. She swayed towards him. Whether to feel more of his heat or because of the last two liquor shots swimming in her veins, she wasn't sure. The silver handcuffs attached to his black belt caught in the light, and her mind ricocheted back to her dream. Heat tingled between her thighs.

He cleared his throat, pulling Quinn out of her reverie. God, what was she thinking? This was the same cop who had been such an ass to her. Twice.

"Well, thanks then," she muttered reluctantly through chattering teeth as she quickly sidestepped him to carry on her way. It was freezing, and she was not firing on all cylinders. She just wanted to get back to the inn and crash.

"Have ye been drinking?" he asked disapproval clear in his lilting voice.

Oh, here we go! she thought, *back to being a jerk.* "Is that the only question you cops are taught to ask?" she snapped sarcastically. "I did just come out of a bar." She gestured overtly behind her. Was he seriously going to give her a hard time again? The glare on his too-handsome face was cool enough to keep ice cream from melting on a hot summer's day, sending a shiver up her spine.

It pained her that despite his being all Mean Cop again, she couldn't seem to stop thirsting after him. Quinn hated that her tipsy brain found him appealing in any way. Her rational mind couldn't stand the beast, but her undersexed, lacking-in-the-man department brain just saw a damn near-perfect specimen of a male who could explode her dry streak into oblivion. Lord, help her.

"Ye best not be driving then." His voice was edged with steel, and his blue stormy eyes were full of warning.

It was a look that was meant to strike fear and leave someone shaking in their boots—or high heels as it were. It was probably the look he'd given those creeper dudes that made them disappear faster than Houdini. Quinn didn't think though. She just reacted and threw him an incredulous look at such a ridiculous remark.

"No shit, Sherlock, " she snapped and then immediately realized she'd said the quiet part out loud. Oh jeez, she'd definitely blame that one on Tanya's washroom shots.

Christ, he would have laughed if she didn't frustrate the hell out of him. In fairness, it was the kind of comeback he'd probably say. Keeping his features schooled, he warned her, "There are few cabs tonight with it being Christmas time. How do ye intend on getting home, Ms. West?"

"I think these legs should do the trick. I'm walking, Mr. Officer," she quipped, patronizingly tapping a hand on the top of her thigh.

The gesture hit Alex squarely in the groin as he noted the soft-looking skin of her curvy thighs. An image popped unbidden into his mind of those lush legs wrapped around his waist as he pounded into her. He blinked it away, stunned at the lightning speed his mind conjured it up. What in the fuckin' name of Mary was wrong with him?

Quinn had started to tromp through the snow away from him.

"Ye cannae be serious," Alex bit out. "Ye cannae walk in those bloody spikes ye call shoes in this snow. Ye're no' dressed properly for this weather. Ye'll catch ye'r death," he snapped with a heavy Scots brogue.

A feminine scoff escaped her. "I'm fine thanks, Dad," she mocked as she slipped and slid, trying to walk on.

Alex was quite certain her stubbornness would either get this woman home or to a bloody morgue. It was infuriating watching her. Surely, her feet were frozen.

"Stop," he commanded.

"What?" she asked, incredulously turning back to face him.

"I'm going to have to have ye come with me." His voice was deep and deadly serious.

"What? Why?" She was incensed. "Is it illegal now to bump into a cop? Did I hurt you, you...you brick wall!" He shouldn't be enjoying her fiery insolence, but when this wee woman riled at him, he felt something akin to admiration. The words just tumbled out of her with a force that belied her tipsy state. Remarkably enough, she didn't seem to have the sense to regret them. Instead, she just scowled at him as if he wasn't the police officer giving her a direct order.

Alex almost laughed though. He'd been called a lot of things in his career, but no one had ever tried to insult him by calling him a brick wall.

"Let's go," he said, putting a strong hand on her upper arm.

"No," she said, stubbornly trying to pull out of his grip.

"Public drunkenness," he said, knowing it would piss her off, but also knowing it was his trump card.

She whipped her head to look at him. "That's ridiculous!" Her deep brown eyes were throwing daggers at him now.

Fuck, she was feisty, but Alex had no intention of letting her walk off in this weather. She'd surely catch her death. Not wanting a sparring match, he chose to be straight with her. "Look lass, I dinnae want to find ye frozen in a snow bank by morn'."

"So you're hauling me to the drunk tank?" She bit out furiously.

Alex stopped in his tracks and released his hold on her arm. He sighed as he rubbed his palms against his tired eyes. This lass was going to drive him mad. It was late, and he wanted to get home to bed. The second he'd let go of her, she loped away from him with surprising agility and speed trying to make her escape no doubt.

"Christ, woman," he growled. "I'll give ye a ride home, just stop already."

Pausing mid-stride, she turned back and looked at him. Her gaze assessed him as he stood with his arms crossed over his chest and his legs spread in a wide stance. Alex knew he was a force to be reckoned with, and the lass should be bloody nervous. But it wasn't fear or nerves he saw in those big brown eyes. It was satisfaction like she'd won an unspoken game.

As if emboldened by the small win, she sauntered back to where he stood, and he couldn't help watching the sexy sway of her hips. Alex stood stone still as she stopped right in front of him, looking up from under thick long lashes, she bit her full lower lip, and Alex felt blood pump to his cock.

"Better be careful." Her voice was surprisingly steady. Alex could barely breathe, never mind respond to her. "Sounds like there may be a heart somewhere in there after all." Her gaze dropped to his name tag, and then her brown eyes drew up to his again as she pointedly added, "Sergeant Mackenzie."

Alex could feel tension gripping his jaw. The comment should have rolled off him—hell, he'd heard far worse. But for some reason, her words pierced something deep beneath the surface. Did she think he was so cold-hearted?

Stepping impossibly close, eyeing him and silently daring him to stop her, she reached up and touched her hand to his chest. Right below his heart thundered, and he was certain she could feel it under his police-issued bomber coat and bulletproof vest. Her slim fingers curled lightly against the fabric of his coat, but he could feel it as if her hand was touching his fiery skin beneath. It was like she was casting a spell on him with the clash of innocence wrapped in desire in the big brown eyes looking up. Those expressive eyes seemed to speak to a part of him he'd long denied. She wanted him to kiss her. He knew it without a shadow of a doubt, and for fuck's sake, if he didn't want to oblige her.

The sounds of laughter and music spilled out into the night air as the big wood door to the Purple Deer opened and snapped Alex back to reality. He stepped away from her, glancing towards the door. A couple of guys came out and headed towards the nearby donair shop, thankfully without even glancing their way. Alex let out a breath and straightened his police cap. What in the hell had he been thinking?

What was wrong with him that this lass was getting to him? It made no sense. Where in the hell was his immunity now? She was attractive. Anyone could see that. But she also was so damn obstinate. If he wanted to kiss a lass, it should be one far less troublesome. And one who wore sensible clothing in the cold and didn't argue with him.

Christ. Perhaps the long hours were taking their toll. It was a good thing his holidays started tomorrow. Well today, he supposed as it was after midnight. Aye, he looked forward to hunkering down in his cottage with Bear and escaping the world for a bit. Getting out of the town, he could ensure he'd not keep running into this damned woman.

"Well, are we going then?" she asked as if she was tired of waiting on him.

Shaking his head unable to believe the gall of the woman, he stepped past her towards his truck. "Come," he commanded.

This time, thankfully, she didn't bother to argue.

Opening the back door and gesturing for her to get in, Quinn threw him a look. "I don't want to go in the back, isn't that relegated to people you arrest?" She peered in the back seat apprehensively.

"Did ye want me to arrest ye then?"

She shot him a scowl.

"Ms. West, get into the truck," he said wearily.

10
Where the Bad Guys Go

GROWLING HER FRUSTRATION, SHE reluctantly conceded to getting in the back seat. He held out his black-gloved hand to help her up. *As if.* Haughtily refusing his help, she instead grabbed an interior handle and lifted herself in, as a wave of dizziness washed over her. Closing her eyes and gathering her composure, she felt relieved to be seated, even if it was in the back of a police truck.

For a split second, a moment in time, she thought she'd finally cracked the cop's code. Found the man under the uniform. She'd even been momentarily convinced he was going to kiss her, but in an instant, Mean Cop made a comeback. Despite alcohol frolicking merrily through her, the rejection smarted, like the crack of a whip.

The warmth of his police truck enveloped her, melting away her agitation, and she sighed contentedly. Despite sitting in the spot reserved for jailbirds, she had to admit the toasty heat was heavenly on her frozen extremities. The comforting warmth was so deliciously distracting that she almost didn't notice the dog eyeing her from the front seat. "Aww, hi, you sweet thing," she said gently as she put her hand to the grate between them, and let him sniff her.

The driver's side door opened, and Quinn sat back in her seat. She silently watched as the tall broad cop slid into the driver's seat. The first thing he did was get on his radio, Quinn couldn't very well pretend not to hear what he was saying, so instead she listened intently. He was telling them about those assholes, and Quinn was surprised at how thorough a description he gave like he had a photographic memory. The one guy had been right in Quinn's face, and she couldn't recall the first thing about what he looked like—only that his smell revolted her. She shuddered recalling it.

"Aye, Barnes and Hanson are on site."

"Calling into them now. Thanks, Sergeant. Enjoy your holidays."

"Copy that. Thank ye, 10/4."

The sudden silence made Quinn glance up, and she caught his stormy blue eyes studying her in his rearview mirror. She wished she knew what he was thinking, especially as he wasn't wearing his usual scowl.

"Where are you off to? For your holidays?" Quinn asked curiously. "Hopefully somewhere warm. God, I'd love to go to the Caribbean and just lay on that white sand soaking in the sun drinking some fruity boozy drink with a little umbrella in it." The vision made her smile. "Have you ever been to the Caribbean? The water in the pictures doesn't even look real it's so turquoise and clear. Do you think it's like that in real life?" She paused to consider it, then continued. "Do you know, I've never even seen a palm tree." She caught his gaze in the mirror, looking at him expectantly. She should have known she'd find nothing more than weary boredom on his annoyingly handsome face.

"Where are ye staying Ms. West?" he asked as if she hadn't just been engaging him in conversation.

Quinn's smile dropped, and she turned her head to look out the window. What an ass. She had to bite her tongue not to give him a piece of her mind, for all the good it would do.

"The Calen Mountain Inn. Down the road," she said through gritted teeth.

"Aye, I know where it is."

Quinn rolled her eyes and crossed her arms. Clearly, he wasn't interested in chatting which was fine by her. Between feeling frustrated and getting to the not-so-good stage of being drunk, she just sat in the back of the truck quietly feeling mildly irritated and also a little queasy. Actually more than a little queasy, and her head was really starting to swim. Even the heat was losing its bone-warming effect.

As he drove out of the packed parking lot, Quinn needed a distraction and asked, "What's your dog's name?" And almost kicked herself because she couldn't seem to hold her tongue for a moment. Why was she trying to engage him in conversation again?

"Bear," he responded.

Ignoring him, she spoke to the dog instead. "Bear, you're so sweet, aren't you?" she said, reaching up to the metal divider to scratch his soft fur through the grates as he leaned in to her touch.

"He's on duty, so it's best to keep your hands to yourself," Mean Cop said bluntly. She got the impression he wasn't just talking about his dog. Bear didn't seem to be on duty, at least based on what she'd witnessed yesterday. His on-duty behaviour had been quite different from the behaviour of the docile dog looking back at her now.

But Quinn immediately dropped her hand, disappointed Sergeant Mackenzie didn't even want her to pet his dog. Perhaps it was reasonable, but somehow, it just felt like she irritated the man by her very presence. It wasn't like she asked for a ride. That had been his idea.

She eyed him in the rearview mirror from the back seat. Even in a truck, he seemed big—tall, broad, and muscular. His dark hair was cut short. She was a sucker for the clean-cut look. Curse him.

"Are you always so mean?" she asked, not wanting to think about how physically attractive she found him.

"Aye," he said matter-of-factly. His eyes caught hers in the mirror, but there was a twitch in his lips right before he said it like he wanted to smile but held it back.

She huffed in disapproval and looked out the window again, trying to breathe through the little waves of nausea that had started to assault her as they drove. She was definitely tipsy, but it would be okay. It was probably just the motion of Mean Hot Cop's truck making her feel worse.

"I'm no' being mean, 'tis my job. Technically, Bear isnae on duty at the moment, but it is confusing for him to huv friendly interactions with someone who is sitting in the backseat of this truck."

She could understand that, but why couldn't he have just said that in the first place instead of making her feel like she was doing something wrong?

"Didn't your mother ever teach you that you attract more bees with honey?" She crossed her arms, looking back up at him in the mirror.

"I've no desire to attract bees." He sounded dumbfounded by her comment.

She laughed despite herself. "All I'm saying is that a little kindness can go a long way."

"Aye, well, I'm saving ye from becoming an ice sculpture aren't I?"

She smiled at that. Maybe Mean Hot Cop had a sense of humour in there.

"It isnae very sensible though, dressing for summer in the dead of winter," he added gruffly.

She rolled her eyes. He just had to say something snarky.

It took longer than she thought to get back to the inn, and she found herself much relieved that the cop gave her a ride. She just might have frozen if she'd tried to walk it. At the same time, she was eager to stop moving and get back into the fresh cold air.

As they pulled up near the glass doors, her head was really starting to spin. As soon as they stopped, she tried to open the door, needing to get out, but it was jammed. Then it occurred to her that she was in the back seat of a cop's vehicle. They wouldn't open from the inside. God, and here she was getting out of the back of a police truck, not the best look. Good thing nobody knew her here.

As he eyed her in the rearview mirror, he almost chuckled watching her try to open the door.

How had this wee stubborn lass been able to push his buttons? He'd made sure to sit her in the back seat away from him after whatever the hell that was that happened between them in the bar parking lot. He knew that it pissed her off to sit where the "bad guys" went, but there was no way he could have her sit up front with him. And all her nattering. He'd never know a lass to blether so much.

Although when she'd talked about the turquoise waters of the Caribbean, he came mighty close to telling her about the beautiful turquoise waters of the sea up in northern Scotland. White sandy beaches and turquoise waters that stretched for miles with the rugged mountains as a backdrop and usually nary a soul to be found. It was heaven on earth.

He might be giving the lass a hard time, but until he could get his cock to remember it was on a diet, it was better to keep her at a safe distance. Currently, that was the back seat.

She caught his eyes in the mirror. "Are you going to let me out?" she asked not hiding her irritation.

"Aye." He sighed more than ready to be done for the evening.

He got out and opened the door for her, standing back. This time, he didn't offer a helping hand as she'd made it clear when she got in that she didn't want it.

"A little help would be nice," she said, looking pointedly at him.

God, this woman. He offered to help her in and she snubbed him, and now she wanted his help out. Forget it.

"There's a handle up there. Ye managed to get in. I'm sure ye can manage to get out," he said bluntly, stepping back to allow her to sort it out herself. It annoyed him that he had to restrain himself from offering his hand. Hell, he had to restrain himself from putting his hands around her waist and hoisting her out.

Big brown eyes assessed him coolly. Apparently, she found him rude. Well too bad. He watched out of the corner of his eye as she tried to maneuver herself out of his truck, but her movements were sloppy. He could see before it happened that she wasn't going to make it. Her high heel shoe slid on the truck rail, and she lost her grip on the handle above her head causing her to fall unceremoniously right into his ready-waiting arms.

That was the second time that night she'd fallen into him. The first time, he had no problems setting her on her feet and letting go. It wasn't even a thought, but this time, *Jeezus hell*, why did it feel like he was crossing a line? He felt hyper-aware of every part of her body touching his. He was wearing a bulletproof vest for God's sake. He shouldn't be feeling a bloody thing. *Fuck. Fuck. Fuck.* Needing to put some immediate space between them, he deftly extricated himself from her.

Quinn's big brown eyes looked up at him, and she took a deep breath as if steadying herself. "Um, thank you for the ride. And for catching me. Twice," she added awkwardly and then huffed. "But I will also say that you should try to be a nicer person." Apparently satisfied she'd said her piece, she sucked in another deep breath and moved to walk past him to the door of the inn, but he stepped out in front of her.

"What? What now?" she grumbled, and he noticed her sway slightly.

"It's not my job to be nice." His tone was level, but his eyes were stormy.

"Fine, but," she stopped mid-sentence taking a deep nasal breath, and then she looked up at him with a hazy look in her brown eyes. Impervious to acting strange, she leaned and little closer and breathed in again. "Mmm, like what is that cologne anyway?" she said as if speaking to herself and not for his benefit.

Caught off guard, he answered plainly, "It's fae Scotland. It's aftershave no' cologne. I dinnae recall the name."

Her big brown eyes widened, and she slapped a hand over her mouth. Had she not meant to say that out loud? And why was he bothering to tell her that anyway? Christ, he just wanted to get home to bed.

Moving away from him, she tucked her auburn hair behind her ear. "Oh. Right." Her eyes scrunched closed, and she pursed her lips before blurting. "I just noticed it. That's all. Um, it smells like my brother's."

He gave her a dubious look but chose to leave it be. "Aye, well if you're going to be sticking around town. Ye may want to invest in some proper winter clothing. Boots and a winter coat." He couldn't keep the sarcasm from his tone. "Ye *are* in the mountains, Ms. West."

"This is a winter coat," she snapped and then let out a little moan as she clutched her stomach. Looking up at the night sky, she started taking quick exaggerated breaths. "Are ye okay, lass?"

Panicked big eyes darted to his. "Oh my God, I'm going to be sick," she whimpered right before the contents of her belly came hurdling out of her with a ferocious force and a primal-sounding retch.

Alex should have recognized the signs. The deep breaths, the swaying. He should have known it was coming, but he stood back shell shocked. Fortunately, she'd managed to turn away from him. It wouldn't have been his first time being puked on, but he was thankful for small mercies that tonight wasn't one of those times. Christ, it sounded like the woman was exorcising the devil from her body. Self-induced or not, he couldn't help feeling bad for her.

With the violent episode at an end, Quinn straightened on shaky legs holding the back of her hand to her mouth.

"Sorry," she mumbled. "I feel better now, I think." She gave him a weak smile and tried to step towards the door, but she swayed heavily to one side before barely being able to right herself.

Alex had two choices. Leave the lass to fend for herself, which at the moment looked like a highly improbable task or he could get even more involved than he regretfully already was.

11
Even If You Begged

Damn it all to hell. He strode up beside her and caught a secure arm around her waist hiking her to him. He helped her through the revolving glass doors. Fortunately, it was late, and only the concierge was about. But he immediately looked up at them from the front desk alarm written all over his pinched face.

"It's fine," Alex reassured him giving him a look indicating that he should not get involved. "She's no' feeling well. I'm just going to help her to her room." The balding spindly concierge looked uncertain but thankfully just nodded.

"Where's yer room, Ms. West?"

"Sergeant Mackenzie." She looked up at him, her drunkenness more apparent in the light of the inn. As if trying to concentrate, her pretty arched brows snapped together. "I have an idea." Her words were subtly slurred.

Lord help him, he did not want to hear her inebriated idea, he could only imagine. Alex adjusted his grip on her as she was fairly dead weight leaning against him now.

"Just tell me yer room number," he ordered, hoping to God the stubborn lass would just acquiesce for once.

She pouted coyly at his gruffness. "I will tell you my room number if..." She stretched out the word "if," and Alex dreaded what was on the other side of it.

"You carry me," she said delightedly albeit drunkenly. She promptly rolled her ankle failing to balance on her high heels any longer, but he tightened his grip on her so she wouldn't stumble. The concierge was watching them intently, and Alex was regretting his decisions tonight. This all could have been avoided if he hadn't gone to The Purple Deer in the first place. But he almost shuddered to think if he hadn't been there when those arseholes surrounded her. Christ, this woman was going to drive him mad.

"Fine," he agreed, deciding it was the quickest way to get this over with. "What's the room number?"

"It's just down the hall, 108," she said grinning up at him like she'd just won a hand at a poker.

Alex unceremoniously dipped down and deftly looped an arm around her thighs while nudging his shoulder under her ribs and standing back up to his full height. She squealed in response, but then thankfully quickly relaxed and fell limp, accepting her fate. She was likely too intoxicated to fight him now, thank God. Alex could only imagine the reaction of the nervous concierge. He could practically feel the feeble man's eyes burrowing into his back.

Noting her skirt had hiked up, with the strictest work mode manner he could muster, he snatched at the hem and yanked it back down over her well-rounded behind. He stalked down the hallway, trying his best to ignore her mumbling about how she didn't mean for him to carry her like Santa's sack of toys or some such thing.

They got to her door, and he placed her down as fast as he'd picked her up. "Where's yer card key?" His tone was terse.

"In my pocket," she replied, playfully making no attempt to retrieve it as she threw him flirty bedroom eyes.

"Which pocket?" Alex was exhausted and struggling with the fact that Quinn West's drunk girl attempts at flirting with him were somehow penetrating through his expert-level lass immunity. Alex's teeth were practically grinding with the tension woven through his clenched jaw.

Lifting her hands in an "I don't know" gesture tugged on Alex's last nerve. Rightly or wrongly, he reached for both coat pockets to feel for the card. Thankfully, he found it quickly. Tapping it on the keypad, he opened the door, and with remarkable dexterity the lass sauntered away from him into the room, peeling off her high heels and jacket, and, lord help him, she casually yanked her blouse up over her head discarding it on the floor as she went.

Alex felt a trickle of sweat slide down his back as he stood at the door. He needed to leave. Now. Scanning the room from the door, looking for anything that would be of concern, he finally said gruffly, "Ye'll be okay then?"

"Mm-hmm," she murmured, not even glancing back at him as she walked into the bathroom. "Don't let the door hit you on the way out, Sergeant Mackenzie," she threw him one last jab.

Seriously? That's what he gets for helping her? The lass was a bloody handful, and Alex had to bite his tongue to hold back a retort. Nothing would please him more than to sprint out of her room before he wrung her pretty little neck, but instead, he waited and then heard what sounded like water and teeth brushing coming from the open-door bathroom.

Satisfied that she wasn't at risk of accidentally drowning in the tub or falling and smacking her head on a nightstand, he was about to take his cue and leave when she poked her head around the corner with a crinkle between her brows.

"You're still here? I may be a little tipsy, but I'm not going to sleep with you if that's what you're thinking," she said as if it were the most ludicrous idea in the world.

Alex would have laughed at her outrageous comment, but he was too stunned. His cocky gaze narrowed on her. "I dinnae sleep with drunk women, and trust me, little lass, I wouldnae sleep with ye even if ye begged."

The last thing he heard was her incredulous scoff as he turned and strode out of her room, savouring the finality of the door slamming behind him.

The concierge's eyes nervously watched as Alex came out from the hallway into the main lobby. "All good, she'll be fine." He tried to sound professional despite the fact the jittery man just witnessed Alex hauling the woman over his shoulder to her room.

Alex peeled out of the parking lot eager to put some much-needed distance between himself and that pain in the arse woman. Christ, what a night.

12
The Morning After the Night Before

When Quinn awoke in the morning with a splitting headache, she immediately looked over and felt relieved to see Meg and Belle safe in the other bed. Last night was fuzzy in her mind, and once her head hit the pillow, she'd slept like the dead. Quinn lay there in the quiet of the morning trying to piece together the events of the night. Ugh, she cringed as the memories trickled back to her. Trying to push them and her pounding headache from her mind, she drifted back to sleep.

Later that morning, once everyone was awake, they headed to the hotel restaurant for a greasy breakfast to chase off the hangovers they were all suffering from. "Sooo, what happened with the guys after I left?" Quinn asked taking a bite of her bacon. "I want details."

"Nothing much for me. We had a good time dancing, but meh. Meg and I left not long after you," Belle said, sprinkling a solid layer of salt and pepper over her eggs Benedict.

Megan was smiling to herself as she absently picked at her scrambled eggs.

"Spill it, Megs," Quinn quipped, having noticed her friend's light-hearted demeanour since they'd gotten up.

"Well," she said, looking up from under her golden brow, "we exchanged numbers, and Travis has been texting me all morning." Her cheeks flushed and she beamed like a kid on Christmas morning.

"Ooh, so it was a good night then." Quinn said, excited for her friend. In fairness, it was a rare occasion if Megan did not exchange numbers with a guy at the bar—if not a few guys. More often than not, it ended at the phone number exchange. The fact that they were still texting the morning after was a good sign.

"We had a fun night from what I remember of it." She laughed. "Ugh, the hangover sucks, but I think I kinda like him." A flush of pink crept on her apple cheeks.

"Shit, I had no idea you were into him. I thought you were just drunk making out. Now I feel kinda bad for making you leave," Belle glanced up between shovelling forkfuls of ketchup-laden hash browns into her mouth.

Meg snickered. "It was probably good you dragged me outta there before the ugly lights came on. I drank way too much." She quivered.

"You were pretty hammered, getting you into an Uber was not fun." Belle grimaced.

"Sorry, babes. Thanks for getting me home safely." Megan patted her leg and leaned a head on her hoody-clad shoulder.

Belle was still grinning. "Yeah, yeah, you owe me, Megan Mitchel."

Meg attempted to gulp down her orange juice and nearly choked on a festive sprig of rosemary. Sputtering, she whipped the offending herb out onto the table. "God-damn Christmas everywhere," she muttered.

Belle and Quinn eyed her and laughed.

Swallowing the last of her juice in dramatic fashion, her eyes narrowed on Quinn. "What about you, Quinn? How did you get back to the inn? I didn't even know you'd left. It was like a blizzard when we got out. I feel kinda bad you left on your own."

Quinn flashed back to the night before and rubbed a hand over her eyes feeling embarrassed.

"I was fine. I ended up getting a ride."

"With who?" Belle asked wide-eyed. Her fork full of creamy eggs Benedict paused mid-air.

"Take a guess," Quinn said, putting her napkin over her plate, deciding she was done eating.

Megan and Belle both stared at her dumbfounded.

"Did you meet someone last night too? The last I saw you, you were dancing by yourself in your own world," Meg teased her.

"Nope, I didn't meet anyone in the bar. Well, unless you count the sweet crazy women in the girl's washroom who fed me shooters." She scoffed.

"Bar washroom friends are the best." Meg grinned knowingly.

"Then who the heck drove you back here?" Belle asked, a perplexed look in her dark eyes.

"I know! I know!" Meg said excitedly. "Hot Cop!"

Quinn nodded.

"Wait, what? Really?" Meg sobered.

"Noo!" Belle said at the same time. Both her girls just stared at her from across the table, wide-eyed.

Quinn laughed at their deer-in-the-headlight expressions. "I know, crazy, right?" She fiddled with a paper packet of sugar.

"Right, start at the beginning. We want every gory detail!" Meg picked up her tiny hotel coffee mug and sipped intently.

Quinn told them everything starting with the guy who spilled his drink on her.

"So the second time he caught you, you think he held his arms around you longer than necessary?" Belle asked, needing further clarification as to every exact detail.

"I don't know. Well, yes, I think so. I mean, it was longer than the first time."

"And it felt good?" Megan grinned conspiratorially.

Quinn rolled her eyes and then scrunched them closed. She wasn't going to lie to her friends. They'd call her out if she even tried. "A bit," she conceded.

"And he smelled good?" Belle's black-brown eyes burrowed into Quinn's, waiting for confirmation.

"Yes." She sighed heavily in resignation. "So good. Like peppermint and cedar wood and fresh yummy spiciness." She bit her lip. "But then things took a turn, I wasn't feeling very well."

"Please, for the love of God, tell me you didn't puke," Meg said her nostrils flared in apparent distaste.

Quinn folded tiny corners on the sugar packet. "I puked," she said in a barely-there voice.

"Uh, God. In front of him?" Meg was incredulous.

"And you are a terrible puker. You always sound like a freight train is roaring out of you. It's kind of terrifying." Belle quivered as she simultaneously ran her forkful of food over the last of the hollandaise sauce and ketchup on her plate and popped it into her mouth.

"Thanks, Belle." Quinn shot her a look.

"It's true, Quinn. We've witnessed it more than once. It's nasty when you puke." Meg waved for the server's attention as she was about to walk by. "Can I get another orange juice and hot coffee? This one's gone cold."

"Right away, hun," the bubbly server said.

"Thanks. Oh, could you leave out the green herb thing from the orange juice this time?"

"Not a problem. Can I get anyone else anything?" she said brightly as she deftly cleared their finished breakfast dishes, expertly stacking them in her hands.

"I'll have a coffee too, with eight creams, please. Oh, and one of those Christmas strudel things," Belle said, sliding her cleaned-off plate to the side. Quinn and Meg gawked at her, wide-eyed. "What?" she shrugged, her silky black hair bobbing.

Quinn shook her head with a smile.

"Where were we?" Belle said after the server walked away.

"Nasty puke," Meg supplied looking pointedly at Quinn.

"Right, fine, whatever, I nasty puked in front of him!" Quinn snapped.

Meg and Belle both looked like they smelled something off, and Quinn rolled her eyes.

"It's okay, Quinn. He's a cop. I'm sure he's seen worse." Belle reached across the table and patted her hand.

"So then what happened?" Meg asked, and Quinn somewhat reluctantly continued the story. In one way, it felt good to talk it through, but it also made her cringe, recalling all the sordid details. What he must think of her. Not that she should care.

"I can't believe he actually physically carried you. I didn't think cops would be allowed to even do that." Belle leaned back in the leather booth seat.

Quinn shrugged. "I don't know, but he didn't carry me in the nice way," she said as if that were the real issue.

"Yeah, Belle, he didn't carry her like a bride to their honeymoon suite," Meg added mockingly.

Quinn groaned, still stinging with the embarrassment of it all. "God, I hope I never see him again." She laid her head on the table.

"You could still change your mind and come with us back to B.C. for Christmas," Belle said, not missing a beat.

Meg shot her a disapproving look and turned to Quinn. "You have to see him again!"

Quinn sat back up looking at Meg skeptically. "I'd rather die."

"What happened when he got you to the room?" Meg and Belle both eagerly awaited her answer.

Quinn hated the memory of it. She'd been so drunk, but his words came back to her. "Nothing happened," she said.

"Nothing at all?" Belle pushed.

Quinn picked up a fresh napkin from the stash at the side of the table, and she tore at it, ripping off little pieces. "I told him he should leave because I wasn't going to sleep with him."

"You said that?" Belle bit out, shocked. The server girl returned with the drinks and Danish.

Once she was out of earshot, Quinn leaned in across the table. "And he told me he didn't sleep with drunk women and wouldn't sleep with me even if I begged."

"Fuck off. He did not say that." Megan nearly choked on her OJ.

"Told you he's an ass," Quinn chirped, crumpling the remainder of napkin in her hand.

Her girls went suspiciously quiet. Quinn looked up at them. "What?"

"Belle and I saw it the other day. There is something between you two. I still think he likes you. There is no way a cop just gives someone a ride out of the goodness of their heart."

"Oh my God! Did you not just hear what I said? He basically told me I'd be the last woman in the world he'd ever sleep with!"

"Yeah, but only after you said you weren't going to sleep with him. He had to save face," Belle argued. "Cops don't just drive people around out of the goodness of their hearts."

"He was protecting me from those guys and the freezing weather," Quinn protested, "Trust me, he doesn't like me. And I told you I puked in front of him."

"Yes, yes, the puke is unfortunate, but he could have abandoned you then and he didn't," she said slyly like she cracked some secret code.

"Megs." Quinn straightened in her seat and looked at her friend with her very best 'I'm deadly serious' expression. "I do not like him, he does not like me. Never mind that I made an utter ass of myself."

"Perhaps you need to stop by the station today. Maybe bring in some doughnuts? Cops love doughnuts." Megan leaned back in her chair and slugged down her orange juice as if she hadn't heard a word Quinn had just said.

Quinn stared at her like she was nuts. Belle piped up then too, "Perhaps take just a coffee. You already know he likes coffee. You could go to that same cafe we saw him at."

"Girls! What? No," Quinn snapped. "Why on earth would I go to the station? Did you not hear anything I just said?"

Meg rolled her eyes. "Oh my God, Quinn." She laughed an incredulous gleam in her eyes. She reached across the table and grabbed Quinn's hands to make Quinn look at her. "Listen to me Quinn. Hot Cop drove you back to the inn, caught you twice, didn't run when you monster puked, and then carried you safely to your room. He likes you."

"And told me he'd never ever sleep with me." Quinn pulled away from Megan's grip slouching back in her seat. "Megs, he's a cop. That's what they do—help people. It's his job," Quinn huffed. She couldn't understand why her friends didn't get it.

Meg shook her head in resignation while Belle inhaled deeply as if to garner patience. "Quinn, cops do not drive people home from the bar. " Her eyes were intense on Quinn, willing her to understand. "They arrest people, they drive them to the drunk tank, they might even hail them a cab. But they do not drive them home."

"So why'd he drive me home then?" Quinn challenged.

"Because he's into you!" Megan joined back into the argument, leaning towards Quinn over the table.

"And you are into him," Belle added pointing an accusatory slender finger at Quinn.

"Well, it doesn't matter anyway. He's going away on holiday, so he's not even going to be at the police station or in Calen at all. Thank God!" she uttered. "I admit that he's hot—and yes maybe I got a little ahead of myself last night—but I'm going to blame those last two vodka shots! Trust me, though, he is not my type. He's not nice, and I told him so. And believe me, even though he drove me back to the inn, I'm 99 percent sure it was to give him more time to berate me. He was so rude about me petting his dog and about my clothes, and about not sleeping with me."

Megan slapped the table. "Quinn Eloise West, you are impossible!"

Quinn shrugged with a cheeky grin. "Meh."

13
It Will Be Okay

"Are you sure you don't want to come back with us? Christmas is only a couple of days away. You know my family would love to see you," Meg said as she zipped closed her hot pink travel case.

"I'd love to see them too, but another time. You know me, I've got it in my head that I want to stay in this little town over Christmas. Something about it just sings to my soul. I want to write and drink Christmas lattes all in this mountainy bliss." Quinn grinned. "I'm used to the solitary life."

"We know damn well there's no convincing you to change your mind once it's set." Belle yanked Quinn into a hug. "We're planning another girl's weekend soon, though," she said as if daring Quinn to argue.

"I can't believe you want to stay here all alone over Christmas." Megs came in for the group hug. Quinn's chin rested on Belle's smooth glossy black hair, as she mightily squeezed Quinn. Belle always hugged like she wasn't going to see you ever again. For such a tiny woman, she hugged like a bear. Meg, being the tallest of the three, wrapped her arms around them both. They all stood embracing in the tiny entry of the inn room. Hugging with her friends always had a way of making Quinn feel more whole somehow. She didn't know what she would do without them.

"At least have Hot Cop." Meg patted Quinn on the back.

"Oh, stop," Quinn chided with a snort. "I'm gonna miss you girls."

"We should make birthday plans. It's the big three-o, this year." Belle gave Quinn a sly grin before turning to the mirror as she smoothed her rumpled hair and checked her red lipstick.

"Ooh that's right," Meg quipped. "Gettin' up there, Quinn."

"Shut it, Megs, you're only a few months behind me." Quinn smacked her butt and she jumped away with a laugh.

"Yeah, yeah, I'm getting up there too. Anyway," Meg sobered, "good luck with the writing and Merry Christmas." She reached out to squeeze Quinn's hand.

Quinn nodded, grateful that her friends understood her so well. "Don't be worried if I'm MIA over the holidays, I'm really gonna try to get in the zone with this. Make it finally happen, you know?"

From the looks on their faces, she knew they understood and supported her fully.

After the girls left, Quinn switched rooms to a smaller less expensive one. The new room felt very empty and quiet without her friends. Snow had been falling on and off all night and she watched from her window as a fairy-like flakes danced about. She considered grabbing her laptop and heading to a coffee shop, but the thought of possibly running into Mean Hot Cop turned her off the idea. Instead, she grabbed her backpack and readied it for a hike. Despite being a bit of a late start in the day for a hike, it felt like exactly what she wanted—what she craved right now. She needed to clear her head, and being out in nature, moving her body was the best way to do that.

Breathing in the fresh mountain air, Quinn let it feed her soul. She continued to hike up the trail, snow crunching beneath her boots. This was exactly what she needed to clear the cobwebs. The snow was falling in masses of fluffy flakes like some kind of Christmas wonderland. Despite thick snow making it tougher to trudge along the trail, Quinn felt alive pushing her limits. Her blood was pumping and her breathing was heavy, but she was in the zone. She felt invigorated. It wasn't even a consideration to turn back. She was determined to reach the summit.

Seemingly out of nowhere, the wind whipped up. Not uncommon in the mountains, but it blew so hard that it made it almost impossible to keep moving. Quinn stopped to catch her breath and decide what to do. It didn't look like she'd be summiting the mountain today after all. She tried to look around, but the wind had become so harsh and biting and the snow so thick that it was next to impossible to see. Disappointing as it was, it was time to head back down and call the hike. She suspected if the weather had stayed good, she'd likely hit the summit within the next forty minutes. It was frustrating, but she couldn't keep going now in this, it would be stupid to push her luck.

She'd barely noticed that the white sky of the day had now turned to the blue-grey of dusk. She looked at her phone. 4:00 p.m. At this time of year this far north, the sun set early. Definitely time to head back down. The cold began to seep into her, which was not ideal as she was a good couple of hours away from the base. Trying not to think of the cold, she tried to move a little faster, but with the fresh thickening snow, it was slow going.

Quinn carefully made her way back down the mountain trail. She had been grateful for the new hiking boots she'd bought as they gripped the snow so well, but now her feet were starting to get cold.

It felt like she'd barely made any progress as the harsh wind and snow forced her to look down most of the way. Her toes were feeling numb, and it was getting dark quickly. All the while, the temperature seemed to be plummeting.

"Shit," she whispered. She stopped again and looked around her not feeling sure of exactly which direction to head in. The trail that she'd been on was whitewashed with snow, she questioned if she was even on a trail at all anymore.

Quinn carefully pulled out her phone from the zip pocket in her coat. She had to lean close to a tree to shelter from the thrashing wind. Pulling off her glove, with shaking fingers she typed *the Calen Mountain Inn* into a maps app. No service. Panic crept to the edge of her mind, and she tried to take some calming breaths. Her fingers were freezing from being exposed, so she quickly shoved her phone back into her pocket and pulled her glove back on. It was impossible to see anything as she tried to look around and get her bearings. The wind and snow bit at her face, and she automatically tucked her chin down into her coat to try and protect herself.

At this point, she was freezing, and it had become clear she was stuck on a mountain in a full-on blizzard. This was not good. A little wave of terror snaked through her. Despite the loud whipping of the wind and snow, she could hear her own breathing rapid and shallow. Her heart seemed to pound in her ears.

"It's going to be okay," she whispered needing to reassure herself. She tried again to look around her to get her bearings. If only she could make out the trail, maybe she could make it down, but every direction was just a white snowy blizzard. Trying to move in any direction could be lethal. If she tried she could literally fall off the side of a mountain. She couldn't tell what direction anything was in.

What to do? What to do? Panic was a heartbeat away, but Quinn fought to keep it at bay. She needed to find some kind of shelter from the wind. Maybe she could wait out the worst of the storm. Her heart was racing, but she did her best to try to stay calm. She concentrated on taking slow deep breaths, but the frigid air didn't help her swirling thoughts. *It will be okay*, she told herself again.

Quinn could just barely make out a nearby dark patch through the blowing snow. Trees. She carefully dug through the snow and got herself under the canopy of the nearby pine boughs. It gave her a bit of shelter from the roaring wind, but she was wet with sweat from the exertion of the hike and now she felt bitterly cold. Pulling out her phone again, she prayed for service. Nothing. She could've cried. This was about survival now. The surreal realization struck her, and she forced herself to wiggle her numb toes in her boots trying to keep them from totally icing up. Then she breathed into her cold hands, the warmth of breath painfully fleeting. She huddled into a tight ball. As much as she tried to be calm knowing that panic wouldn't help, she felt scared. With every passing minute, her fear grew. Her mind raced, trying to think what she could do and feeling regret that she hadn't turned back sooner. What had she been thinking?

It felt like she sat huddled for ages. Time seemed to stand still, and all the while her anxiety grew exponentially. Her efforts to stay calm were futile. The cold wind was savage despite the shelter of the tree boughs. Tears stung her eyes as she hunched up shivering, praying for a miracle.

A distinct sniffing sound snapped her out of her anxious-ridden reverie. Darkness had settled in, and all the while, the snow and wind were relentless. Her ears strained towards the sniffing. Quinn sat stone still except for her heart which pounded like a beating drum in her chest. A Bear. She didn't think things could get worse, but apparently they could. This was the Canadian Rockies. Bears were a very real threat.

"Fuck, fuck, fuck," she silently breathed. With frozen hands that didn't seem to want to work, she desperately dug through her bag to find her bear spray. She felt its cool smooth cylinder in her bag, and a brief relief washed over her. She quickly grabbed it and held it ready.

Her heart was pounding furiously in her ears. Her body shook with cold and adrenaline. Why hadn't she just stayed at the inn and worked on her book? What she wouldn't give to be back at the warm cozy inn now. Regret stabbed cruelly at her.

The sniffing became more intense. She'd never been so terrified in all her life, and she tried in vain to steady her frayed nerves. Something snapped inside her and fear suddenly rolled into anger. *Not today Bear*, she thought, ready for battle.

14
Santa's House. Somewhere in the North Pole.

QUINN WAS NOT GONNA go down today. She had too much life left to live, damn it, and she had a novel to write. More scared and more determined than she'd ever been in her life, she waited.

Holding steady on the trigger, her finger itching to press and let it fly, the sniffing grew closer. When the sniffing gave way to raucous barking, she nearly flew twenty feet in the air. For a brief moment, Quinn's panicked mind jumped to a wolf, but then sweet relief washed over her when she realized it was a dog. *A dog*. She could have cried. The bear spray dropped out of her hand as her body slumped with relief. It was a dog barking, and just like that, fear was replaced with hope. It suddenly dawned on her how stupid she'd been. It was winter. Bears hibernate in the winter. The cold must be numbing not only her body but her brain.

A tawny masked face with a black snout poked through the pine boughs sniffing at her and then the head of a German Shepherd nudged past the boughs and excited golden brown eyes took in the sight of her. Quinn's heart nearly burst. Never had she been so glad to see a dog, and he looked as if he'd found a missing toy, he was so pleased with himself. The sweet furry beast barked excitedly at finding her. She laughed as her body coursed with pent-up adrenaline. Reaching out, she let him sniff her before she ruffled his ears.

"Hello, Beautiful," she cooed.

"C'mon, outta there." She heard a man's voice call. Another wave of relief washed over her. Oh, thank God, a person! Her furry newfound friend rushed off at the call of his master. The wind and snow were still swirling like a tempest, but Quinn quickly got herself out of her makeshift shelter.

"Wait," she cried out, hearing the panic in her voice. The blessed dog bounded back to her. She could just make out a large dark figure coming towards her. Her mind briefly flew to Mean Hot Cop, but there was no way in hell she'd run into him up here.

"I'm lost," she called out over the roar of the wind.

The figure approached her, but it was hard to see much other than his size in the blowing snow and darkness of the evening.

"Come." His voice was calm through the whipping of the wind. It didn't matter to her that he was a total stranger and could be an axe murderer for all she knew. He was her only hope tonight, so she followed him without question.

The world had become a dizzying snow globe with no clear direction, but somehow, the man seemed to know where he was going. It wasn't easing keeping up while he moved almost stealthily through thick snow, but Quinn worked hard to stay close on his heels. She wasn't going to risk losing sight of her only hope of survival tonight.

It felt like they trudged through the blowing snow for ages. Her toes had lost feeling, and she felt exhausted. Quinn looked up as they came across a log cabin. It seemed like a mirage after the hellish hike. Emotion swept through her at seeing a warm light glowing through the window. She could've wept at the site. The past couple of hours of her life had been so intense, so surreal. She'd genuinely wondered if she'd freeze to death if this would be her last day on this earth. She shuttered thinking about it. It was hard to process all that had occurred.

"Oh, thank God." She let out a shaky breath.

The man got the door open and let her in. Quinn almost lost her footing as her dog saviour barrelled past her. The first thing her eyes took in was a modest fire crackling in a stone fireplace. From her current perspective, she was certain that it was the most beautiful and welcoming sight she'd ever laid eyes on. Despite being colder than she ever knew was possible, the relief of being inside this warm inviting cabin spread over her like a drizzle of hot caramel on an ice cream sundae.

"Here come, take off yer coat and warm by the fire. I'll make ye a hot drink." *Oh, shit.* That voice. That accent. The cop. *No way.* She thought he was supposed to be on holiday. Her stomach sank. God, she was an idiot. She spied him as he pulled off his snow gear. How did she not recognize him sooner? That tall broad frame. *His* dog. Good Lord, her brain really must be frozen.

15
The Thaw

PART OF HER BRAIN cringed, but a bigger part was too damn cold and fragile to care. God, what were the chances though? She watched his broad form as he walked to the kitchen and memories of the night before jumbled in her mind.

Feeling too many things all at once, her body shivered still not accepting the warmth of being inside. There was a wooden bench at the front door. She slid down onto it and tried to will her frozen fingers to work so she could get her boots untied. Fingers fumbling, she was not getting anywhere. Mean Hot Cop approached her, towering above her where she sat fighting frustrated tears.

"Ye're freezing lass." He knelt in front of her, taking her frozen hands in his. He cupped his large hands around hers and blew warm breath onto them. Quinn welcomed the warmth, but his gentle compassion overwhelmed her. It was the last thing she expected from him.

She felt spent and on the edge of a tidal wave of emotion, barely contained.

Hot Cop continued to blow hot breath onto her hands and gently rubbed them in his. Sweet relief began to trickle through her as her hands thawed under his ministrations.

"Thank you." Her voice shook. Tears pricked her eyes. She could've died out there, the thought was sobering. The cold still seemed to have its grip on her, but it was getting better and she felt safe now. Safe with him.

He glanced up at her face for the first time, and Quinn saw in his intense blue eyes the instant he recognized her. She braced herself, fearing he'd turn into Mean Cop again—disapproving and cold. She felt so frayed and was already so cold. She'd probably crack if he did.

"Where are your friends?" he asked concerned, tension etching between his dark brows.

"Oh no, they weren't with me." She assured him realizing he must have assumed she'd been hiking with her friends, and they were still out there. Thank God, that was not the case. "They headed home this morning. I was hiking alone..." Her voice trailed off. Regret bit at her, she should have stayed at the inn. Worked on her novel. She should have known better than to hike alone, not to have turned around when the snow got thick.

He didn't say a word as he let go of her hands. Quinn felt a harsh stab of disappointment, but then to her surprise, he went to work untying her boots. She tried to contain the flood of emotions that were threatening to consume her. Perhaps it was all the pent-up adrenaline, but his kindness was hitting every emotional cord in her.

Exhausted and cold, she just watched him as he silently worked. It was strange to see the hulking muscled man kneeling before her. He wore a dark long-sleeved fitted shirt, and she could make out almost every detail of his perfectly sculpted shoulders and biceps. His head was down as he focused on the task of her boots which allowed her to take in his thick clean-cut dark hair with a little extra messy length on the top. Even now, she couldn't deny that she found him stupidly hot. This time, it was maybe his kindness that made him even more appealing though. He seemed far from the jerk cop she'd witnessed. When he realized it was her he'd rescued, she'd half expected him to kick her out of his cabin. But instead, he was seemingly taking care of her, and she found herself truly grateful.

Quinn had always been a strong independent woman. She'd had to be. Despite everything life had thrown at her and all she had faced, she always found the silver linings. But she had never experienced anything like tonight. On that mountain under the branches, while the wind and snow were a torrent around her, she genuinely feared that she might freeze to death before getting out. To be so completely at the mercy of her environment, with her very existence on the line, left her feeling as tenuous as an icicle in the late winter's sun.

The man kneeling in front of her had rescued her—saved her life. Overwhelmed by a vulnerability that shook her to her core, she found herself completely surrendering to his care. She'd done her best to stay strong on that mountain, but now she felt the strength she'd held onto so tightly begin to melt away under his touch and kindness. For once, she let go of the need to be strong. Her energy was zapped, and her strength felt depleted. Somehow, instead of feeling weak though, she felt herself mindlessly relax into his warm care. Until this moment, she wouldn't have known how to allow someone to take care of her, but she had nothing left to resist his help—and she didn't want to.

He gently held her leg as he helped her slide one foot at a time out of her winter hiking boots. She whimpered as the pain of frozen toes bit at her. They throbbed as they now slowly began to thaw.

"Ye were out there for quite a while," he stated matter-of-factly, handling her frozen feet with care to avoid worsening her discomfort.

Alex could tell the lass had been through an ordeal. In the brief interactions he'd had with her, this was the quietest he'd known her to be. He could sense that she was processing the experience she had gone through. Likely she was in a bit of shock. It disturbed him to think what would have happened if Bear hadn't found her. Alex felt a wave of protectiveness. He had to fight the urge to wrap his arms around the lass. God, he was relieved that she was there safe with him. He silently vowed that he'd take care of her and not let any harm come to her.

Being as careful as he could, he gently slid off her thick wool socks from one foot and then the other. Her bare frozen feet rested on his thighs just above his knees. When he pressed his warm hands onto them, it struck him how fully his hands engulfed her wee feet. *Good*, he thought, *all the better to warm them*.

The lass's feet were vivid red and white in some parts. To his chagrin, Alex also noted the cherry red polish that adorned the feminine feet in his hands, reminding him of his unbidden attraction to her.

"I dinnae think they are frostbitten. Do ye huv any pain, lass?

Quinn nodded. "A bit, they feel burny and like they are throbbing."

"Likely ye'll be okay once we get ye warmed through," he said as he took care to gently rub each foot.

"That feels good." She sighed, and Alex glanced up at her face still wrapped in the hood of her coat.

Her eyes were closed and she had the most beautiful pleasure-filled expression on her face, and without warning, Alex envisioned her under him looking similarly as he slowly glided in and out of her. Swallowing, he forced his eyes away and set her feet gently back down as he stood up. Thoughts like that were dangerous, and he needed to leash them in immediately. The woman needed his help, and he'd be wise to keep his focus on that.

"Come, lass, let's get ye by the fire." He held out a hand to help her up, and it felt impossible not to notice how delicate and distinctly feminine her hand felt in his. Christ, it brought out every masculine urge in him to protect her like some kind of gallant knight from the fourteenth century. When she faltered with a whimper of pain and grabbed onto his arm to steady herself, somewhere deep in his core, he intuitively understood, like trusting the sun rises in the east, that there was nothing he wouldn't do to protect this lass and keep her out of harm's way.

Not letting himself think on it, he instead focused on the task at hand. "Let me help ye," he said, and she nodded trustingly. It broke him that she stood about as stable as a newborn kitten.

Alex didn't ask. He just took control and scooped the lass up into his arms. Perhaps he should have thought it through as he had to steel himself not to appreciate the feel of her petite, curvy body nestled so perfectly against him.

They looked at each other face to face.

"It's easiest, aye?" he asked, belatedly realizing he hadn't cleared it with her.

16
Alex's Cafe

Quinn immediately felt bereft as his arms released her. The absence of his warmth and strength around her felt visceral. God and his scent. She could happily keep her nose shoved in his neck until the New Year. That fresh woodsy spicy scent did things to her and her lady bits. Regretfully, he'd already stepped away from her, so she tucked her legs up under her and sank into the chair that hugged her like a well-worn glove.

It felt as though the chill in her bones would never ease. As he added logs to the fireplace, Quinn was mesmerized. The man looked like he could be a model for a sexy spread in *Woodsmen Magazine* or something. All ruggedly handsome with a full day's stubble on his strong jaw and muscles bulging under his fitted long-sleeve T. This was the first time she'd seen him without his intimidating black uniform, and the woodsy guy effect was downright delicious. All that rugged gruffness was hot. And he'd been kind to her. Not something she would have expected from him. Quinn watched him, realizing that perhaps he wasn't so bad after all. Had she misjudged him?

The new logs he put in the grate crackled and snapped as fire licked at them. The glorious heat radiated blissfully through her. Quinn willed herself to finally pull off the hood of her coat and her toque. Then she unzipped her coat, and a fresh shiver quaked through her. It was wet from all the snow, but at the same time, it was a warm wetness that made her reluctant to pull it off of her chilled body even though she knew she needed to.

Steeling herself, she peeled off her coat and snow pants as quickly as her cold limbs would allow. Left with her teeth chattering again as she sat in her long-sleeved shirt and black leggings, she was still glad to be rid of the wet outer layers. He must have noticed her shivering because he pulled a blanket from a hall closet and strode back, handing it to her.

"Thank you," she said, looking up at his face as she greedily pulled the blanket up under her chin. He caught her eye and held her gaze, and something seemed to pass between them. Quinn half feared he'd say something to make her feel even more stupid than she already did or that the spell of kindness would be broken, but as he looked at her, she saw no disapproval in his stormy blue eyes. Instead, there was something more akin to concern.

"I'll make us some coffee," he said, breaking the moment as he strode back to the kitchen.

"Um, or maybe do you have tea? I'm more of a tea girl. Weird right? Everyone loves coffee, but not me. I think it tastes like mud." She scrunched her nose. "The only way I drink coffee is in a latte. Mmm, like an oat milk eggnog latte—those are divine." She groaned. "Can't even taste the coffee."

"Right, tea it is then," he muttered ignoring her cheer-filled little tirade.

"Thank you." A smile curved her lips as she thought about how delicious a mug of hot tea sounded right now. "Do you have oat milk by any chance and maybe a bit of honey?"

"This isnae a bloody Starbucks," he bit.

"Sorry," she said, fearing his kindness was going to evaporate and Mean Cop might make a comeback. She hastily added, "It's just that dairy makes me sick. I can't have it at all and honey makes everything nicer, but I don't need anything in the tea if you don't have it. I can take it as is. That's fine."

"No dairy, as in no cheese? No ice cream? Ye poor unfortunate soul." He looked at her like she was some kind of alien.

Quinn giggled relieved at his teasing. It was far better than his wrath. "I know, it's heartbreaking, right?"

"I might die without a sharp cheddar in my life," he deadpanned, and Quinn almost snorted.

"I think I do huv some honey somewhere," he added, digging through a cupboard.

"Thanks." She smiled, leaning in towards the fireplace and trying to let its delicious warmth envelop every body part at once. Quinn felt relieved again. For a second, she worried she'd poked the bear. She couldn't handle confrontation right now, she craved the kindness and care he had been so openly giving her. Bear, his German Shepherd, laid his head in her lap, and Quinn absently petted his soft black-brown ears and stared into the fire basking in its heat. It felt like she was finally thawing out from the bitter cold that had gripped her in its icy embrace.

Alex filled the kettle for the lass's tea and peered out the window at the blowing snow. He had been out for a hike with Bear when the blizzard had whipped up. They were calling for the "storm of the decade," so he wanted to get in one last good hike before it hit. In the mountains, the weather was unpredictable at the best of times, so he shouldn't have been surprised when the storm arrived in all its fury a good twelve hours ahead of schedule. He was heading back to his cottage when Bear found her. Thank God for his furry beast. It wasn't the first time he'd been deeply grateful for his pup.

When he joined the police force in Canada, he had been given little choice in his partner. The force wanted the advantage of a dog, and, being the new guy, he'd been first in line to take on the duty. At the time, it was far more responsibility than he wanted, but it turned out that Bear was the best partner he could ever have. The dog had crazy instincts and had saved Alex's arse more than once. Glancing back at Quinn, he saw his loyal pup had his head nuzzled right in her lap. Apparently, his dog was oblivious to the troublemaker he was cuddled up with. Where were those killer instincts now? Alex sighed. Poor lass. He had to admit he was relieved she was safe and sound.

Since his trip to Scotland was cancelled and knowing this storm was coming, he'd gone for a large grocery shop this morning. Aside from doubling up on staples, he found it rather satisfying to splurge and buy some of his favourite foods for Christmas. *Why not?* he'd thought. Now, his cupboards and fridge were very well stocked—and a good thing too, given his unexpected house guest.

Alex had been invited to a friend's for Christmas dinner. As much as he appreciated the offer, he was almost relieved the impending weather forecast gave him an excuse to stay home. Time spent up here on the mountain with no work or people always helped clear his mind. The Canadian wilderness had become a part of his soul almost as much as his homeland. It was bloody ironic though that just last night he'd been reflecting on how getting out of town for a week or so would also thankfully quash the chances of running into Quinn West again. But low and behold, here she was…in his cottage. Christ, what kind of shenanigans was the universe playing at?

Pouring himself a hot cup of coffee and throwing in a hearty splash of baileys, he felt a bit bad, reflecting on the fact she couldn't have dairy. No Bailey's for the lass. 'Twas a downright shame. As he let the tea steep on the counter, Alex looked back at the lass huddled up in his favourite leather chair staring pensively at the fire.

Where had she come from? In a few short days, he'd pulled her over and given her a bloody useless ticket, gotten her safely back to her hotel room (something he did not want to think about), rescued her in the "storm of the decade," and now, here she was sitting in his home with his normally incredibly perceptive police dog loving her up like she was the one who paid for his food.

It seemed like an odd set of coincidences. All he knew about her was she was headstrong, talked too much, and that her big brown eyes and full lips were mesmerizing. He swallowed, tearing his gaze from her as he pulled out the tea bag from her mug, squirted in a small blob of honey, then reconsidered and squirted in some more. If she couldn't have Bailey's, she could at least have sweet tea. He stirred it and carried the steamy mugs into the lounge.

She looked up at him as he handed her the tea. Aye, she did have beautiful eyes. He couldn't deny it.

"Thank you." She said softly and Alex's eyes dropped momentarily to her pink full lips. God that mouth. He did his best to clear his head as he sat in his second favourite chair across from her.

"Mmm, it smells like Christmas." She swooned, holding the mug close to her and savouring its warmth.

"It's a Christmas spiced orange tea," he provided by way of explanation.

She eyed him, curious how this big brawny cop who appeared to live alone had a fancy Christmas tea. Somehow, he didn't seem the type. The steam wafted its warm festive scent and Quinn sighed contentedly.

"My mam sends the tea to me every year for Christmas. It's the only tea I have."

Ah, mystery solved, Quinn thought, taking a sip. "It's a Scottish tea then?"

"Aye, I suppose so."

Taking a tentative sip, her lips puckered from the excessive sweetness. "Mmm," she croaked, covering up a cough. The honey completely overwhelmed the flavour, but she wasn't about to complain.

"'Tis good then?" he asked, appearing almost hopeful, and somehow she felt obliged to say it was.

"Mm-hmm," she lied, reasoning that the tea was likely great without the overwhelming amount of honey. "You haven't ever tasted it?"

He glanced at her and raised his mug. "I prefer mud."

She laughed at his reference to her earlier comment about coffee tasting like mud. "But your mom sends you the tea, and you never drink it?" Her full lips were pinched, and her brows knitted together as if she couldn't understand how he couldn't have at least tried it.

He shrugged. "I dinnae throw it out either. I have three boxes of the stuff in the cupboard. If ye like it ye can fill yer boots as they say here."

"I don't know anyone who says that." She scrunched her nose in disapproval and again Quinn noticed a slight quirk in his lips, like he was holding back a smile.

"Are you always so objectionable?" he asked, his lips settled back in a serious line.

"I'm not objectionable!" she huffed frustrated as she'd been trying hard not to be objectionable.

He arched a disbelieving brow.

Quinn ignored it. "You should at least try the tea. Your Mom sent it," she argued, but he didn't look persuaded. "It's like a taste of Scotland," she added, digging her heels in. She took another sip and tried to focus on the flavour beyond the excessive honey.

The low rumble of Mean Hot Cop's laugh took her off guard. "Och, lass, that is no' a taste of Scotland."

She shrugged indifferently, and he looked like he was about to say something but held back. Instead, they both fell into a companionable silence as they sat sipping their warm drinks and watching the logs burn and crackle in the fireplace.

17
The Will of the Snow Gods

Quinn let out a contented little sigh that stole Alex's attention. While she seemed deep in thought staring into the fire, he took the opportunity to study her. It was no wonder Alex found her attractive. Physically, the lass was very bonnie. Auburn brown hair fell just past her shoulders. In the firelight, the glistening strands of rich bronze and copper appeared to be shimmering. A pert nose fit perfectly against the backdrop of soft angled cheekbones and full rosy lips. He was mesmerized as she took a sip of tea, and her pink tongue darted out to lick her lips. As if sensing his eyes on her, she glanced up at him. When he didn't look away, her big brown eyes turned sheepish.

"You must think I'm an idiot." She exhaled, looking down into her mug. "For getting stranded out there." She closed her eyes, and he had no doubt she was reliving the events of the day.

"I dinnae think yer an idiot lass, far from it," Alex replied honestly.

Quinn looked up at him with surprise on her pretty face. Her eyes searched his. He could tell she wasn't sure if she believed him.

"My girls left in the early afternoon to go back to B.C., and I don't know... I hadn't intended to go hiking. I knew it was late in the day, but I guess I just craved getting out. And these mountains are just so dang gorgeous. It's like they beckoned me." She swirled the tea in her mug and stared down at it as if it was showing her the playback of her harrowing day.

Alex could relate to the need to get out in the fresh mountain air. He'd felt the same way today. These mountains often beckoned him too. He stayed quiet though and let her be with her thoughts.

"Well, and you know about my night." She looked at him awkwardly, a moment later.

Recalling what he'd said to her the night before, he felt like an ass. Shite, he shouldn't have said what he did to her. It was a low blow, and he knew it. Memories of the night before flickered in his mind—their almost kiss and all the other parts that should have never happened. Just recalling it made his pulse kick up a notch. It was dangerous territory. He definitely did not want to talk about last night, and he was silently grateful when she didn't elaborate.

"I think I just needed to move and get some fresh air," she said, "and it was so sunny and gorgeous earlier in the day. I didn't even pay attention to the fact it was snowing pretty hard when I started the hike." The remorseful look in her big brown eyes made him wish he had the power to steal away her regrets.

"I was so in the zone. You know?" she said as more of a statement than a question, but he did know. Nothing better than the zone.

"Then the weather seemed to turn bitter in a flash. I should've turned back sooner." She shook her head. "The snow had been coming down thick for a while. It was stupid of me to keep going."

There was remorse in every pretty feature.

"I got caught in it too," he said with a dispassionate shrug. "The storm was expected but no' until well after midnight. The weather can change in a flash in the mountains, but this storm kicked from zero to sixty faster than I've ever known."

Alex was disarmed when the lass looked up at him. Her big brown eyes were filled with warmth that seemed to spread over his skin.

He could've scolded, he could've disapproved, or he could've agreed with her assessment of her stupidity. She half expected him to, but he did none of those things. And she found her heart a little lighter.

"Proper winter clothing." She grinned, gesturing to her pile of winter gear.

"Aye," he said as his lips tugged in a smile obviously catching her reference to his comment from the evening before.

It was the second time she'd seen him smile, and it was like the sun bursting through the clouds after a storm. There was absolutely zero possibility now of denying that the man was ridiculously hot. Breathtaking really. Wow. He was far from the intimidating Mean Cop now.

To her surprise, he actually seemed likeable. Perhaps out of uniform, he let that cold Mean Cop guard down. Although she hadn't forgotten his jerk comment when he'd left her room last night, nor would she. It stung more than she cared to admit. It felt good that they seemed to have found a truce, but she'd be wise to remember that he wasn't attracted to her like she was to him. So be it.

For now, Quinn was feeling toasty and contented. Her worries were at bay. It seemed she had all the feeling back in her feet and hands too. Thank goodness. She'd gotten used to the sickly sweet tea and found it had kind of grown on her by the time she took her last sip. Mug empty and as pleasant as the situation had somehow become, she decided it was time to head back to the inn. Unfolding her stiff legs from beneath her, she gingerly stood up, getting to her feet, she stretched out her arms above her.

"I should get back to the inn. Do you have a landline so I can call an Uber?" she asked, not wanting to put him out.

Alex laughed. "Uber's dinnae come up here."

"Oh right." She bit her lip, concern winding through her as she contemplated how she would get back to the inn.

Not moving from his chair, he sat back looking amused. She had a feeling he knew what she was about to ask. She just hoped their newfound civility would hold.

"Would you possibly be able to drive me back then?" she asked him sweetly.

Without a word, he lifted himself out of the chair and took her empty mug from the tree stump end table as he did. Standing facing her, Quinn felt a little shiver of awareness race through her.

God, he was big, and when he stood towering over, for some reason, it tickled her horny side. She felt her cheeks heat as her mind flickered back to him carrying her to the chair and how his thickly muscled arms lifted her like she weighed nothing even in all her wet winter wear. That was when she caught his piercing blue eyes on hers, and her stomach did a little flip-flop as she felt certain that he knew where her thoughts had gone.

"I'm sorry, lass, but nobody is going anywhere for a while."

The words were exactly what her perked-up nipples and tingling nether regions wanted to hear, but from the look in his eyes, she knew the intent was far different from her body's interpretation.

"How long is a while?" she asked, feeling her stomach knot.

He shrugged casually oblivious to the emotions whirring inside her. "Hard to say exactly."

"Mm-hmm. Right." She tried to comprehend what that meant, and then in the next breath, she completely dismissed what he'd said. "Obviously, staying here is not an option. I need to get back to the inn tonight, so how do we make that happen?" She looked at him expectantly.

And there it was, his disapproving cold, Mean Cop look. The one that made her want to kick him in the shins. Without a word, he turned and casually strode back to the kitchen. Quinn felt frustration bubbling in her as she noted that clearly the uniform had nothing to do with the attitude after all.

"There must be a way to get back into town." She didn't even try to keep the exasperation from her voice.

Was the woman mad? She'd just narrowly been rescued from freezing to death in the worst blizzard in a bloody decade, and now she expected to be somehow magically transported back to her inn?

"Have ye looked outside?" he said in a clipped tone.

"Yes, but can't we drive? You must have some kind of four-by-four. This is the mountains. The weather gets bad. You must have a way to get around. Surely things don't just come to a standstill." She ended on a shrill little laugh that made him want to ring her perfectly creamy neck and kiss her senseless all at once.

"We would get stuck before we even started, and it's no' like being in town. We are halfway up a mountain. Visibility is next to zero. Nobody is going anywhere."

"Well, when do you think we can get back to town?" He could see she wasn't going to give up easily.

Alex looked out the kitchen window as if assessing, but he knew the answer without looking, "Depends on when this finally lets up and they get the ploughs going."

"You mean I'm probably going to have to stay the night?" she asked indignantly as if the thought was completely unacceptable.

God, this woman. He took great pleasure in his next statement because he knew it would irritate her pretty little head. "I'd count on staying at least three nights, maybe more."

"*What?*" she shrieked. "Don't be ridiculous! It's the mountains. It snows. We are not in the dark ages, you know. We're not just at the mercy of the snow gods."

He had to hide a smile. The lass was bonny, but when she was fired up? Christ. For such a tiny thing, she was feisty, and the flush on her cheeks made him want to push her farther.

"Last time it snowed like this, it took them five days for them to get up here and do some clearing. So aye, little lass, we are at the mercy of the snow gods."

Those big brown eyes gave away her every emotion, and right now, she looked as though she was going to cry. Alex certainly didn't want that.

"But it's almost Christmas." Her argument was futile, and they both knew it. A growl of frustration erupted from her as she seemed to finally accept the reality of the situation. "And don't call me little."

Alex barely held in a laugh. "Did ye have plans for Christmas then? Ye have a laddie waitin' on ye?" He was mocking her, but something about the idea that it might be true bothered him. Did she have a man in her life?

"No, no, it's just, well, I…" She seemed flustered. Then she abruptly walked over to where she'd abandoned her backpack at the front door. Unzipping it, she pulled out her phone looking at it with sudden desperation, and then she slumped.

"There's no signal up here," he stated, to her utter annoyance.

"Yeah, got that," she said with more sarcasm than she'd intended. Her mind was racing. Was she seriously stuck here with Mean Hot Cop? While he may not be a complete jerk as she'd originally thought—he had rescued her after all—she still found him to be annoyingly mean. Worse yet, he was definitively hot, like superhero hot. Much too hot to be stranded in a cabin with for God only knew how long.

She studied him with a crinkle between her brows. Sergeant Mackenzie now stood in his kitchen, washing their mugs like some kind of domesticated Adonis. It was impossible not to be impressed with his incredibly broad muscular shoulders and those massive biceps tight in his shirt. Jeez Louise. If he were any other guy, she'd jump at the chance to be stuck here with him, but no, this was Mean Hot Cop. The mean part was not to be forgotten about!

"You never said if you had a landline or not. I'd like to make a call," she huffed, less than impressed with this whole ordeal.

He pointed to a phone on a table beside the couch. Immediately, she went over and picked it up. "There's no dial tone," she said in disbelief.

"Guess the storm must have knocked down the phone lines." He shrugged as if it was insignificant.

"How are we supposed to get a hold of anyone to let them know we are here?" she asked, feeling her stomach clench, as anxiety pricked at her.

"The ranger knows there are a few of us that live up the mountain, and he knows that we all stay prepared for a snow in."

"A snow in?" she repeated, still trying to comprehend the full extent of the situation.

"Aye, when there is so much snow you have to stay in." He spoke as if he was explaining the concept to a small child.

A frustrated growl escaped her lips, and she flopped back down on the chair in front of the fireplace crossing her arms. Resignation set in. Like it or not, she was stuck here. With him.

"Trust me, I'm no' thrilled with this situation either," he declared as if reading her mind.

18
Maybe It's the Whisky

THE LASS WAS EXCEPTIONALLY quiet from what he knew of her. She sat staring at the fire, her perfectly arched brows knit together in worry.

"Is someone expecting ye lass?" Alex didn't make any reference to a so-called boyfriend this time, but he realized that maybe someone would wonder where she was, especially being Christmas time.

"No. Not really." She sighed.

Her response seemed odd to him. Given the current circumstance though, perhaps it was a good thing that nobody would be worried about her whereabouts. "What about the lassies ye were with the other day? They won't expect to hear from ye?"

She looked back at him. "No, they'll be busy with their families. We weren't planning to connect again until the new year." There was a sadness in her tone. Why was she alone at Christmas? Realizing that was a can of worms he did not want to open, he pushed the thought aside and didn't question her.

This time, when he came back from the kitchen he brought over a glass of scotch and handed it to her. Nothing like sipping on a wee dram to calm a situation.

"What's this?" she asked.

"An actual taste of Scotland," he said, plopping down on the chair across from her.

She eyed the golden liquid with suspicion.

"'Tis a single malt whisky from the highlands," he added.

"Hair of the dog," she said before shooting it back like a bar star. "Ugh," she huffed with her face scrunched up.

Alex was stunned. "Ye dinnae shoot whisky lass, fer the love of fuckin' Mary."

Her eyes went wide as if she was surprised he'd sworn. "Oh. Right. Well, that didn't taste very good." With a skeptical look on her pretty face, she set the empty glass carefully on the table between them. "I think the Christmas spiced orange tea would be a much better representation of your country. That stuff burns." She rubbed her chest.

Alex stared at her and then took a deep breath to stop himself from saying something he shouldn't. God, what a woman. How the hell did she end up in his home? And why was he wasting good whisky on her? He didn't know what possessed him to forge on.

"Scotch Whisky is the very essence of Scotland, and this particular one, well, 'tis from a distillery near my home. Close to the sea."

She seemed to look at him thoughtfully. Alex lifted his glass to his nose and breathed in its essence before taking a sip. *This is definitely a taste of Scotland*, he thought as he closed his eyes to savour it. "Ye can smell the salty sea air in it," he said proudly.

She guffawed, and he snapped his piercing blue eyes open to glare at her. Why was she so infuriating? "Smell it, lass." He handed her the glass wondering why he didn't just give up.

Eyeing him with suspicion, she tentatively sniffed at the glass of golden liquor. "Oh God," she moaned. "It smells like rubbing alcohol."

The little quiver of disgust is what threw him over the edge. He looked up at the ceiling in a silent prayer for patience. Not that he was a religious man, but he needed all the help he could get. The lass was painfully obstinate. "Right. What is it you'd like to drink then?"

"I don't know. What else do you have?" she said reluctantly.

"Beer?" he asked, getting up and heading back to the kitchen.

"Wine?" she countered.

"Beer," he said, brokering no argument as he pulled a bottle from the fridge and twisted it open.

Alex strode back to her as she cuddled up her legs beneath her in the chair, getting comfy. Her gaze was drawn back to the fire. He handed her the open bottle of beer.

"Thanks," she said, and he clanked his glass to her bottle before lumbering down in the chair across from her.

They both sat for a time in silence.

"I didn't mean to sound ungrateful earlier," she said thoughtfully, not looking up.

Alex glanced at her.

"I suppose I just hadn't considered things. I don't know what I thought really. I've never been snowed in anywhere. This is a new experience for me. It's weird to be stuck somewhere because of the weather," she said, taking another sip of her beer.

"It's nothin' to worry about lass. It's part of life in the mountains."

She nodded, and Alex sensed that she seemed to relax a bit.

"What's your name?" she suddenly blurted out.

"Sergeant Mackenzie," he stated pointedly, sipping his whisky. *Keep it professional*, he thought until he saw her exaggerated eye roll.

"I'm in your home, and you don't want to tell me your first name, *Sergeant*?"

What was it about this woman that both infuriated him and made him want to kiss that disdainful little look off her face all at the same time? Glaring at her for a moment, he replied stonily, "Alex."

"Quinn West." She grinned with her dimples on full display like the cat who got the cream.

Lord, help him. "Aye, I know that," he said, reminding them both of their rocky history to date.

"Oh right." She bit her lower lip, snagging his attention before taking a long slug of her beer.

Alex swallowed, wishing he'd stop noticing her full lips. He shifted in his chair quelling his untoward thoughts. "Are ye warmed now?" he asked in an attempt to stay on safe ground.

"Oh, so warm and toasty." Those lush lips curved up into a smile. "The fire is heavenly." She sighed blissfully.

"Aye," he agreed, tearing his gaze away from her and back to the fire. He never knew someone to find such pleasure in the simplest things. When he pulled her over, she'd had that same dreamy look in her eyes about the snow. Pensive, he sipped his scotch. God, it was good. Took him back home. He wondered what the lass would think if she actually gave it a chance. Would she appreciate it like she seemed to other things? Would she get that blissful look in her eyes?

"I need to thank you." Her softened voice pulled him from his reverie. "If you and Bear hadn't found me..." Her voice trailed off.

There was worry etched on her pretty face. He didn't want her to think about what could've happened. Protectiveness surged through him, and he had to remind himself that the feeling that roared through him was likely because he was a police officer. That, and his parents raised him to be a good human. As much as he might be swearing off women, he certainly still had a heart. He hated the thought of what could've been, but he also hated that she felt the heavy weight of it too. The lass had been through a lot tonight, and he could see it troubled her.

Needing her to know she was safe with him, he reached over and put a reassuring hand on hers. "It's okay, Quinn. You're here now, safe and sound."

His hand was warm and comforting on hers. She knew what he said was true. She was safe now, safe with him. He was a cop, after all. That was their duty, to serve and protect. At least she didn't have to worry that she'd been rescued by some opportunistic axe murderer or sexual predator. Nope, even if he was a rapist, she'd be safe because he'd already made it crystal clear she was the last woman he'd ever want to sleep with. With that thought, she slid her hand out from under his and changed the subject.

"I love your cabin," she said, sweeping her eyes around the open space. Despite being an open layout, it was cozy with the log walls and rug-covered slate floors. The river rock fireplace was floor-to-ceiling, making it a ruggedly beautiful focal point.

"Aye, 'tis pleasant, I suppose," he said as if it never occurred to him before how nice it was.

"How long have you lived here?" she asked curiously.

"Two years."

"It must be heavenly to be able to escape the world to this wonderful cozy cabin." She sighed contentedly at the very idea. What a great place this would be to just sit and write. Dang. She wished she had her laptop with her.

"So what brought you here? To Canada, I mean." Quinn found her curiosity budding. He'd tentatively answered her questions which she took as a good sign. Hopefully, they could actually have a proper conversation for a change.

"That's a bit of a long story, lass." Alex deflected, standing up to take his empty glass to the kitchen.

Quinn recognized his stonewalling immediately and decided there was no point in pushing. She yawned, feeling a deep weariness in her bones.

"I guess we should call it a night then," she said, coming up behind him with her empty beer bottle.

He took it from her and put it under the sink in a bin. When he stood back up, she moved in closer to him and wrapped her arms around him in a bear hug well aware he'd hate it, but she didn't care. Quinn needed to hug the man who'd saved her life.

Pressing her face against his chest, she settled her arms around him even though he stood stock-still, his arms hanging awkwardly like he didn't know where to put them. It didn't deter her though. Instead, she savoured his solid warmth. God and his scent. She suspected she could hyperventilate, trying to breathe in all his yumminess. Never had someone smelled this good. It was next level. Realizing she was bordering on sniffing him like an airport drug detector dog, she lifted her face to look at him.

"I just wanted to thank you." Her breath caught under his stormy gaze. She cleared her throat and forged on, "I— You— Well, if you hadn't been there..." She bit her lip, feeling her eyes sting. "Thank you." Her voice was barely a whisper.

"I am glad we found ye," he said gruffly. He lifted his hand to her face, but he seemed to think better of it, dropping it away.

It sobered Quinn. He didn't want to touch her, or if he did, he schooled himself not to. Either way, it sucked. He likely came to people's rescue often given his job. This wasn't a big deal for him like it was for her. He was a cop, duty-bound. Hastily, she released her arms from around him and turned to walk back into the living room.

"Guess you're used to being all hero-like," she teased, trying to quell the small stab of disappointment.

"No' bloody likely," he grunted and turned back to the sink to wash his glass.

Quinn watched him curiously. For a guy who came across as cocky and overly confident, it surprised her he didn't relish the hero reference. Could it be that Mean Hot Cop was humble? She noted he'd gotten uncomfortable under her praise and with her hugging him. What was under all his gruff facade? She'd caught glimpses. Moments of kindness and good humour. Jeepers and that smile. What would he be like if he let down that guard that he kept so high? Then she bit her lip and wondered what was it that made him keep a guard up in the first place.

"I'm sure ye must be exhausted. Ye can sleep in the bedroom, and I'll sleep on the settee." Not that he wanted her sleeping in his bed, but his mam had taught him manners. As a guest in his home, wanted or not, it wouldn't be right to make her sleep on the settee. Christ, but the very thought of her lying in his bed made him want to do bad things. *Very* bad things. Wrapping her arms around him, giving him a wee bosie, shouldn't have had him mentally arguing with his dick to calm down. One of the few occasions he'd have preferred to be wearing his bulletproof vest. Instead, he was tortured with the feel of her large breasts pressed hard against him. Their unmistakable soft fullness relentlessly taunting him.

"Settee?" She grinned, raising her brow playfully pulling him from his spiralling thoughts. She was teasing him, Alex realized belatedly.

"Aye, the settee, or how do ye Canadians say it, the couch." He emphasized the vowel sound.

She giggled, and he felt the corners of his lips twitch.

"It's fine. I'm not going to push you out of your bed. I can sleep here." She flopped down full out on his settee to make her point. And holy fuck, she looked incredibly inviting as she lay there.

Alex crossed his arms over his chest uncomfortable, he did not want to be thinking about *that,* especially not with this particular lass. She was trouble. A feisty, chatterbox with big innocent eyes and a sinfully tempting mouth, who didn't know danger even when it towered at six foot four in front of her.

"Besides, I suspect you wouldn't fit very well on here," she added oblivious to his randy thoughts. She stretched right out to demonstrate the length of the settee.

Alex's mouth went dry as eyes ran the length of her. Oh, he could fit on. Tamping down the arousal that threatened his senses and reminding himself that he needed to stay immune to the bloody lass, he agreed.

"Fine." He wasn't about to argue. The sooner he could get to his room and put some distance between them, the better.

"Right then, I'll bring ye another blanket and a pillow," he said practically stomping down the hall.

Alex wasn't sure what had gotten into him. Quinn West was undoubtedly an attractive woman, but she'd half driven him crazy since he'd met her. He'd been around plenty of appealing, willing women, who were far less frustrating, and he'd had no problem keeping any kind of arousal at bay. So why on earth was he fighting base urges left, right, and centre with Quinn West?

Perhaps it had been a bit too long since he'd last been with a lass. Not that he was some kind of animal, he could live without sex. He'd sworn off women when he'd left Scotland. It wouldn't be forever, but at this point in his life, he had no desire to complicate his world. And if he was going to complicate everything, it certainly wouldn't be with the headstrong stubborn woman lying on his settee.

19
Discipline and Boundaries

Quinn slipped to the bathroom to get ready for bed. When she came back to the living room Alex was back puttering in the kitchen, but he had set out a sheet on the couch with a couple of pillows, and he had a thick cozy quilt laid on top turned down ready for her to get in. Quinn's heart squeezed at the sight. He might not like to show it, but it seemed like Mean Hot Cop had a sweet side.

"Perfect," she groaned sleepily sliding her weary body under the quilt.

"Comfy then?" he asked, avoiding eye contact as he flicked out the kitchen light.

"Mmm hmm." She nodded sleepily.

"Right, well, I'm down the hall if ye need anything." His voice had that gruffness to it again.

She smiled closing her eyes. "Good night, Sergeant Mackenzie."

Oh, she's a handful, he thought to himself. He stood there for a moment, brooding. Her breathing deepened, and she was already asleep. Alex shouldn't be surprised. The lass had quite the ordeal today. That was his cue to get himself to bed, but instead, he found himself moving towards her. Standing by the settee, he studied her. Her full lips were gently parted as she took deep slow breaths. The sight of her silky auburn hair scattered across the pillow gave Alex the urge to run his hands through it. Stiffening, he realized his thoughts had once again gotten away from him. He turned and strode to his bedroom.

After trying to get comfy and flipping from one side to the other, Alex finally lay on his back throwing his forearm across his head. Every time he tried to clear his mind and willed sleep to come, thoughts of her skittered through his brain like a pigeon flapping around a warehouse not knowing the way out. He kept replaying the memory of carrying her to the fireplace. When he picked her up, his only thought had been to get her close to the heat of the fire, but with the way she wrapped her arms around him and leaned in, her face was near his neck. He'd felt her soft intake of breath. Christ. It haunted him.

Not only was he frustrated having to fight erections around her, but he also felt perturbed that she seemed to think of him like he was her bloody knight in shining armour. He wasn't going to be anyone's Lancelot. Yes, he felt the need to protect her and didn't like that she'd gone through what she had, but that was simply because he was a cop. Protection was an instinct, or so he told himself.

Alex sighed heavily and rolled over. A lass had been his downfall in Scotland, and he'd be damned if he'd ever let that happen again. As much as he wanted to fuck Quinn West or at least his cock did, he knew better. He knew that even casual sex could lead to disaster. Coming to this country was a fresh start for him, and there was no way in hell a pretty face lush-lipped pain in the arse lass was going to wreck it for him.

One day, he'd likely move back to his homeland. It was where his family lived after all, and when he did, maybe then he'd settle down with a woman. Maybe. Or perhaps he'd enjoy a peaceful life akin to a monk's. His semi-stiff cock seemed to snicker at the idea.

Alex originally came to Canada on a work exchange, but one year had now led to two. In all the time he'd been here, he'd steered clear of any kind of love interest. He knew the trouble it could cause.

Living in this remote area of the mountains served him well. Close to town, but not too close. He spent a lot of time in the backcountry. He and Bear hiked these mountains together. His pup was all the companionship he needed.

tight against the line of her jaw. Holy shit was that a gun? Quinn flashed back to the black gun she'd seen in his holster the day he'd pulled her over.

She could barely breathe, never mind move, and it wasn't for lack of trying. All she could do was feel the utter terror that snaked through her.

"One move and I'll pull this fucking trigger." His voice was as cold and menacing as the hard steel pressed against her jaw.

"Alex, no!" she screamed frantically from under him.

"Jesus Christ!" he bellowed, releasing her and flying off her like she'd scalded him. "What the hell are ye doing sneaking around in my room like that?" he boomed. His breath was ragged.

Quinn quickly scrambled off the bed, shaken. Was he blaming her? In an instant, her fear turned to anger. "I wasn't sneaking." Her voice was quivering, but she stood before him a combination of fury and fear thrumming through her body. "This place is freezing," she said accusingly. "I came in here to see if you had a heater and then you pounced on me like some crazed prize fighter!" She was breathing in and out so heavily like she was in the final minute of a spin class.

attention and ask if he had a heater, maybe he could just tell her where it was and then he could go back to sleep. She was happy to find it herself. Quietly, she padded further into the room and towards his bed.

"Alex," she whispered. No response.

She hated to wake him, but she couldn't keep from shivering she was so cold. His covers were pulled up snugly around him, and then suddenly, he moaned something in his sleep, making her nearly jump out of her skin. Was he having a bad dream?

"Sergeant Mackenzie," she said, thinking maybe his cop title might stir him awake. He didn't respond except for the incoherent tortured-sounding mumbles. Quinn bit her lip with worry. She didn't know what she should do. *Probably best to try and wake him*, she thought and nudged his shoulder through the blankets.

Before she knew what was happening, she felt her body being yanked and then slammed face down onto his bed. Vicelike hands gripped her wrists and yanked her arms above her head. Alex's rock-hard body pressed down on the back of hers, pressing her into the bed, her cheek flattened against the mattress. He had her trapped, and she struggled to breathe under his weight.

Still trying to comprehend what was happening, her terrified mind registered the feel of cool steel wedged at her neck to discover a linen closet. There were towels, but no other blankets that she could see. At this point, it didn't feel like an extra blanket would do the trick anyway. She didn't see a thermostat. Although, it was dark, and she didn't know exactly where to look. Maybe he had an electric heater somewhere.

Quinn turned towards the middle door. Mean Hot Cop's bedroom. Her heart started to beat faster in her chest again. He did say to go to him if she needed anything.

Taking a breath, she raised her hand and gently knocked on the door. On the other side of the door, she could hear Bear stir with his paws on the hardwood floor as he got close to the door, but she didn't hear anything else. Gingerly, she turned the handle and carefully nudged the door open.

"Hello?" she said, quietly peeking her head in.

It was very dark, but she could make out Bear sitting like a very well-behaved pup. He eyed her but didn't seem disturbed by her presence. He'd saved her life. Maybe that meant they shared an unspoken bond. Quinn adored all animals, but this dog would live forever folded deep in her heart. Without him, she would likely still be out there.

The moon made a silvery blue path across the bed in the darkness. Quinn watched for a moment, but Alex didn't stir. Her chilliness kept her on her mission. She didn't want to wake him or disturb him, but if she could quietly get his

20
More Than She Bargained For

QUINN AWOKE IN THE middle of the night to the howling sound of the wind whipping around wildly outside. Her heart was racing, and she felt cold as ice. Panic filled her. Pulling the blanket tighter around herself, she lay there. She was safe in Alex's cabin now. She wasn't out there. It was okay. She tried to calm herself. Shivering, her eyes darted to the fireplace, where she couldn't even see an ember. The air in the log cabin felt arctic. Wasn't there heating in this place other than the fireplace? She pulled the blanket over her frozen-tipped nose, but it was no better than cling wrap on an ice cube. She felt chilled to the bone all over again.

Needing to get warm, she willed herself to get up off the couch to see if Alex had more blankets or a thermostat. The icy slate floor tiles only added to her cold hell as she stood up. Wrapping the quilt tighter around herself, she crept to the small hall. Recalling that the bathroom was on the left, she noted that there was also a door to the right and one in the middle. Slowly, she opened the one on the right only pass by sooner than anticipated. However long this situation lasted, Alex needed to set some boundaries. Perhaps he'd allowed too much tonight. Let his guard down. He didn't need to spend the time getting to know her and vice versa. He could tell she wanted to know more about him, but he was not interested in all that. Best if they stayed as companionable strangers.

It pissed him off that his body had reacted to her though. In the early days after arriving in Canada, he'd been tempted by a few lasses, but he'd stuck to his guns. He taught himself to be immune, to not let them penetrate his senses. At first, it was almost like a game for him, a challenge and Alex loved a challenge. It had surprised and pleased him how disciplined he'd become, and he maintained it knowing it served his purposes.

All he had to do was get through the next few days—hopefully less. Keep her at a distance. He could do that. Discipline, he reminded himself. The woman who'd put him through hell back in his home country drifted into his mind unbidden, but it served as the reminder he needed. He'd not let any lass into his life.

Compared to his policing career in Scotland, being a cop in Canada was a piece of cake. Most of the crime was small kind of stuff. Although occasionally, he'd get involved with some big shake-ups in the larger nearby city. The occasional adrenaline rush of those jobs was just enough kick to his otherwise peaceful existence. Alex had found a haven here in Canada, and the last thing he wanted was for a lass to ruin it.

He suspected he knew what the problem was with Quinn West. She was attracted to him and had that subtle way of flirting with him. It was no wonder he was reacting to her. The last thing he wanted was for her to get the wrong idea about this situation they found themselves in.

Christ, from what he'd gathered about the lass, she was probably dreaming of sugar plums and fairies right now with him as her hero come to the rescue. Alex shuddered at the thought. There would be no fling, no romance, none of that shite. There was attraction. He could admit that, but he'd be sure to keep the lass at a distance. Easier said than done with her right under his roof, but he'd put his foot down if he had to. He had no intention of being her bloody knight in shining armour.

The moonlight reflected bluish shadows of gently falling snow on his ceiling. It snowed hard earlier, but at least the wind had died down a bit now. Hopefully, the storm would

Alex shook his head looking down at her in the darkness of the room. "God, I'm so sorry lass. I'm not used to anyone being in my place."

"Clearly," she snapped, snatching her blanket off the floor. It dumbfounded her. She had been standing, wrapped in the blanket, and then in the blink of an eye, she was trapped under the hulking man held in a vice grip with a frickin' gun to her head. In her mind, he'd flung himself squarely back into the intimidating cop category. This was the intimidating dangerous cop she'd first seen approaching her vehicle, all in black—tall, broad, and fucking lethal.

Feeling equal doses of fear and anger, she escaped in the darkness to his door, needing to get the heck out of his room. In two quick strides though, he met her there. Blocking her from opening the door with one strong arm pressed against it.

"Wait," he said.

And there he went again with his damn commands. Quinn stood ramrod straight, refusing to look at him.

He dipped a finger under her chin and lifted it to look at him. It surprised her to see concern in his eyes in the pale of the moonlight, but she refused to be swayed by it.

"Did I hurt ye?" he asked with a worry in his low timbre.

Quinn wanted to be mad at him. She should be infuriated. He'd put a gun to her head for crying out loud, but his gentleness and nearness were quickly crumbling her resolve. Not to mention that accent. Ugh, that accent made her weak. She shook her head no.

Relief seemed to flood through him as his shoulders relaxed and he let out a breath. "I'm truly sorry, Quinn. I was having a bad dream." He sounded gruff. "It was instinct. I thought you were an intruder. I didnae mean to frighten ye. I'd never hurt ye lass. I promise ye that."

She could hear the anguish in his voice, and what was left of her anger dissipated. She believed him. Somehow, she trusted that he wouldn't hurt her—not intentionally at least. He'd scared the life out of her. But he hadn't hurt her.

"I pity the fool who tries to break into your house," she scoffed.

"Aye," he agreed gravely.

Her attempt at lightening the mood fell like a lead balloon. An involuntary shiver skittered down her spine as she considered anyone who made the mistake of crossing Sergeant Alex Mackenzie.

"If it makes ye feel any better, I wouldnae huv shot ye. My gun is no' even loaded."

She looked at him incredulously. "Oh right, very reassuring."

He almost smiled. "Can ye forgive me?" His thumb had joined the finger under her chin and moved to lightly caress her jaw.

It was both calming and arousing. This gentle touch was such a juxtaposition to the danger she'd glimpsed. Quinn couldn't help the tiny sparks that lit inside her at his light caress on her chin.

Despite being momentarily petrified, there wasn't a doubt in her mind that if he'd known it was her, he'd never have reacted like that. In retrospect, if she was being honest, it was insanely impressive. Like he was the real deal kind of cop. The one who'd fuck you over if you even attempted to cross him. *Hot Cop*, her brain quipped.

"I'll forgive you on one condition," she said, standing a little taller before him although her face only reached the height of his well-chiseled chest.

He arched a brow. "I'm listening."

"Teach me."

"Teach ye what?" he asked dumbfounded.

"Teach me how to defend myself," she breathed, looking up at him.

That was the last thing he expected the lass to say. Even in the pale moonlight of the room, he could see the determination in her big brown eyes. He didn't want to admire her, but he found that was what he was feeling. Fucking admiration. She was a clever lass. It was a good idea really. Every woman should know how to defend herself. The asshats who leered at her outside the bar popped into his head.

"Aye," he agreed not allowing himself to think on how her nearness was already fucking with his head. No. This was business. The least he could do was teach the lass to defend herself after pouncing on her like a trigger-happy numpty. He cringed inwardly.

"Good." He didn't miss the satisfaction in her voice.

Still standing at the door in front of him, he noticed her shiver slightly, and he belatedly recalled his own state of undress—certainly not ideal at the moment. Either the lass hadn't noticed or didn't care that he was as nude as Michelangelo's David. The bedroom was dark, so likely it was the former; she probably assumed he was wearing boxers or something. It briefly crossed his mind that maybe he should throw something on, but then again, how could she be that oblivious? He was second-guessing himself. Perhaps it wasn't prudent to draw attention to the fact that his ill-behaved dick was mere inches away from her, especially after just having calmed the situation between them. He didn't want her getting all blustery with him again—he was too fucking tired to deal with that. He was still doing the mental math, when she spoke again.

"Your house is freezing," she stated flatly.

"Aye, I ken it," he agreed.

Her eyes drew up to his, and in the dim moonlight, he could just barely make out her full lips that were pinched together in disapproval. And her eyebrows crunched in consternation.

Alex sighed. "Log cottage. Not the greatest insulation. I keep the fire going in the day. It keeps things warm enough, but it can get cool at night. I'll chop more wood in the morning. It's getting low."

"Well, thanks for the forewarning," she muttered sarcastically, pulling the blanket tighter around her.

It was a bad idea, but what else could he offer her right now? The lass was freezing, and there wasn't enough wood to even get a good fire going again. With no other feasible option and against his better judgement, he strode to the bed.

"Come lass," he said.

Quinn stood stone still, and Alex sighed as he looked back at her. "It'll be warmer in the bed together. Come, you're shivering."

"Ha!" she bit out. "As if! I'm not getting in bed with you!" She was incredulous at the suggestion.

At that point, he was certain she was well aware of his state of undress. He knew more than a few women who would jump at the chance to get into bed with him. It shouldn't have pricked his pride that she was so opposed to the idea. He was tired though, and he felt his mood darken.

"Listen, Quinn, lovely as ye are," his voice dripped cynically, "I'm not interested in doing anything with ye in this bed aside from sleeping." In the back of his mind, he fought the idea that his pronouncement might not be altogether true. "I'm simply suggesting we share the bed and share some warmth. If ye'd rather freeze by yerself on the settee, be my guest."

He'd clearly said his piece and was done now. He got into the bed turned away from her and pulled his blanket up around him.

"Right, I believe you made it clear last night how egregious it would be to sleep with me. Don't worry. The feeling is mutual."

Her barb hit its mark and Alex gritted his teeth, holding back a retort.

"Don't you have an electric heater?" she asked, and he could hear the desperation in her voice, like getting in the bed with him was repugnant.

"Naw," he snapped, leaving no room for discussion on the matter. "Trust me, lass. I dinnae like this situation either, but 'tis the one we find ourselves in. If ye dinnae want to freeze, then get in the bloody bed."

Quinn stood there not knowing what to do. He had felt incredibly warm against her when he had her in the intruder death grip. If it hadn't been so terrifying, it might have been nice. The man was ridiculously big and strong. And warm. She shivered again. *Oh eff it*, she thought and quickly stalked to the bed, sliding in beside him before she changed her mind.

Laying ramrod straight so she didn't accidentally touch him, she pulled the blanket up and tried to get comfortable. Then she crunched her knees to her hoping to ward off the cold as she shivered again.

"For crying out loud woman," he muttered, rolling over towards her. Then she felt his strong arms wrap around her and easily pull her back up against him as he yanked the covers over them both. Quinn was afraid to breathe. She considered pulling away indignantly, but then his warmth began seeping over her cold tired body. She quickly lost the will to pull away from him and his delicious heat even though he was Mean Cop...Hot Cop. Oh God, she shouldn't be in his bed wrapped in his arms, but she didn't move away. Instead, she found herself greedily melting into him stealing his warmth.

She was so tired and so thankful to start warming up that she relaxed surprisingly quickly. There was a bit of blanket wedged between them, creating a slight barrier. And though Quinn still wore her leggings and slim-fit running shirt, by morning, she'd wonder how in the heck she hadn't realized that Alex was completely naked behind her. She would blame it on the dark room, the drama of a gun to her head, and being distracted by the cold. Who knew how she hadn't noticed? Or maybe, deep down, she had known.

But in that moment, she only basked in his warmth and the feel of his incredibly solid body at her back—protective and safe. Her conscious mind was blissfully unaware of his nakedness. His muscular arm held her securely to him. At first, her brain was lit up with the awareness of being wrapped in the embrace of Sergeant Mackenzie—in his bed. Mean Cop. Hot Cop. Alex. His strong, rhythmic breathing behind her lulled her senses. A secure, grounded feeling seeped into her bones as lucid thoughts drifted away, and a dreamless sleep claimed her.

21
Morning Glory

Alex awoke to a faint floral vanilla scent, and he breathed deeply as he pulled her warm body close to his. He was aroused by the soft fullness of her behind pressed against his morning erection. He ran his hand over the rounded curve of her hip, and awareness cut through his senses like a bullet.

Fuck, what was he doing? He lifted his arm off her like he'd just brushed his hand over a bomb, but she was still pressed against him and her head was laying over his other arm with her satiny hair sprawled over him. No sooner had Alex pulled away, then she nuzzled her backside tighter up against him and reached back for his free arm pulling it around her again. He would have laughed except his erection was throbbing painfully, distracting all his senses.

Careful not to wake her, he disentangled himself. He should have known having her in his bed would be trouble. In the middle of the night though, he didn't have any better solutions.

Rolling onto his back, his mind reeled right before he felt her turn towards him, pressing against his side, her leg sliding over his and her hand coming to rest on his bare chest. If that wasn't bad enough, she sighed as her slender fingers absently stroked his skin. *Not immune now are ye, Alex?* he chided himself swallowing hard. He needed to remove himself from this situation before he did something he'd sorely regret.

Releasing a deep contented sigh, she stretched against him nestling further into him. It was sweet torture. He recalled how she looked the night she came out of the bar and slammed into him. Her curvy legs. Truth was, he wanted nothing more than to roll her over, rip off her leggings, and slam his throbbing cock into her full hilt. He wanted to watch those big brown eyes fill with desire as he slid slowly in and out of her. Jeezus. Alex gritted his teeth.

Thankfully, she tipped herself the other way and not a moment too soon. Alex took the opportunity to get the hell out of the bed and reach for a pair of sweatpants he had thrown on the chair in the corner. Quinn's eyes cracked open. She wore sleep well. Her hair was slightly mussed, her eyes heavy-lidded, her cheeks rosy, and her lips plump. It was a good thing Alex was no longer in that bed with her.

"Oh my God!" she squeaked, hiding her head under the covers. "Why aren't you wearing clothes?" Her panicked voice was muffled by the quilt.

"Well, I am now," he stated flatly, yanking his sweatpants on. While he couldn't stop looking at her and fantasizing about her curvy body, she acted horrified to see his. It had been a long time since a woman had looked upon his cock, and her reaction grated. Christ, he was extremely well proportioned to his muscled six foot four frame. Shouldn't she like what she saw?

Quinn peeked her head back above the covers, and her big brown eyes widened, this time in obvious appreciation as she slid her gaze over his bare chest and down his abs to where his sweats were slung low on his hips. *That's better*, he thought with a wave of masculine satisfaction. *Good.* Then he rebuked himself. *Not good*. He shouldn't be so damn pleased with her blatant perusal, but God help him, he had to remind himself not to flex for her.

"Should I skip the shirt?" he asked unable to resist toying with her. She flushed being caught staring and then rolled her eyes and let out a feminine little huff. He smiled as he pulled on a t-shirt.

"Do you sleep naked?" she asked, biting her lip worriedly.

"Always," he answered definitively.

"Oh. Right," she said seeming to consider his response. "Sorry, so were you naked last night?" She scrunched her eyes closed in consternation.

"Always," he repeated.

Her eyes snapped open, and he threw her a wolfish grin that he'd intended to make her tits tingle. Those big eyes were so expressive; he could practically read her every thought. She was thinking about his nakedness and all that had occurred between them. He was sure of it. When he'd thought she was an intruder and was stretched out on top of her when they were talking by the door, when she'd slept in his arms, and the entire time, he'd been naked. Completely fucking naked. It was immensely satisfying watching the flush that arose on her creamy skin. This was dangerous territory and he knew it. Discipline. He needed to exit. Now.

"I'm going chop some wood," he stated, heading for the door. "Give it fifteen minutes or so and I'll have the fire going again."

"Wait," she called. He looked back at her from the bedroom door. He almost hoped she'd ask him to get back into bed with her. Fuck, he needed to get out of the cottage.

"I wondered if I could borrow something to wear, like a hoodie and some sweats. Oh, and some socks. I'd like to take a shower, and I don't have any clean clothes to wear."

"Socks are in the bottom drawer. Clothes are in the closet. Take your pick. Towels are in the hall closet. There are new toothbrushes in there too. Help yourself to whatever ye need."

Without another word, he strode out of the bedroom, leaving her all alone in his bed. For some reason, she felt abandoned. Did she expect him to pick out everything for her? She found she would have liked it if he'd stayed and they could talk for a bit. It felt like he couldn't get away from her fast enough. Well, what did she care anyway? It was not like they were dating. Quite the opposite. She was just stuck with him for who knew how long.

Maybe the snow might be cleared enough today that she could get back to the inn. She craved writing. It sucked that she didn't have her laptop with her.

Quinn pulled up the covers around her shoulders. It was already cooler without Alex in the bed. He'd taken Bear with him too. Dang. Not even a pup to keep her company.

The details of the middle of the night played out in her mind. She had been petrified at first when she found herself face down under him a gun to her head. It took her a second to even register what had transpired. God, what an insane moment. She was genuinely relieved to know that the gun wasn't loaded. Alex wouldn't have hurt her, she knew that, but it was scary when he'd mistaken her for an intruder.

She knew it was ridiculous, but there was a piece of her that also found it sexy. With his split-second reflexes and the strength of his perfectly sculpted body, the man was lethal. His dangerous look wasn't a facade—it was reality.

Yet, he'd been so gentle with her when he realized his error. The stark contrast between brute strength and kind heart had her more intrigued than she'd like to be.

She'd slept so deeply wrapped in the warmth of his protective arms. It was unfathomable to think that ever could have happened. Not only being in Mean Hot Cop's home, but in his bed and in his arms all night long. It was crazy. A smile played on her lips as she tried to imagine how Belle and Megs would react to her current situation. They'd probably have to pick their jaws up off the floor.

Stretching, she wondered when she'd ever slept so soundly. From his perspective, he was doing his duty and keeping her from freezing to death, but for Quinn, it was more than that. She had felt so safe in his arms with his body protectively holding hers to him. It was heaven if she was being honest. She'd never felt protected by anyone in her life. She'd always done life pretty much on her own. No one to wipe her tears or tell her it would be okay. No one to chase away the cold while she slept.

Quinn had been alone most of her life. No siblings. No Dad and an absentee mother. She was used to taking care of herself. She didn't rely on anyone. She didn't even know how to rely on others. Since she was young, she was very independent, and the truth was, she liked it that way.

But last night in Alex's arms, she'd felt herself let go in a way. It was like she surrendered to his warm safe embrace, like she could completely relax and let go of any worry. She pondered the thought for a time, trying to wrap her brain around it, and she couldn't. All she knew was that she liked being in his embrace much more than she should.

"Well get over it, Quinn. He's not interested," she muttered to herself. If he was interested, he wouldn't have been so quick to rush out of the bedroom.

Quinn sat up and looked around Alex's bedroom. It had bachelor pad vibes. Nothing on the golden log walls, but it still felt cozy. The log walls didn't need dressing up. The dark wood chest of drawers where he said she could find the socks had a Christmas cactus sitting on the top. It was in full bloom, covered in cheerful fuchsia flowers. It made her smile. Cold Lethal Cop had a very definite soft side. She would have never expected this manly Scot to have a spray of pretty Christmas flowers in his bedroom. She was very curious about the softer side of him and wondered if she might see more of it.

There was a tall narrow window on one side of the bed. She leaned over and peered out. The snow was blowing and thick. It looked bitter out. She shivered, feeling glad to be inside safe and sound.

It crossed her mind that she would have still been out there if it weren't for Alex and Bear. It was an unsettling thought that she quickly pushed out of her mind. Quinn wasn't one to dwell on bad things. Though the stormy weather that continued its battering rampage didn't bode well for her hope of getting back to the inn. She sighed, snuggling back down under the thick down cover.

Hard to believe, but tomorrow was Christmas Eve. How she loved Christmas. Being stuck here was not part of her plan, but when life gives you lemons... *Hmm*, maybe being stuck in this cabin wasn't so bad really. She always adored the Christmas season, and here she was tucked away in a cozy mountain cabin. It was kind of poetic really. Right there and then, she decided that she was going to make the best of her situation of being marooned with Mean Hot Cop.

Quinn forced herself from the cozy bed. The cold skittered through her as her bare feet touched the slate floor. As she hurried to the bathroom, for a hot shower, she could swear she could see her breath in the cold of Alex's cabin.

After yesterday's hike and then with all the shivering, her muscles were achy. It made the steamy hot water feel heavenly as it enveloped her. She spied his shampoo and body wash. The thought of smelling it set off a flutter low in her belly. As if fearing she'd be caught, she slowly picked them up and opened each taking a hearty sniff. Mmm, God, they smelled nice. So very nice. She luxuriated in their scent as she cleaned herself with them.

Next, she washed her bra and underwear in the shower too, rung them out, and hung them over the shower curtain bar to dry. It was maddening not to have any extras, but hopefully, the ones she had would dry within a few hours.

Stepping out of the bathroom, she noticed the air in the cabin felt warmer. Wrapped in a fluffy grey towel, she poked her head around the corner from the hall. She could see a good fire going in the fireplace, but looking around, she didn't see Alex or Bear.

Back in Alex's room, she slid the black barn door to the side and stepped into his closet. Even though he'd given her permission to help herself, she felt uncertain because she was standing in Sergeant Mackenzie's closet. It seemed the kind of thing that he wouldn't like. She was being silly though. He'd told her to help herself.

There were two rows of neatly hung clothes. On a top shelf, there were formal police caps as well as a couple of baseball caps. Under the clothing racks were shoes, a duffle bag, and a suitcase. What struck her most was how tidy and organized it all was. Somehow, it didn't surprise her though. The rest of his place seemed clean and organized too.

Slowly, she inched forward feeling both timid and intrigued. She gently touched the dark black police shirts that hung on an upper rack, and a vision of him in his police uniform popped into her mind and sent a tingle between her thighs. Biting her lip, she moved on. Next, she came across two bulletproof vests. She reached up and let her fingers run over one of the vests, and she couldn't help thinking how dangerous Alex's work was. Yet, he, himself seemed almost bulletproof—so tough, so solid.

On one hanger, she discovered a deep blue and green kilt with a sporran. She pressed her hand to the soft wool. It was so authentic and made her curious to know more about Alex Mackenzie. What was his life like back in Scotland?

Her mind suddenly conjured up an image of him in his kilt and nothing else, and it sent a delicious little shiver dancing down her spine. *Oh, stop that*, she scolded herself. But then she considered whether or not it was true what they said about the Scots and their kilts. What did Alex wear under his? That question led her to the memory of the view she had first thing that morning.

The first sight she'd caught of him when she'd opened her eyes was of his massive member. It looked lethal. Thick and long as it bobbed. She'd wanted to stare, but at the same time, it had shocked her. She shouldn't be looking at that. And then the view with sweatpants on was just as good. With his dark sweatpants hanging low on his hips, she hadn't been able to stop her eyes from feasting on his perfectly chiselled torso. His muscles were smooth taut ribbons from the strong curve of his biceps and triceps to his thick capped shoulders, his pumped chest, and his ripped abs... Dear God. He was utterly glorious. She swallowed away the memory and continued on her mission.

Looking at the sporran, she wondered if there was anything in it. What did Scotsman keep in their Sporran anyway? She stared at it for a moment before curiosity got the better of her. Carefully unsnapping the metal button on the sporran, she opened the fine leather pouch and peered in. She couldn't really see into its dark leather, so she slid in her hand and pulled out its only contents: a small photograph.

There were no other photographs that she'd seen in Alex's home, which made this one all the more intriguing. Peering at it, a small pit formed in her stomach.

22
Secrets and Secret Places

THE PHOTO CONFUSED HER. Alex was in it, handsome as ever. Although he looked maybe a couple of years younger and not as muscular as compared to now. There was a proud look in his slightly crooked smile with his arms playfully wrapped around a grinning beautiful blond woman. Quinn bit her lip. The love between them almost jumped off the picture, but that wasn't the part that struck her most. The woman held a bundle in her arms. A baby. And a second child, maybe three years old was standing beside them grinning up at them. Adoration in his cherub features. It was obvious. Plain as day. The child's look of love was for his parents.

Quinn swallowed hard. There was no doubt it was a family photo even as her mind rallied against it and tried to find alternative answers. Alex was married? With kids? She frowned, staring at the photo. They looked like the perfect happy family.

But it didn't make any sense. Where were they now? They obviously didn't live in this cabin. What happened? It wasn't any of her business, but she couldn't help wondering. Was he divorced? Had he left his kids back in Scotland? Or maybe they were here in Canada? Could something have happened to them? That possibility disturbed her.

The distinct disappointment and sadness that crept over her made her realize that she was hoping for something to happen between her and Alex. Shit. Her friends were at least partially right. She liked him.

It sucked to come to the realization now because this photo changed things. She'd assumed he was single. Although, he'd never given her an indication one way or the other. But there had been moments that definitely felt flirty. She'd slept in his arms last night for crying out loud, but nothing had happened between them. The only reason she was in his bed was for warmth. He'd made that very clear.

Still, she couldn't imagine he'd hold her in his arms all night if he was married. Would he? Maybe what felt intimate to her, was simply doing a duty to him. He had torn out of the bedroom the first chance he'd gotten.

Quinn would never want to get involved with a married man. She looked back down at the photo, willing it to tell her the secrets it held. It was not like she was looking to get involved with anyone at the moment anyway, but certainly not with a man who was married with children. The thought made her queasy.

Quinn took a breath. She was being silly. They had not exactly hit it off anyway. Well, there were moments though. She thought back to him carrying her to the fireplace. *Oh, Quinn*, she chided herself. *You're reading into things*. He was helping her. It wasn't like he was making a move or hitting on her.

At best, they were tentative friends. Stranded together and making the best of a difficult situation. She sighed, wondering how her heart had already wanted something so much that her mind was only just catching up. The disappointment was real.

Quinn stared at the photo. They looked so happy, and the little boy was so damn cute. Of course, he made cute kids. She sighed. She supposed somewhere deep down she wished that for herself. To find love and have a family.

Quinn blew out a frustrated breath. *Enough*. It was Christmas time, and she was being ridiculous. She might be stranded there, but she intended to make the most of it and that did not include any kind of romance or anything with Alex. No, nothing like that, but she could make things festive for them both. She was good at festive.

Carefully, she slid the photo back into its place in the sporran and snapped the button closed, leaving it as she'd found it. Quinn was still mightily curious. Perhaps he might let his guard down enough to tell her more about himself. Maybe she'd learn his story yet.

Walking past the rows of hanging clothes, she stopped at a column of open shelving that contained neatly stacked t-shirts, jeans, and the like. She tried to put the photo out of her mind as she found a pair of black sweatpants and a matching hoody on one of the bottom shelves. The hoody had *POLICE* written in caps on the back in black lettering over the black jersey material. Black on black. Her rogue brain conjured an image of Alex in it, and she immediately pushed the thought aside and threw on the clothes before heading to the dresser for socks. She needed to stop lusting after the man. Pulling out a thick pair of socks from his bottom drawer, she yanked them on. His clothes were huge on her, but they were cozy and clean so they'd do.

She padded out of his bedroom and into the great room. "Alex?" she called, but there was no answer. How much wood was the man chopping?

"Wow," she breathed, taking in the sight of the little cabin by daylight. She hadn't paid that much attention last night, but in the light of day, it was downright charming. The ceiling vaulted high over the living room and kitchen. How could she not have noticed that there was a loft? It didn't look big, but it did look cozy and inviting.

It sat above the kitchen, facing the large picture window in the living room. She would definitely need to explore up there. It looked like the kind of loft that held treasures and secrets. She smiled. *The perfect place to write*, she thought again frustrated that she didn't have her laptop. The river rock fireplace went all the way up the side wall. It was ruggedly beautiful, especially against the backdrop of the log walls.

Quinn stood and looked out the large front window at the snow still whipping about in a frenzy. Now that she was safe indoors she found the snow majestic and she felt a coziness being tucked warm inside. Although she began to wonder about Alex, she hoped everything was okay. Peering out the window, she looked for him, but it was just a flurry of white. She bit her lip feeling a prickle of concern, and she glanced over her shoulder to the kitchen. There was a window at the back over the kitchen sink, she made her way to it, but before looking out, she noticed a sticky note on the counter. She picked it up. *Out shovelling snow with Bear, make yourself at home.*

It was short and to the point. She expected nothing less from Sergeant Mackenzie, but it was sweet that he thought to leave her a note at all—and that he wanted her to make herself at home. Quinn sobered, reminding herself not to get caught up in fantasy about Alex. She stood with her back leaned against the counter and smiled as an idea came to mind.

Alex was relieved to put some space between himself and the woman in his cottage. He felt all tense and needed to blow off some steam. The wind was biting and shovelling snow was a waste of time except for the release of energy. Alex decided he might be better off chopping some more logs.

Thoughts of the night before taunted him. He'd felt so badly about tackling her, but she handled herself better than many of the "tough guys" he'd encountered in his career. The lass had been rattled, but her small frame and pretty face belied the lioness underneath. He was glad for it. Any other lass might still be cowering. She definitely wasn't timid.

He wondered what in the hell he'd been thinking when he invited her into his bed though. He'd have been better off getting up in the middle of the night and chopping some damn wood. He had not been thinking. At the time, it just seemed like the easiest solution to her freezing was for him to warm her. He shook his head, still wondering how he thought it was a good idea.

The feel of her curvy body pressed against his... And she just seemed to melt into him like she belonged in his arms.

Fuck. He didn't want to feel anything towards her. He wanted to feel immune, damn it! Slamming his axe through a log, he relished the satisfying splitting sound it made as it snapped in half. It felt good to work his muscles and try and ease out the irritation that gnawed at him. It frustrated the hell out of him how affected he was by the lass in his cottage.

He supposed he shouldn't be surprised that his body responded so blatantly to hers. It had been a long time since he'd been with a woman. God, the way she'd felt in his arms with her lush arse pressing against him... His cock tugged just thinking about it. He slammed the axe clean through another thick log.

Now was not the time to break his dry spell—and not with this lass. She was already a handful. If he slept with her, it would just make things way too complicated. No, he had to keep things platonic. He had to stay disciplined. He was good at that. In what felt like no time, he'd chopped enough wood to last a week or more.

Loading up the logs back in the cottage and starting a fresh fire, he was relieved the lass wasn't about. He could hear the shower running, and he forced himself not to think about the lass naked in his shower. Christ. He needed to go back out again. Maybe shovel some snow.

Leaving her a quick note—his mam had always ingrained in them to be courteous—he headed back out. The snow was blowing hard, so he decided against trying to shovel. Instead, he and Bear made their way to his shed. He took a deep breath once he got inside and shook off the snow that clung to him. His trusty pup shook off the snow from his coat too and proceeded to his dog bed in the corner.

The room wasn't big but enough that he'd turned it into a small workout area. He had a bench press, stationary bike, and some weights inside. He'd also installed a small heater which he was especially pleased about on days like today. Time to let off some real steam. He threw himself into a hardcore lifting session.

Hours had gone by, and the snow continued to fall and swirl about. Alex was feeling better though. Physical exertion worked wonders on his mind. Not only did he feel physically strong—he felt mentally strong. He was beginning to find it laughable that he'd been rattled at all by Quinn. He knew damn well the lusty feeling he'd had had more to do with his deprivation than it had to do with her. Perhaps he'd need to take care of a little business in the shower. That should help temper his undersexed imagination.

With a clearer mind, it now seemed ridiculous that he'd been so worked up about Quinn staying with him through the snow blizzard. Yes, the lass would be his house guest for a day or two, but so what? It was not such a big deal. He'd been through harder things—far harder things. His muscles burned in his chest and arms, but it felt good. His stomach growled. Feeling hungry, but also more clear and grounded in himself, he supposed he should get back in and get something to eat.

23
Hot Shower and Warm Cookies

Alex came through the door looking like he'd just dug himself out of an avalanche.

"Jeepers!" Quinn quipped taking in the sight of him. "How'd the shovelling go?"

He looked up at her as if she were nuts to even ask. "An asinine task in this." He nodded towards the window where the snow was drifting up on the sill.

Guess we won't be going anywhere today then, she thought.

"I was getting a little worried. You were gone for a long time. I thought you might have shovelled your way to the town," she teased.

He looked at her under his brow. "I huv a shed in the back with some workout equipment. I chopped some wood, then did a wee workout. We willnae run out of wood again."

Quinn felt a pang of disappointment. Did that mean she wouldn't need to cuddle up in his bed? Then she reminded herself of the photo. She bit her lip. "Oh right, good." She was quiet before she added, "I'd like to see your shed. I've always thought I should learn to lift weights and go to the gym, but then I end up doing yoga instead. I love yoga." When he just looked at her blankly she added, "Maybe you can train me in your shed. You know, to defend myself and all that."

She had a hunch he didn't like the idea, but she wasn't about to let him forget their deal. She'd always intended to learn self-defence, but it was one of those things that she never seemed to get around to.

"Aye," he said casually, and she could guess he'd forgotten their middle-of-the-night agreement or maybe hoped she'd forgotten. Grabbing an apple from a fruit bowl on the kitchen table, he strode to the bathroom not giving her a second glance.

Quinn watched after him feeling slightly disappointed by their interaction. She hoped they could at least be friends. She wished he didn't seem so on guard with her. That and she had been feeling excited to have him come back to show him what she'd been up to while he was out.

Alex pulled open the curtain on the shower, and his mouth went dry at the site before him. A red lace bra and matching thong hung off the shower head. What kind of girl goes hiking in that? Shouldn't she have some kind of sports bra? And why on earth were they hanging in his shower?

He stared for a moment, unable to deter his thoughts from what she'd look like in the ensemble, and then it dawned on him. She was in his kitchen, in his clothes, with nothing underneath them. His cock thickened. Damn her all to hell.

Tentatively, he reached up and touched the offending thong. It was damp. Of course. It appeared she had washed her underclothes and had hung them to dry. It shouldn't get to him, but it did. Seeing her red lacy bra and thong had him imagining what it would be like to plunge his cock into her, to feel every part of her luscious curves, to hear her whimper as he drove into her. Heat coiled around him. Swallowing hard, he carefully removed her skimpy underwear from the shower head and put it on the vanity.

Stepping into the shower, he let the hot water hit him and grabbed his rock-hard cock, needing to find some relief. He wasn't going to think about her. All he needed was a quick release. He braced himself, putting one hand up on the tiled shower wall as he let the other pump him.

Immediately, his thoughts turned to the way her arse felt snug against him last night. He growled. *Stop.*

And her full breasts as she pressed into him at the kitchen sink. *Don't.*

Her tight nipples beaded through her sweater when he pulled her over. *Christ.*

His body spasmed in sweet release, and the second he could breathe again, guilt rolled over him. God, he shouldn't have noticed her body while he was on duty. And he certainly shouldn't be fantasizing about it while he… Jesus. Enough. He'd found his release. Now he could calm the fuck down around her. Letting the water spray over him, he cleared his mind and then washed up as he thankfully began to feel more at ease.

Alex strode into the kitchen and Quinn thought she was ready for him this time, but she was thrown off guard by how damn good he looked all clean-shaven with his dark hair still damp from his shower. He looked at her from under his dark brow, and it made her knees go weak.

Tearing her gaze away, she focused on pouring a fresh mug of coffee that she'd made. Before her grandmother had passed she always told Quinn, *kill 'em with kindness.* That was her plan. If they were going to be stuck here together during Christmas, she was going to make sure it was pleasant at the very least.

"Coffee?" she asked, and without waiting for him to answer, she handed him the steamy mug.

"Thank ye," he said taking it. Alex seemed refreshed after his shower and much more amiable. Taking a sip, he looked down at the coffee in his emerald green mug and took a second sip as if testing it. A subtle smile touched his lips. It was his coffee, so it shouldn't taste different. But maybe having someone else make it for him made it better? Quinn didn't know, but either way, it was nice to see an agreeable expression on his too-handsome face.

"Good?" she hedged.

"Aye, for someone who doesn't like coffee, ye make it well enough."

She smirked, leaning against the kitchen counter. "I used to make it for my Grandmother, and she was very particular about the water-to-grounds ratio."

"Canny woman," he said savouring another sip. Then his blue eyes squinted suspiciously as he scanned the kitchen like it was a crime scene. "Smells good in here." He concluded.

Ahh, finally he notices, Quinn smiled inwardly. "I made shortbread cookies," she said over her shoulder as she pulled a batch out of the oven. "I was going to make sugar cookies, but I saw you had icing sugar, so I decided to do whipped shortbread instead. Plus, you didn't have cookie cutters or a rolling pin, so sugar cookies were pretty much nixed as an option."

Alex looked over at the fresh cookies sitting on a cooling rack and his stormy blue eyes widened with interest. It pleased her more than it should.

"Help yourself," she said, sweetly noticing he'd already moved and was hunched over the rack inspecting which cookie to snatch up and try.

Taking one from the cooling rack, Alex examined it briefly and then popped it into his mouth. Quinn watched him with a tentative look on her face as she awaited his verdict.

"Mmm," he groaned and then grabbed another. "They huv a familiar sweet buttery taste, ach God, and they just melt in your mouth." He took a sip of his coffee after making short work of a second cookie. "They remind me of the ones my Nan used to make."

That felt like high praise coming from Sergeant Mackenzie. Perhaps her Grandmother was right. Kindness was the key—or maybe it was baked goods.

"Here try this one." She held the cooling rack to him with the final batch. A little thrill ran through her that he actually liked her cookies.

He eyed her curiously as he took one and popped it whole into his mouth. His stormy blue eyes rolled back in pleasure.

"Och, what is that? I recognize that taste. Mmm. God lass, ye could make a fortune if ye sold these."

She grinned delighted by his praise. "Thank you." She hoped he'd like them, but she didn't expect such compliments from Sergeant Mackenzie. "I added a splash of your scotch to this batch."

"Ye put my single malt scotch in yer cookies?" His eyes narrowed.

Oh shit. Was he angry? "I-I—" She didn't know what to say.

"It's fine, lass," he said, reassuring her as if sensing her unease. "But I thought ye dinnae like my whisky." His dark brow raised in a challenge as his blue eyes bore into her with a knowing twinkle in them.

God, he could make a nun stray with that look. She grinned, relieved he wasn't angry. "I don't like your whisky," she said, pointedly scrunching her face up, "but cookies make everything taste better. And I don't know... Somehow scotch and shortbread seemed like a good mix." She shrugged.

His deep chuckle disarmed her. God, she'd almost forgotten how shockingly hot he was when he smiled.

He bit into a second scotch shortbread cookie. "Mmm, I honestly cannae believe you wasted single malt whisky in a bloody biscuit, but damn, they're good lass."

It was a backhanded compliment, but she'd take it. She was pleased that he was enjoying them. She giggled. "Glad you approve, Sergeant Mackenzie."

He threw her an arched brow. "Are ye a baker then?" he asked between bites.

"Oh heck no." She snorted. "But I do enjoy a little Christmas baking."

"Maybe not such a bad thing having ye stranded here wi' me after all," he remarked.

"I can earn my keep with baking." She smiled, glad to have an easy light interaction with him.

"Aye, ye can." Alex leaned against the counter and sipped his coffee. "So what is it ye do Ms. West, if ye're not a baker?"

"I'm a writer." She smiled, shyly tucking a strand of hair behind her ear.

"What do ye write?" He watched her intently as she moved cookies from a baking tray to a cooling rack. Then he snatched a warm cookie from behind her, making her feel a fluff of pride flutter in her chest that he liked them so much. She'd never had someone to bake for before, except for herself.

"I write lifestyle articles for a couple of magazines and online publications. It pays the bills, and, for the most part, I enjoy the writing," she said. "But it's not really where my passion lies."

"Oh?" he said curiously.

It was the first time he seemed interested in something about her, but still, she was hesitant to tell him—nervous to share something that meant so much to her. Writing a novel was her dream, and it was still early in the process. She didn't want him to judge her.

His stormy piercing blue eyes were looking at her expectantly.

She bit her lip as she contemplated whether or not to open up about her novel.

"Where does your passion lie?" His voice seemed to have dropped an octave.

Her heart fluttered at the heat in his gaze. She quickly turned away, trying to tamp down the tingles that pricked her senses. Plunging her hands in the hot soapy water, she began to wash the dirty dishes from her baking. "Um, I'm working on a novel right now," she said tentatively and then threw caution to the wind. "Writing stories with characters and a plot, that's what truly sings to my soul." She sighed dreamily, not daring to look back at him.

"What's it about, your novel?" It surprised her to find he sounded genuinely interested.

She glanced at him shyly, wondering whether or not to tell him. She hadn't even told her girls what it was about. Why would she tell Mean Hot Cop? Husband Cop? Dad Cop?

Her mind went back to the photo of him with his wife and kids. Why did he want to know about her novel? Why did he care? What about his secrets?

His blue eyes seemed to be studying her. She didn't know why she felt compelled to tell him about her writing. Maybe it was that they were stranded together all alone. Maybe it was because if she shared her secrets, perhaps he'd share his. Or maybe it was just the way he was watching her, so intently, like he actually cared.

Continuing to absently scrub the dishes, she said, "It's a mystery novel that takes place in Budapest." She felt a little thrill saying it out loud. She hadn't told anyone about it yet.

"Hmm, I'm intrigued already. Budapest is one of my favourite cities."

She felt a nervous tension she hadn't even realized she'd been holding, begin to melt away and she eyed him over her shoulder. "You've been?"

"Aye, many years ago now," he said, and for a moment there was a distance in his eyes, almost a sadness. He moved alongside her, picked up a dishcloth, and began drying the dishes she'd washed.

Quinn wondered if Alex had been to Budapest with his wife. A honeymoon perhaps. That was a sobering thought.

"I'd love to go. I've researched it for my book. The history is fascinating and the architecture," she paused sighing, seeing it in her mind's eye. "One day, I'll walk the Danube and take it all in."

Alex smiled. "'Tis an intriguing city. I can imagine it to be the perfect choice for the backdrop of a mystery novel."

Quinn was pleased Alex saw it that way too.

"Have ye been to Scotland, lass?"

"No, unfortunately, I haven't done much travelling outside of Canada. I will. though. I love learning about different cultures and seeing new places."

"Aye, well, ye should add Scotland to yer list then. 'Tis a different kind of history and architecture. I suspect ye'd be fascinated with all the ruins with their stories and legends."

She could hear the pride in his voice. "Sounds dreamy." She sighed.

He chuckled lightly. "Aye, and 'tis ruggedly beautiful much like Canada."

Quinn tried to imagine what it would be like to go to Scotland and then found herself wondering if muscular gorgeousness was a common trait in Scottish men. She snuck a look at him as he stood drying the mixing bowl she'd used. The domestic side certainly added to his hotness.

"I'd like to read your book when it's done if ye'd allow me," Alex said, pulling Quinn from her thoughts.

A flattered smile tugged her lips. "Well, you may have to wait a while. I had hoped to be working on it over the holidays, but instead, I'm here—baking cookies."

"Ah right, I see." The compassion in his tone surprised her. "Mother nature is unleashing some kind of winter fury." He looked out the window kitchen window as the snow continued to blow about.

"It's all good." She said absently handing him a cookie sheet to dry. "I'm grateful to be in a warm cozy cabin. There are worse things."

"Aye, 'tis true."

"I am gonna hold you to teaching me some self-defence though while I'm stuck here. It's something I've always wanted to learn but never seemed to get around to."

"It's an important skill to have. Perhaps tomorrow then."

"Perfect." She felt lighter, liking that they'd reached a new level in their relationship. Friendship. Whatever it was.

"Right, I'm going to go grab some more logs so we dinnae run out tonight," Alex announced, walking to the back door and putting his coat and boots back on. "We dinnae need ye frozen like an ice cube and crawling into my bed again."

"I did not *crawl* into your bed!" Quinn snapped, instantly irritated at his implication. "I had no intention of getting into your bed. If you recall, *you* were the one who insisted I get in," she said haughtily.

Alex looked at her with a tired expression. "I was only teasing ye, lass."

"Oh," she muttered, regretting that she'd been the one to get snappy this time. She turned away from him to start transferring her cookies from the cooling rack to a platter she'd found. "I'm just about all washed up here, I can come and help you," she offered, trying to make peace.

"It's okay. I willnae be long." And with that, the door slammed behind him.

24
Married

ALEX CAME IN A little while later with a couple of bundles of wood. He put them in the iron log rack near the fireplace. "Quinn?" he called not seeing her in the kitchen or living room.

"I'm up here," she called down from the loft.

Climbing up the wood ladder that was attached to the kitchen wall, he stepped off into the loft and saw Quinn sitting on the old tufted love seat with books surrounding her. When She looked up at him, her big brown eyes were filled with childlike wonder that almost knocked the wind from his lungs.

"You have the most amazing library up here!" she gushed.

"Aye," he said, moving a couple of books to the trunk coffee table to sit down beside her. "Most of them came with the cottage," he said. God, the lass was lovely when she was excited about something.

"Wow, that's a pretty sweet deal. I've been sifting through the greatness. Did you know you have *A Christmas Carol*?" She grinned from ear to ear.

Alex was struck at how her face lit up in pure pleasure. Without thinking, he reached out and moved a stray strand of hair that had fallen forward against her rosy cheeks. He didn't think about it; he just did it. His hand lingered, and he allowed his knuckles to gently brush against the soft skin of her cheek.

The subtle sound of her breath hitching caused desire to tug at his senses. Reeling, he dropped his hand away. Her eyes had dropped to the book in her lap, and he noted she seemed to grow uncomfortable. It made him question whether she'd wanted his touch and was disappointed or whether he'd made her uncomfortable touching her at all. It was a subtle touch, but they both seemed to recognize its intimacy.

"Sorry," he grunted leaning away from her.

Quinn felt confused. This was the gentle side he kept tight to himself. God, but when he unlocked his chains, she melted. *But you shouldn't be melting* Quinn, she reminded herself.

He's married. Or perhaps divorced. Not knowing meant Alex Mackenzie was off-limits.

"Are you married?" she blurted, peering into his stormy blue eyes.

"What?" The question took him off guard. "No, of course no'." He ran his hands over his face, and he looked almost remorseful. "I am no' married lass, rest assured, but I'm no' looking for anything either. I dinnae mean to give ye the wrong impression."

Quinn searched his eyes and realized there was truth there. So he wasn't married, but then what about the woman in the picture? She couldn't make sense of it. And for a guy not looking for anything... God, for a split second sparks were flying. The intensity of his gentle touch scorched her. Couldn't he feel that too?

Alex leaned back and ran a hand over his clean shaven chin. After an awkward silence, Quinn took a breath and opened the book in her lap, believing him that he wasn't married. She was even more curious about what his deal was, but she chose to leave it be. For now.

"We should read it," she said, gesturing to the little red book. Without giving him a chance to respond, she flipped it open and began aloud, "'Marley was dead: to begin with. There is no doubt whatever about that.'"

The sun was setting, and the light in the cabin was dimming. They'd been sitting in the loft for about an hour as Quinn read. At first, Alex thought he should put some space between them again, but the cottage wasn't big and he couldn't keep avoiding her. Once she began reading, he decided that sitting with her and listening wasn't such a bad thing. The truth was he loved *A Christmas Carol*, having watched many versions of it, but he had never read the book itself. He found himself relaxing and getting into the story. Quinn's voice was animated but at the same time calming. The only problem was that he kept getting mesmerized by her full pouty lips as she read. Reminding himself that he was immune was quickly becoming an asinine strategy when it came to resisting the lass. Everything about her was taunting him, provoking him much like the ghosts taunting Scrooge into changing his ways.

"'Stave Two. The first of three spirits.'"

"Maybe we should take this downstairs, and I can get started on making us some dinner," Alex suggested.

"Mm, good idea. I could definitely eat," she responded. With the book still in hand, she stretched her arms up over her head.

His police-issue sweatpants and hoodie never looked so good. They were big on her, but when she stretched, everything seemed to pull a bit tighter on her in all the right places.

Inconveniently, that was when he remembered that her bra and panties were in the bathroom and not on her personage. His eyes drew to her well-endowed chest, pushed out proudly as she arched back with a satisfied groan. How easy it would be to yank up the hoodie and free those delectable breasts. Shite, he needed space. Now. He stood up and moved to the ladder to climb down and get himself out of the loft that now felt way too small. Christ, it frustrated him that even blowing his load in the shower had done little to curb his carnal desire.

To his chagrin, she came down right after him, and he got a prime view of her curvy sweat pant-clad ass as she made her way down the ladder from above him. God help him.

Alex quickly busied himself with preparing dinner. Opening the fridge, he pulled out some steaks.

"Can I help?" Her voice was sweet as she sidled up alongside him at the countertop. Was she trying to torture him? His cock stirred at her nearness. For a moment, he imagined bending her over the countertop exposing that tempting ass to him so he could... Bloody hell, what was wrong with him?

He did not want her help. What he wanted was for her to get the hell away from him so he could stop feeling this way. Unfocused, undisciplined. Like he was out of control. *Fuck.*

It was all wrong. In two years, he hadn't been tempted by anyone as much as he was right now, and he didn't like it. If she would just stop getting so close to him.

"I got this," he murmured, intentionally avoiding her gaze.

"You're sure?"

"Aye," he growled impatiently. "Ye're just in the way."

Quinn bristled at his abrupt response. "Right. Got it," she said tight-lipped, and he could hear the hurt in her voice.

A piece of him knew he should apologize. But what could he say? *I just need you to get the hell away from me so I can stop imagining fucking you!* Christ.

No, let her think he was an arse. That was a better option. He needed a little space. She could be mad at him. Perhaps it was safer that way.

He could feel her eyes boring into him as he purposefully ignored her and continued gathering ingredients.

"I'm going to lie down for a bit. Is it okay if I go in your room?" she asked, and he could hear the apprehension in her voice.

He nodded curtly without looking up.

Quinn made her exit, feeling irritated at the return of Cold Mean Cop. It had all been going so well...or so she thought. What had changed from in the loft to coming down to make dinner? She was dumbfounded and disappointed. Bear plodded in behind her as she walked into Alex's bedroom.

"Come on boy," she encouraged him onto the bed with her, and he happily obliged, cuddling up next to her. Alex might hate that she was here, but at least Bear liked her company.

Quinn absently stroked Bear's soft ears. There were moments when things were so easy between them. She even found that she liked their time together, but then he'd get all cold and mean again. It was frustrating. She wondered how much of the way he was with her had to do with the woman in the photograph. He'd said he wasn't married, and she believed him. He had no reason to lie, and somehow, she just felt like she could take him at his word. But what was his story? None of it made sense to her.

Quinn bit her lip. It didn't help anything that she was very attracted to him, and it seemed that he was to her too. But if he wasn't married, why did he seem to fight their chemistry? They were stuck alone in this cabin. How bad would it be to have a fling? The thought sent heated tingles straight to her core. *Don't go there, Quinn,* she chided herself.

Maybe his reluctance had something to do with the woman and kids in the picture. Perhaps they were dating, and they were the woman's kids from before him? Except the toddler had a definite resemblance to Alex. She rolled onto her side pulling the thick cozy duvet around her. A terrible thought came to her. What if he was widowed? Had something happened to his family? The thought alone made her heart sad for him. Could that be it? Her thoughts eventually turned lucid as she drifted to sleep.

With time to think while he prepared the food, Alex started to feel bad for how he'd behaved. She didn't deserve his wrath. It wasn't her fault that he couldn't seem to get a grip on his base urges. As much as he didn't want anything to happen between them, he realized that it was ridiculous that he couldn't just enjoy her company with no strings attached. She wasn't so bad to have around if he was honest. Minus the damn horny thoughts that barraged his mind, but he could keep that in check. He *needed* to keep that in check. Perhaps a few extra showers would be required over the next couple of days to help keep his sex-starved cock quiet. Lord help him.

Having a clearer mind, he allowed himself to appreciate that he'd have some company for Christmas. Even if it was Quinn West. She still talked too much and made him crazy, but he also kind of enjoyed her company. He liked that she'd busied herself today baking. If she could make the most of being stuck here together, he could too.

Dinner ready, Alex strode into his room where Bear popped a lazy eye open from the bed. The bedside lamp cast a warm glow. Quinn looked cozy curled on her side, blankets pulled around her. She must have drifted off. She lay with her hands slid together and tucked under her cheek. He'd tried so damn hard not to notice her loveliness, but as he looked down at her now, he was almost taken aback. God, she was achingly beautiful.

Awareness and desire collided in his body. It seemed an unrelenting combination. He should've turned and walked back out of the room. Gone to take another shower. That would have been the wise thing to do. Instead, he sat on the edge of the bed beside her. Those innocent big eyes opened, sleepily landing on him and a sweet smile touched her pouty mouth.

"Hi," she said softly.

Christ, she was irresistible. He shouldn't have done it, but he couldn't seem to stop himself. He reached down and ran his hand over her hair that lay across the pillow, letting the silky strands slip between his fingers. His resolve slipped away faster than steam from hot coffee. His eyes slid to her face as she watched him with those big curious brown eyes lined with thick sooty lashes. Her rounded cheeks narrowed as they rode up to her temples giving her the look of a magazine model. Her nose was pert and adorable and God help him, those lips. Berry pink, full, and pouty. They practically begged to be kissed.

And he wanted nothing more than to taste them, take them in his, conquer them, and kiss those lips that had given him grief since he first saw them...surrender to them. Without thought, he cupped her jaw in his hand and ran his thumb over those soft plump lips. She allowed him to. Her innocent brown eyes were fixed on his, and he could see desire growing in them. His cock thickened, begging for her. That mouth of hers had taunted him since the moment she'd stepped out of her car the day he'd given her the defunct ticket.

Unable to stop himself, he leaned down closer to her, and a rush of pleasure hit his groin as her eyes widened in anticipation. His eyes dropped to her beckoning sinful mouth, and her rosy pink lips parted, ready, longing to be kissed.

Every fibre in his being wanted to plunder those full lips and give her what she desired. Like Santa's reindeer hurdling through the sky on Christmas Eve, Alex was helpless to stop himself, and his mouth dropped to hers. The touch of her full warm lips against his set every nerve ending in his body on fire and need roared through him as intensely as the torrential winds whipping around outside the window.

Despite the light touch of his lips on hers, the hitch of her breath nearly scorched him. He wanted to reach up into her thick auburn hair and pull her firmly against him, to open those sweet torturous lips with his and taste her.

The blissful sigh against his mouth as her lips parted slightly for him, allowing him to kiss her more deeply, made him feel feral, and he knew he had to stop. Now. He pulled back from her, refusing to play with fire—refusing to lose the control that he clung to like a thread of Christmas tinsel. Giving in and kissing her how he wanted to, letting his tongue touch hers, the thought alone made his cock jerk painfully. Giving in to his hunger would open floodgates that were never meant to be opened. God but pulling back was a herculean feat.

25

The Accidental Confession

One minute his mouth was pressed to hers in the sweetest kiss of her life, the next Alex stood up abruptly, and she was sure she heard a growl as he strode to the door.

"Wait," she pleaded, scrambling to sit up in his bed. Her mind rolled with a hundred thoughts as her body still clung to desire.

The tension was thick between them even as Alex stood with his back to her, but he waited.

"I-I, well, you said you aren't married…" she finally got the words out.

"I wouldnae huv kissed ye if I was married." He whipped around to face her. His voice was tight.

"But, I-I saw the picture with you and…" her voice trailed off, realizing she'd spoken without thinking.

His eyebrows snapped together as his lips set in a grim line, and it sent a shiver down her spine.

"And who? What picture?" He eyed her suspiciously his voice clipped.

"Um..." She bit her lip, knowing that anything she said would sound bad, but she couldn't un-bake the cake now. And the truth was she wanted to know. Even if he got angry with her. Pulling her knees to her chest, she said, "The one with you, the blond woman holding the baby, and the little boy." She swallowed. "You all looked so happy."

He stared at her, but she couldn't read his expression. "And where exactly did you see this picture?"

She swallowed scrunching her eyes closed. "I found it in your sporran. In the closet." She confessed, cringing at her own words. "But it's not what you think," she added feeling overwhelmingly guilty.

Alex looked at her stunned, like she'd slapped him in the face. Then his brows dropped, his jaw tightened, and she could see the look of betrayal right before his stormy eyes turned dark and a menacing expression overtook his handsome features. She realized then and there, he was no stranger to betrayal.

She could practically feel him seething, but it didn't stop her. Clambering off the bed, she grabbed his strong arm. "Please, it's not what you think, I was looking for clothes and I saw your sporran, I never meant. I-I was curious. I didn't know what was kept inside. I've never seen a sporran before. I didn't mean to go through it." It sounded bad to her even as she pleaded her innocence.

Alex snatched her waist and spun her around slamming her firmly against the closed door. His hands hammered down on either side of her, locking her in place. His angry handsome face inches from hers.

Quinn shook nervously, half hating herself for the hint of arousal that rippled through her even as his stormy blue eyes pierced her with their intensity. She should fear for her safety with the anger emanating from him. She gripped her hands against the door behind her trying to find her courage. "Alex, I honestly wasn't trying to snoop, I promise. I came across the picture by accident." Her voice quivered.

"By accident?" His lip curled menacingly, his face so close to hers.

Her heart was racing, and with him seething down at her like she'd committed some grave atrocity, her own anger spiked. "You know what? You big brute! I don't care what you think," she snapped. "I would never snoop through someone's things in the way you're implying." She poked her finger into his hard muscled chest. "Yes, I opened your sporran, but not because I was trying to spy on you, you big oaf! I'd never seen a sporran before, and I simply wondered what in the heck people keep in them. Maybe it was wrong to look, but excuse me for living!"

Alex was completely taken aback by her fiery little rant and had the strangest urge to kiss the tip of the slim finger that had poked angrily at his chest. Did nothing scare this woman? He'd made grown men beg for mercy with less. At five foot five tops and trapped in front of a pissed off six foot four man, she raged at him like a lioness. Bloody hell, he shouldn't be admiring her right now.

"I saw the photograph. I'm sorry. I didn't mean to, okay? But it's done now. I've seen it." She crossed her arms over her chest.

Alex didn't even know what to say as he continued to stare down at her. Her big brown eyes were breathtakingly disarming.

"You can tell me if you have a wife and kids or what happened to them. I'm a good listener," she said, softly biting her lip.

He heard her, but he was wholly distracted by her lips. God, he wanted to kiss them again, properly this time. Letting out a groan, he ran his hands through his hair and turned away from her, going to the window and looking out into the darkness. The snow was still coming down, but now, it fell in big quiet flakes. At least the wind had died down. The lass didn't move, she stood waiting and he could feel her hopeful gaze upon him.

Alex believed the lass—not that he wanted to. It would be easier if she were a liar. He'd never fuck a liar again, but he'd encountered enough lying sons of bitches in his career and lifetime that he could spot them a mile away. And Quinn was not one. Far from it.

But she was a complication for him right now. He struggled to fight off his desire for her, but if he gave into it, it would not end well for either of them. He recalled how she'd shied away from his touch in the loft, and it made sense now. She thought he was married. Before the idea was even fully formed, he knew it was terrible, but it might just save them both some grief. He'd told her he didn't have a wife, but if he left the photo a mystery. Perhaps it would help them both to resist anything physical. Then there would be two of them fighting against their off-the-charts chemistry. He didn't have to lie per se, but maybe not tell her the entire truth.

She tentatively came up behind him, and with her soft touch on his arm, he made his decision. He couldn't look at her. "I dinnae want to talk about my family, Quinn." It was not a total lie.

"Are they here in Canada?" she asked.

"No." Also, not a lie.

He turned to her. "Leave it be, lass," he said heavily. She searched his face before nodding her agreement.

"Okay," she said, reluctantly looking like she wanted to say more. Alex knew the lass had questions, but for now, he'd let her make her own conclusions. He just hoped it would be enough to prevent them both from giving into the desires that seemed to be growing unbidden between them.

"Dinner's ready," he said matter-of-factly.

"Good, I'm starved," she said, before turning away from him and marching towards the door. "I hope you're a decent cook, Sergeant Mackenzie," she called to him over her shoulder as she made her way to the kitchen.

A smile pulled at Alex's lips as he shook his head and followed her out of the room.

26
Ice Cracking and Pleasantries

The smell of dinner made her stomach growl. She padded down the hall to the kitchen with Alex behind her. She was far too aware of the man, and she couldn't help but think of the moment before all hell broke loose when his lips had touched hers so tenderly. She was sure she could relive that moment a thousand times and not tire of it.

"Have a seat." Alex gestured to one of the chairs at the old wood kitchen table. Quinn took in the sight before her as she sat down. Their meals were plated, and in the middle of the table, Alex had lit a new red candle. It felt romantic, or maybe more charming than romantic. She was certain he didn't intend to woo her.

He sat across from her, and they briefly looked at each other over the candlelight.

"I'm sorry, lass, for getting so angry. It wasnae fair of me."

Quinn felt an instant relief hearing his apology. "I'm sorry, too. I truly didn't mean to go through your private things.

That's the only thing I looked in. Otherwise, I was a perfect angel." She grinned at him.

Alex scoffed as if he doubted the angel part. Clearing his throat, he added, "I'm sorry too for when I first came in." His voice was strained. "I didn't mean to…" he paused, looking up at her. "It willnae happen again," he said with finality.

Nooo. Quinn's mind rebelled against his words. Her most feminine parts desperately wanted it to happen again and then some. She couldn't help the stab of disappointment. If she thought he was actually married, she'd feel guilt and his lips would not be on hers again, but there was something fishy about the photo and his reaction.

She was certain that he wasn't married to the woman, at least not anymore. And the kids? Well, she really had no idea. But why was he so secretive about it all? It wasn't like he had to divulge every detail, but could he not just give her the *Coles Notes* version of events?

Although she still didn't know the situation with the woman in the photo, she did believe him when he said he wouldn't have kissed her if he was married. Which was a giant relief, because the fireworks she felt would be very hard to keep at bay.

She cut a small piece of steak, picking it up with her fork. "I wouldn't mind if it happened again," she said quietly as she slid the fork into her mouth without looking up.

She felt his eyes shoot to her. Good. She'd surprised him. She guessed he'd thought he'd thrown her off track.

"Quinn." He sighed.

As she chewed her cooked-to-perfection steak, she noted his brows had knit together in frustration. "Well, it wasn't the best kiss," she fibbed, pinning her hands together under her chin, "but I suspect if we tried again... I mean we are stuck here together."

Alex could hardly believe what he was hearing. She wanted a fling with him? And the kiss he'd barely begun, but Christ, his blood had roared. Was she that unaffected? There was a part of him that wanted to show her exactly what he wanted to do being stuck here alone with her.

God, he'd love nothing more than to strip her of his clothes, handcuff her to his bloody bed, and kiss every square inch of her body before he slid his cock into her slick, tight wetness. Jesus. What was he thinking? *No. No. No.* No good would come of it. He knew that damn it.

He cleared his throat. "I dinnae think that's a wise idea."

"Why not?" she challenged, her big brown eyes sparking. "You're not married, right?" she said casually, to confirm once and for all.

His eyes shot to hers. He wasn't used to someone pushing back, and the truth was, he didn't have a good answer for her. Before he thought better of it, the lie was out of his mouth. "It's because I'm not attracted to you that way."

She threw her head back, rolling her eyes. "Oh right, I remember now, you wouldn't sleep with me even if I begged. How could I forget? I suppose that explains the shitty kiss," she added as she nibbled a carrot off her fork, appearing unbothered.

Alex didn't know what to say. He was damned either way, so he kept his mouth shut. It irked him, though, about the kiss.

At a standstill, they silently ate.

"Mmm, that was delicious," Quinn said satisfied as she finished the last bite of her steak. Alex noted she'd eaten everything on her plate. "Guess you are a good cook after all." Her grin was sly.

Alex eyed her, amazed at how easily she could let things roll off her. It seemed she wasn't one to hold a grudge or stay angry. It was another trait he found he admired in her. It was like she couldn't be bothered wasting time with bad moods.

"Aye, I'm no' so bad in the kitchen. My mam is a great cook, she taught me a few things."

"You must miss her cooking. I assume your parents are back in Scotland?" she hedged. He could tell she was testing to see if he'd shut down the conversation. It seemed like a safe one, so he answered.

"Aye, they are still in Scotland."

"Have they come to see you here?"

"No. Maybe they will one day. I know they'd love it here."

"Oh, I bet they would," she said as if she knew them firsthand. "Who wouldn't adore these mountains? They are otherworldly with the sheer size of them! Gosh, and you could take them on gorgeous hikes; I bet you know all the good places to go. Or if they don't hike, even just wandering around the town would be so much fun. Calen has so many cute local shops at least from what I've seen so far." Her features were lit up like a Christmas tree and Lord help him if he didn't find himself liking it. "Are your parents from Scotland originally?"

She looked at him expectantly. He supposed it wouldn't hurt to chat with her a bit. Maybe it would distract him from his wayward thoughts.

Alex leaned back in his chair and crossed his arms over his chest. "My family has been Scots for many generations. Although my mom's side has some Irish too. My sister Orlagh was named after my mam's gran, she was Irish."

"So I wasn't off when I guessed Irish the day we met," Quinn said with a smug little grin that Alex wished he didn't find so intriguing.

He rolled his eyes. "Perhaps a wee bit off, lass. I'm about as Scottish as they come."

"Fine. Scottish. Except a little bit Irish." Her dark eyes flashed with humour, and Alex felt his lips twitch in a smile.

"I love the name Orlagh," she said as if to herself before looking back up at him. "Is it spelled O-r-l-a?"

"Ye want to use it as a character name in yer Budapest book?"

She blinked. "No, I-"

"O-r-l-a-g-h," he interrupted before she could worry her pretty little head about it. "She wouldnae mind if ye did."

Quinn nodded, the corners of her full lips turning up in a soft smile. "Good to know." She shifted in her chair. "Do you have more siblings or just Orlagh?"

"Two brothers and two sisters." He paused, feeling tension lace his jaw. It never got easier talking about Helena. "My oldest sister, Helena... She died when I was seventeen."

Quinn regarded him. The lass wore her heart on her sleeve; he could see the empathy in the depths of her expressive eyes. "I'm sorry. I can't imagine."

Alex took a sip of beer, the familiar feeling of the loss digging into his chest. He rolled his shoulders back trying to release some of the tension. "She was thrown from her horse and broke her neck." He swallowed back the familiar lump in his throat, then quickly finished without looking up. "Losing her was one of the hardest things my family has had to face, but we've gotten through. I suppose time makes it all more bearable. Life goes on."

Quinn nodded, and Alex had a feeling she truly understood. But before he could ask her about her own life, she asked him, "Are you all still close? I mean as a family?"

"Och, aye. We are lucky, I think. We have always been close. My one brother Drew went through a bit of a rebel spell. Actually, he was a complete arse for a time, but he's come back around." Alex smiled thinking of his family. "They will all get together tomorrow night for a wee feast and some Christmas cheer."

"You must miss being there."

"At Christmas, in particular, I suppose I do. I can see it now. They'll have the fire going, and my da will be the one to start the round of carols. He loves to sing." Alex smiled nostalgically. "Then on Christmas morning, they'll cook up a big Scots breakfast, open presents, and then they'll all head down to the seaside for the Christmas Day polar dip."

"That all sounded completely dreamy right up until polar dip!" Quinn chirped.

He chuckled. "My brothers and I always do it. People come from counties all around. There's upwards of a hundred people all freezing their arses off."

"And you go into the ocean, in the dead of winter?" she said skeptically, looking uncomfortable at the very idea.

"Och, aye, we run in and huv a wee swim about."

"Nooo!" She shuttered.

"It's no' as cold as it is here in Canada. Although it can be nippy. Ach, lass, the swim is a blast. Ye'd love it."

Quinn snorted. "What makes you say that? I've pretty much been freezing my ass off since I met you, and believe me, I don't love it!"

His chuckle was a deep rumble. "I watched ye try and trudge through snow in bare legs and high heels. I huv no doubt that ye've enough sass and stubbornness to do a polar dip."

Quinn smirked, seeming to appreciate his estimation of her. "Maybe," she agreed. "Are you supposed to be going home?" Her perfectly arched brows knit together in concern.

"Naw." He sighed still feeling some regret at his cancelled trip. "I was supposed to fly out yesterday morning, but my work schedule changed. I had to cancel it."

"Shitty," she said matter-of-factly.

"Aye," he agreed. "Probably a good thing it got cancelled, I wouldnae huv been able to get to the airport anyway with all this snow."

"Right," she said, throwing her gaze towards the window.

"Ah, 'tis fine. I'll go another time. I would huv liked to see my nephews though. What about ye, lass? Do ye huv family?" He had wondered about how it was that no one expected to hear from her at Christmas.

"Not really. I am an only child." Quinn bit her lip, and Alex realized it was something she did when she was uncertain. Christ, it set him on fire every time though.

Alex watched her intently and then she looked across the table at him decidedly. "Mine was not exactly an idyllic childhood." She picked up her fork and absently fiddled with tines. "My mom was in her forties when she had me, and she was an alcoholic. It wasn't a great scenario."

"I'm sorry, lass," he murmured.

"She died when I was fourteen," she said, sounding emotionless. Either she'd gotten past it, or she was like him and knew how to keep the emotion contained. She rattled out the words like she was reading off a shopping list. "Complications from years of alcohol abuse. I ended up living with my grandmother, which was for the best really. And I never knew my father. He was non-existent."

Alex sat back trying to take it all in. Christ, she'd been through a hell of a life. The strength he'd recognized in her made sense now. She was a survivor, a fighter. That protective feeling surged through him again.

"I was the fancy product of a one-night stand." She tried to make light of the moment that had grown overly serious.

"Fancy indeed." His lips quirked in a half smile. "Thank God for one-night stands," he added, quickly realizing how crass it sounded, but before he could take it back, the lass burst out laughing and clinked her beer bottle to his.

"Thank God for one-night stands," she pronounced jovially, and he felt a warmth in his chest as he took a sip of his beer, his eyes not straying from her.

They chatted with a newfound ease as they cleaned up the dishes.

"Another beer?" Alex offered as Quinn did one last wipe down of the countertop.

"You have anything other than beer?" She bit her lip and he had to remind his cock to behave.

"Ye want to try the whisky again, lass?"

He looked at her hopefully. He didn't know why, but he wanted her to like it.

"Sure, what the heck." She smiled. "I suppose it must have some redeeming qualities if you Scots like it so much."

He chuckled as he poured two glasses. "The key is to sip it slowly, Quinn. Dinnae guzzle it down."

They sat in the great room in the chairs in front of the fireplace. "We could watch a movie if ye like?" Alex offered.

"We could, but maybe later. I want to hear more about your life in Scotland and what brought you here." She turned in her chair to face him, her big brown eyes imploring him to spill all his secrets.

He threw his head back and rolled his eyes.

"Oh, don't be so dramatic Sergeant Mackenzie," she teased him, shoving her foot playfully at his shin. He was tempted to grab it, tear off her sock, and massage the pretty foot with those red-painted toenails. *Shite.*

"Oh, come on," she cajoled, clearly having no idea the direction his thoughts had gone. "We are stuck together alone in this cabin—and you've made it clear sex is off the table—so we may as well get to know each other."

Alex was taken aback by her blunt assessment, but then he chuckled despite himself. She made a decent argument, he supposed. Standing up, he walked to the kitchen bringing his phone back with him, and she watched him curiously. Christmas music began playing, and then the Bluetooth kicked in, playing from speakers in the living room.

"Christmas playlist" he explained with a twinkle in his eye.

She giggled lightly. "You have a Christmas playlist on your phone?"

"Of course." He grinned unabashedly. "I hope ye dinnae mind a bit of Celtic Christmas music."

"Not at all." She stretched with a contented sigh and relaxed back into her chair. He watched as she took a tentative sip of the scotch.

"Bahh, my God," she huffed, as if she'd just drunk fire.

He laughed. "So ye'r telling me ye practically raised yerself, making ye strong as fuck, but a wee bit of scotch is too much fer ye?"

Her lips quirked eyeing him from under her pretty brow, and he realized she knew damn well that she was a strong lass. And God help him if he didn't like her all the more for it.

Quinn never shied from a challenge, and clearly, he was proposing one. She would master this damn whisky and learn to like it if it killed her.

As they sat chatting, she took tiny little sips of the scotch. It did seem to get better as the night went on. She surprised herself saying yes to a refill later in the evening.

"I can't believe the time," Quinn quipped with a yawn at midnight. It had been an unexpectedly pleasant evening. Alex seemed to have let his guard down, at least a bit and he definitely seemed more at ease with her now. It was Christmas Eve Eve and Quinn realized she'd actually had the best time with Mean Hot Cop tonight—though she wouldn't admit it out loud.

"Aye, I'm ready for bed." He yawned, stretched his arms above him, and then groaned. "I'm a bit stiff from all that wood chopping."

Quinn's eyes were drawn to the sex line *V* that peeked out from under his shirt when he stretched. Good Lord, that little snippet alone was completely swoon-worthy.

Alex caught her eye and for the briefest moment, the tension crackled between them. Quinn knew that, despite the chemistry, the man said he was off-limits. Not that she believed that, but she didn't want him to get all weird with her again. Especially after they seemed to have made headway tonight, so she stood and headed for the bathroom.

"I'm just going to wash up."

Alex sat in the chair, staring into the last glowing embers of the fire. He'd felt her gaze on him, and when he looked at her, he saw desire in her eyes big brown eyes. It stoked his own desire. He'd kept it all in check the whole evening, distracted by surprisingly great conversation. He'd actually found himself rather engrossed in talking with her. But that look she just gave him? Fuck. He needed to keep it together.

Glancing over to the settee, Alex considered their sleeping arrangements. If he built up the fire, she could sleep out here again, but it would only last so long before she'd need to add a log. She'd be up and down all night adding logs. Shit. He couldn't very well make her sleep here tonight, and he didn't want to sleep here either. Memories of the night before crept into his mind.

The evening had felt safe between them. He'd actually managed to have a conversation with her without wanting to either throttle her or kiss her, so that was encouraging. Shockingly, he enjoyed the company of Ms. Quinn West. Wonders never ceased. The bathroom door opened, and as Quinn stepped out, Alex went to go in behind her.

"I'm not going to freeze my ass on your couch tonight," she said matter-of-factly as she strode past him to his bedroom.

Alex swallowed, staring after her. She didn't look back, just went into his room, and closed the door.

"Right, that settles it then," he muttered.

wasn't part of our everyday life anymore, but he was everything to my parents."

"Aww, that's hard." Her voice was soft and soothing.

"They did end up taking in a stray tabby cat a few years back though. Talisker."

"Talisker?"

"Aye, he's a golden orange cat so Da named him after his favourite whisky."

Quinn snorted a laugh. "Of course he did." Quinn's easy humour had a way of making Alex feel at ease with her, and in the darkness, it was easier to keep his unbidden attraction at bay.

"I told ye whisky is very important to us Scots."

"Talisker," Quinn repeated as if trying the name on her tongue.

Something about laying in the dark with her and talking reminded him of the nights he used to stay up late with his brothers when they were kids. When they were supposed to be asleep, they'd often stay up half the night, hidden under the blanket, blethering about cars and girls. Their parents none the wiser. Alex rolled over to face her now.

"What about ye? What was your favourite Christmas present?" It surprised him, just how much he wanted to know.

"Well, any Christmas I got a Barbie doll I was happy." He could tell she was grinning, and for a moment, he wished blanket lay a little white Scotty puppy with a red ribbon tied around his neck. Angus."

Quinn chuckled. "Aww, of course. Angus, so Scottish. Did you have any idea you were getting a dog?"

"None whatsoever. We didn't think we were allowed to have any pets. It never even occurred to us to ask for one. It was the best Christmas," Alex said reflecting back.

"Gosh, I can't imagine. That is like every kid's dream!" Quinn tucked her pillow a little snugger under her head.

"It was pretty great. Angus was the best little dog, too. He lived for seventeen years." Alex's mind drifted back to the happy times of his childhood with his trusty pup always in tow of himself or his siblings.

"Wow, that's a long time for a dog. He must have had a good life with you and your family."

"Aye, he was spoiled." Alex found himself smiling. "Da was always giving him bits of meat from dinner when mam wasn't looking." Despite the darkness of the room, he could tell Quinn was smiling too.

"Do your parents have any pets now?" she asked, and he could feel her gaze on him.

"They never got another dog. I think it broke their hearts when Angus died. It was hard on all of us, but I think worse for them as my brother and I no longer lived at home. Angus *pline*, he reminded himself as he walked back out of the closet.

"Boxers," he said gesturing to the black boxers he was now wearing as if showing her this barrier would ensure they were both safe from so-called unwanted sex. God help him.

"Good call." She smiled sweetly as he quickly got under the covers, unable to handle her eyes on his body. He liked it far too much.

Laying in the bed beside her, Alex felt his heart actually thudding in his chest. What was with him? He was like a nervous schoolboy on a first date. Flicking off the lamp, he felt far from sleepy now. Damn it.

In the quiet darkness, Quinn rolled to face him. "What was the best Christmas present you ever got?" she asked brightly, seemingly unaware of his inner turmoil.

For once, he was grateful for the lass's need to blether. It would help take his mind off things he shouldn't be thinking about. "Ach, that's an easy one," he said. Putting an arm behind his head, he began to relax. "When I was about eight years old, my parents got us a dog for Christmas."

"Really?" she asked, and he could hear the grin in her voice.

"Aye. We woke up Christmas morning and tore into the living room as ye do, and there, under the tree on a tartan

27
Pillow Talk

AFTER WASHING UP, ALEX poked his head into his room and saw Quinn was already snuggled up in his bed. The lamp on the nightstand was on.

"I'm sorry, but I don't like being cold," she said rather unapologetically as she peered up over the blanket at him. "I know you chopped all that wood..." She bit her lip, and frustratingly, it alerted his cock. "But I feel like I'd be up half the night putting logs on the fire. But you don't have to worry, it's completely platonic. I won't try and make a move on you or anything." She giggled lightly.

Alex wanted to laugh at how ridiculous it was that he would worry about her making "moves" on him. The truth was he was more worried about himself.

"Fair enough," he muttered as he strode into his closet.

Alex hated wearing clothes to bed. They felt too bloody constricting, but there was no way in hell he could sleep naked tonight. Last night, he wasn't prepared, but tonight, he'd keep a barrier— both physically and mentally. *Disci-*

there was enough light to see those lush lips and the dimple on her cheek.

"Oh, I get that. That was me with Lego. Just wasn't Christmas without a new Lego set." He found himself relating.

She laughed. "Exactly, but for me it was Barbies."

"Aye, my sister Orlagh always got Barbies too."

"The best present I ever got was when I was seventeen." Quinn's voice grew nostalgic. "It was from my grandmother." He could hear Quinn take a shaky breath before she continued, and without thinking, he laid his hand over hers on the mattress between them.

"She'd passed away two weeks before Christmas that year, but she'd already scoped out a present for me. A typewriter. It was old, secondhand, and weighed a tonne." Alex had to stop himself from reaching out into the darkness to stroke her face. The way she spoke, he could hear the heaviness of the memories and God, help him, he wanted to hold her, comfort her. Instead, he silently listened and kept his hand covering hers, letting his fingers wrap around the small expanse of her palm.

"I found it in her room on Christmas Eve. It was hidden under a towel in a corner of the bedroom ready for me. It had a simple handwritten tag and two little metallic green star bows stuck to the top." Alex gently squeezed her hand beneath his and he could hear her the unevenness of her breathing.

"It felt almost like a gift from beyond the grave. One final loving memory of my Grandmother for me to treasure. God, I loved that typewriter," she said wistfully.

Alex wanted to pull her into his arms. He could hear the tears in her voice. "Do ye still have it, lass?" he asked gently.

"I do." Her voice was quiet emotion. "And the tag and the bows." She paused, "I even kept the towel." Her light laugh was tender and full of emotion.

"I cannae blame ye."

"The towel feels somehow almost as important as the typewriter. I can see her in my mind, putting it over the typewriter and hiding it from me until Christmas. It is just such a sweet thought. I can't bear to get rid of the towel."

"Makes total sense, lass," he said reassuringly. "Ye obviously loved yer Gran verra much." He felt her fingers gently grip at his. Alex understood far too well. He'd wanted to hang on to everything his sister had ever touched when she died.

"Do ye use the typewriter for yer writing?" he asked genuinely.

"Oh heck no. As much as I adore that typewriter, it would make me crazy to try and do my work on it." She snickered.

He chuckled. "Aye, I suppose laptops are the way of it now."

"It is where my love of writing began, though," she said through a yawn. "Thanks for a great evening," she said quietly, and Alex was surprised when she leaned in and gave him a quick peck on the cheek in the darkness. Chaste as it was, it made his blood stir, but he quickly tamped it down.

"Goodnight, lass," he said and she rolled away from him. He lay there for a few minutes not liking the gap between them. It was chilly in his room. The lass would get cold if she wasn't already. Against his better judgement, he wrapped an arm around her and tugged her curvy body to him. Christ, if it was wrong, he didn't want to be right. She sighed contentedly as she nestled against him, pulling his arm tighter around her.

28
Red Lace

Quinn awoke with a smile on her face. It was Christmas Eve. Never in her wildest dreams did she imagine she'd be in a beautiful log cabin with Mean Hot Cop on Christmas Eve. Rolling over in the bed with a delicious stretch, she was disappointed to discover that Alex wasn't there. She hoped it wasn't an attempt to avoid her. Maybe he'd woken up early and didn't want to disturb her. Ooh, or maybe he was making her breakfast in bed. She almost laughed out loud at the thought because she knew better. There was no way Alex would do that, but it was a fun thought.

Not wanting to waste a minute of the day, she hopped out of bed and headed to the kitchen. To her disappointment, Alex was nowhere to be found, and Bear was gone too. Quinn checked the counter for a note, but this time, there wasn't one. She sighed, supposing Alex was probably out trying to shovel snow again or working out—or doing anything to avoid her.

There was a roaring fire in the fireplace though, and the cabin was surprisingly hot for a change. Well, if he was going to get his exercise in, she could get hers in too. She headed for the bathroom and changed into her bra and underwear. The hot air was perfect for a yoga practice.

She briefly contemplated her attire in the bathroom mirror. If Alex came back in, he may get the wrong idea, but she wasn't going to wear bulky clothes for hot yoga and she'd likely be done before he came back anyway. He seemed to need his alone time. She straightened her bra strap, and the devilish thought occurred to her. Would it be so bad if Alex did come back to the cabin before she was done?

She moved the chairs away from the fireplace, laid a towel down on the deep red Persian area rug, and found her yoga playlist on her phone. The acoustic music was calming as she lay on her back on the floor and began to breathe deeply. The heat of the fireplace was so perfect for hot yoga. Lifting her backside high in the air, she pressed her hands and feet down moving into a down dog. The pose felt divine on her body, and she began flowing through several poses deepening her breath and feeling her muscles release. In no time, her mind and body were one, where time and place ceased to exist.

Standing tall on one leg while lifting her other leg behind her, her hands tipping to the floor, she moved into a standing split, feeling the stretch. The heat from the fireplace warmed her muscles and helped her extend her leg up in the air. Focused on her breathing and holding the pose, she didn't notice Alex come in.

Bear woke Alex, needing to go outside, and Alex was glad for a reason to detangle his body from Quinn's. When he'd awoken, he became enticingly aware of her body snuggled up to his side. Fuck, it felt so good, and just like yesterday morning, his erection was like a lead pipe. Bear nudged at him again, and he sighed getting himself out of the bed.

The snow had stopped when he'd taken Bear out, so he worked on shovelling while his pup bounded around. It started to whip up again though, so Alex decided to head in. He closed the door shaking off the snow before he pulled off his hood, and that was when he saw her. Jesus Christ. What the hell was she doing? Mother of Mary and what the fuck was she wearing?

Alex stood mesmerized as she lowered her leg and brought herself into a down dog. She breathed deeply and lifted one leg high in the air in a split. Her red lace panties pulled as she stretched her leg up. He could almost see her...*Christ*. Lowering the perfect curvy leg, she swooped her arms up and she stood. His eyes landed on her barely contained mouth-watering breasts as she stretched her arms overhead. Good God, the lass was hot as hell.

"Oh, you're back." She grinned brightly as she grabbed a towel and patted it to her rosy-cheeked face.

"Where are yer clothes?" His voice was tight, and he didn't trust himself to move. He'd have her bent over that settee in a heartbeat.

Quinn was oblivious to the dangerous temptation she'd become. "It was so warm in here. I decided to do hot yoga. The less clothes the better. In fact, hot yoga is best practiced naked," she stated matter-of-factly. "The heat of the fire was so perfect. My practice was excellent today. I've never been able to get my leg so high in split," she said excitedly. "Did you see?" Quinn started to bend over again to show Alex her achievement like it wasn't an open fucking invitation to do all the things he wanted to do to her.

"I dinnae want to see," he bellowed, angry that he couldn't seem to control himself.

She flinched, bristling, and he could see she finally recognized something was amiss.

For a moment, she looked like a kicked puppy, and he felt a stab of guilt. Fuck, the problem was he did want to see and touch and taste and… God help him. He was about to apologize when she straightened her spine, her gaze narrowing on him. The little lass looked completely pissed off and painfully fucking hot all at the same time. She strode towards him, cool, calculated, and sexy as hell. Alex stood stone still except for the tick in his jaw.

Standing before him, she was brimstone and hellfire. Her big eyes were blazing.

"Does my body offend you?" She didn't mince words.

"Quinn, I— No, no, of course not." Alex suddenly felt like an arse.

"Good. After all, I believe you told me rather clearly yesterday that you weren't attracted to me, so I shouldn't think seeing me in my bra and panties would be a problem." Her smile was cool and calculated. "Sergeant Mackenzie." She raised her brow to him challengingly.

And there it was. There was zero doubt. Quinn West knew damn well that he'd lied through his fucking teeth when he said he wasn't attracted to her—when he said he wouldn't sleep with her if she begged. *Fuck.*

Alex could barely breathe, never mind speak. When he didn't say a word, she turned her heel and sauntered to the bathroom. "I'm going to take a shower," she said.

As she walked with perfectly rounded hips swaying, she reached behind her, unclasped her bra, and let it slide off onto the floor.

Jesus Christ. Alex's cock proudly saluted her, making it impossible to ignore the lust that was torching his body and clouding his mind. If an avalanche came through the door, he still wouldn't be able to tear his gaze away from her.

Then she stopped in her tracks, slipping her thumbs into the waistband of her red lace panties and bent over as she pulled them down over her perfect ass and down her shapely legs until she flicked them aside with a toe and carried on into the bathroom without looking back.

Alex watched her, spellbound. Desire drowning him. Holy fuck.

Trying to pull it together, he stood for a time not sure what to think anymore. On the spectrum of being immune to not, the scale had completely tipped to not. Not immune. Not even a little. The reality was he was lucky if he could hang onto a thread of discipline when it came to Quinn West. How the hell had that happened? She was beyond what he ever knew he wanted or needed. He couldn't possibly deny the chemistry that sizzled wildly between them. There was no doubt that he wanted her with his every fibre, but did it change the situation?

Alex knew that sex with Quinn would be mind-fucking-blowing, but then what? The reality was that even if they had off-the-charts sex, in the end, it wouldn't be good for either of them. Quinn was the kind of woman to take home to meet the family. And Alex couldn't let his life derail again. Was it even possible to just fuck as friends?

The thought didn't sit well. Somehow, he already knew that they were too involved for sex to just be sex. He ran his hands over his face, feeling frustration. What was he supposed to do? With the snow still coming down, he knew they were going to be stuck here together for likely days to come. Maybe he should just talk to her, be honest, and set the record straight. She was a smart lass. He was sure she would agree that sex would just make things complicated between them. Maybe if he levelled with her, she'd understand and even agree.

Quinn went to Alex's room for clean sweatpants and a hoody. For a moment, she stood at the door, contemplating going to see what he was up to, but thought better of it. Quinn had hoped or maybe daydreamed that he'd join her in the shower, but no such luck. It was obvious to her that he was attracted to her, despite his denial about it, but something held him back, for some reason, he seemed hell-bent on keeping their attraction from becoming anything more. The picture with him and the blond woman came to mind, and she again wondered about it. Was the woman in the photo the reason Alex kept himself in check with Quinn?

Quinn had snuck up to the loft the day before and found a book to occupy her next time Alex went AWOL. Now seemed like a good time to start it. She pulled it out from under the bed where she'd stashed it, fluffed up the pillows against the headboard, and hopped into bed.

For the rest of the afternoon, Quinn read a surprisingly juicy historical romance novel she'd found in Alex's loft. It made her smile inside, knowing he probably had no idea there were smutty romance books up there. Good as the book was, it certainly wasn't doing her any favours while being cooped up in this cabin with Hot Cop.

When Quinn finally put the book down, she was surprised to notice the room had become dim. Looking out the window, dusk loomed in the snow-filled sky. Realizing Alex hadn't even come to check on her, she sighed, biting her lip. The man was a mystery. Deciding not to hide out for the evening too, she ventured out of Alex's room and padded down the hall to the kitchen.

Alex stood at the counter preparing dinner. God, he was a delicious sight with his broad muscular back and shoulders showing through his t-shirt as he chopped vegetables. And his ass? *Frick*. She could bounce quarters of it. Damn that book. It had her all stirred up.

She considered offering her assistance when she thought better of it, remembering how he'd brushed her off the day before. Quinn decided to go up to the loft and see what other book treasures she could find. Alex seemed to pay her no attention until she began up the ladder.

"I'll join you in a few minutes," he called after her, not looking up.

"Okay," she answered. *Hmm*, she hadn't expected that. Perhaps he wanted to read more of *A Christmas Carol*. Quinn sat on the little couch up in the loft and looked out the picture window at the gently falling snow. It was a picturesque Christmas Eve. And despite all the things that seemed wrong, so much just felt right.

Alex climbed up the ladder, and they locked eyes as he reached the top. Looking at her tentatively, he asked, "May I?" gesturing to sit beside her.

"Of course." She nodded.

"I think we should huv a talk," he said.

Oh boy, he sounded all cop-like again. Quinn had the distinct impression that this wasn't going to be a festive Christmassy conversation. She watched him as he settled on the couch beside her and stared out the window before turning to her.

"The snow isnae letting up, so we may be stuck here for a few days yet," he said, apprehension lacing his voice.

"I noticed," she said calmly, holding her hands in her lap.

"I feel I wasn't totally honest with ye yesterday." His expression grew serious.

"No?" She tried to think back to everything they'd talked about and what he might not have been straight with her about. Without a doubt, he wasn't forthcoming about a lot of things, but she hadn't thought he'd been outright dishonest with her.

Clearing his throat as if it pained him to speak, he said, "I've come to realize that perhaps we do have some chemistry between us."

He looked so uncomfortable that Quinn could have laughed. "Ah, so you're crushing on me then," She said bluntly, purposefully making him squirm.

"Aye," he muttered.

She looked at him from under arched brows.

"But, I'm no' looking for anything right now," he said with a sigh.

"Mm-hmm," she said in understanding. Although truly, she did not understand at all. She bit her lip, and for a split second, she thought she saw a spark in his stormy blue eyes. But he looked away. *Too bad*, she thought.

"I just dinnae think it's a good idea for ye and me to..." he paused unable to find the right words.

"To?" she asked, wanting him to say it.

"Well to anything really," he said awkwardly.

She looked at him quizzically. "To anything?"

"Ms. West, ye know what I mean," he said, getting all cop serious on her.

"Do I?" She challenged, stifling a laugh.

Suddenly sounding irritated, he said, "The truth is there is a wee bit of chemistry between us, but it is only due to circumstance. Of course, we're going to be affected by each other being stuck here together. It's human nature."

Oh my God. Is that what he thought? Their chemistry was simply due to being alone together? Quinn was silently nonplussed that this was how he was justifying the sparks that flickered between them.

"The thing is, I am not looking for a fling, and I suspect ye feel the same," he said as if that explained it all.

"I see. And what if I am looking for a fling?" she asked pointedly.

Heat careened through Alex at the possibility, and he let himself ponder it. Was that what she wanted—to just go at it?

"I mean, we are stranded here. We could make the most of it," she said as if she'd heard his silent questions.

Alex's mind raced at the very idea that he could fuck her senseless for the rest of the evening and into the next day and maybe the next too. For a brief scintillating moment, he permitted himself to contemplate the possibility before he swore in his head. It would only cause trouble in the end.

The last woman in his life had fucked him over and nearly destroyed him. It would be a cold day in hell before he'd risk ruining all the work he'd done to rebuild his world. Absolutely nothing was worth risking going down that path again. And despite being nothing like the woman who haunted Alex's past, even the vexing ever-present temptation of Ms. Quinn West was not powerful enough to sway him. He'd learned his lesson well. Canada was a fresh start, and he had made a good life here. Screwing it up was not an option.

The woman who had a knack for firing up his cock looked at him expectantly with her tempting brown eyes. Even worse, Alex found he was beginning to like her more than just sexually. It surprised him all to hell to realize her presence here with him somehow made him feel more Christmassy with a little less longing in his heart than he usually felt these past couple of years missing his family over the holidays. She'd been surprisingly pleasant company making it that much harder to let her down.

"Quinn, I think 'tis best if we dinnae complicate things," he said more softly.

Quinn searched his face and must have realized the battle was lost. "No 'stuck in a cabin, Christmas sex fest' eh?" she teased half-heartedly.

Alex's lips tugged in a smile appreciating how Canadian she sounded. There were turns of phrases and nuances that Alex found to be distinctly Canadian, but Quinn's Canadian-ness hit differently. Hers was laced with a soft twist of sexy.

"I think 'tis best that way," Alex said. His resolve was challenged when her lush lower lip tucked worriedly under her teeth.

"Okay," she agreed lightly. "No sex. Even if you beg," she joked referring to his comment to her only a few short days ago.

A half grin pulled at the corner of his mouth. Shite, he was an idiot. Alex should have felt relief, but he didn't. What he felt was something more akin to disappointment. What on earth was wrong with him? Did he want her to put up a fight? Beg him to slide his cock into her.

Oblivious to his internal battle, Quinn smiled brightly. "I still think we should make the most of this time though being Christmas and all." She regarded him painfully diplomatically. "We don't need sex, but we can still enjoy each other's company and celebrate the season. I mean honestly, look out that window. Hallmark would beg to put that snowy mountain scene on their Christmas cards."

Alex chuckled even though inside he still wared with himself. Despite being the one to shut down any chance of sex, it still grated how easily she acquiesced. Although he supposed she was right they should make the most of this time. It was Christmas after all.

He smiled at her. "So what do ye suggest then lass?"

Picking up *A Christmas Carol* from the trunk coffee table, she asked, "Shall I read some more?"

Nodding, he settled back on the couch and crossed his feet up on the trunk coffee table. "Aye." If he couldn't make mad, passionate love to her, then just hanging out was a surprisingly decent backup plan.

29
Shin Kicking

THIS CHRISTMAS EVE WOULD be burned into Quinn's mind forever. Sitting in Alex's ruggedly cozy mountain cabin while snow fell outside, talking, laughing, and "making rather merry" as Dickens would say. Their rocky start felt like a distant memory. It seemed the "we will not have sex" conversation was exactly what Alex needed to let his guard down, and Quinn couldn't feel happier about it.

Quinn wished this conversation had gone differently though. But if she was honest, she also knew deep down that he was right. The truth was, she didn't want just a fling with him. Somewhere along the line, she'd started to develop real feelings for Alex. Things she would have never expected to feel especially for Alex. It was playing with fire to think she could do "friends with benefits" with him. It wasn't the one little kiss that had her heart fluttering. It was that and literally everything else—their conversations, the moments of quiet companionship, the way she felt safe in his arms. The kind of safe feelings she'd never known before in her life. It was sobering to realize that if they did have sex, there was no way she'd be able to walk away unscathed.

The ease of their conversation made her wonder how she'd ever thought he was a jerk. Relaxed Alex was light-hearted and funny, and Quinn couldn't imagine better company. Those gorgeous smiles came easily now and with a heart-thumping frequency. It was like hanging out with one of her best friends minus the fact that she had to tamp down her urge to just nestle into his arms and kiss every square inch of his handsome face.

It was well into the evening when Quinn decided to press her luck. "Okay, so what I really want to know is what brought you here—to Canada?" She knew he'd been reluctant to talk about it before, but maybe now after the evening they'd had together, he'd be willing to open up and talk to her.

"I told ye, it was an exchange."

Quinn didn't miss the tension that suddenly laced his voice, and she could see the tick in his chiselled jaw, but she refused to be deterred. "Mm-hmm, and..." She looked at him pointedly.

He knew what she wanted to know. Without a word, he stood up from the couch and stepped towards the ladder.

Quinn stared at his back wondering if he was honestly going to shut down and walk away over her question.

As he stepped onto the ladder to go down, he glanced back at her. "Come on, lass. 'Tis a long story. I'll add some logs to the fire and get us some whisky."

"Cookies, too," she said as she got up to follow him down. "Cookies make everything better."

A warm smile touched his lips, and her insides quivered.

Alex brought the bottle of scotch and two glasses to the little table that sat between the two chairs in front of the fireplace. Quinn set out some of her shortbread on a plate and brought it over as well.

"Ooh, you know what we need?" Her brown eyes lit with excitement, and Alex felt his heart grip in his chest. The lass was stunning.

Without saying more, she went to where her backpack sat near the end of the settee and dug around in it. A moment later, she triumphantly held up two candy canes. "Ha, ha!" she said jubilantly as she headed towards where Alex was already seated in one of the chairs by the fireplace.

Swallowing hard as he recalled the last time he'd seen her with a candy cane, he leaned towards the table in front of him, added a healthy splash of the amber scotch to each of their glasses, and downed his in one gulp.

Glancing at him wide-eyed, Quinn put one of the candy canes on the table in front of him. She sat down in the chair across from him, and unwrapped her own candy cane, and popped the end into her mouth. The way her lips tugged at it appreciatively made Alex have to adjust himself in his seat. *Christ.*

"I thought you said you never shoot scotch." She looked at him with a perfectly arched brow as she tucked her legs up on the chair, getting comfortable.

"Aye, unless the occasion calls fer it," Alex stated bluntly. He would let her assume that the occasion he referred to was their pending conversation and not the habit she seemed to have to suck on candy canes like she could make them come. Pouring himself another splash of scotch, he swirled the glass in his hand and stared into the warm glow of the crackling fire, silently begging it to distract him away from her mouth.

Alex had already downed his second glass of scotch, but instead of relaxing, he could feel tension building in him. Thankfully abandoning the candy cane, Quinn picked up her glass of whisky and sipped at it. Big innocent eyes looked at him expectantly.

Alex had kept his past to himself for so long that it was hard to know even where to start. Many were aware of his story, even though he'd never spoken of it to anyone. As much as his muscles clenched just thinking about it, there was a part of him that felt almost giddy to finally be able to speak it all out loud. He didn't have an answer as to why he was willing—no, wanting—to tell the woman seated across from him. Perhaps it was the situation, being stuck here alone with her. Just Quinn West and himself. He eyed her over the rim of his glass. Not knowing the why of it, he took a deep breath and started to tell Quinn the thing that had changed his entire life.

"There was a lass," he said. "Kate." After all these years, he expected her name to be bitter on his tongue. It wasn't though. Now it was just a name. A name of someone who was long gone.

"The one in the picture?" Quinn asked gently.

Alex looked at her big brown eyes watching him intently. "No," he said without explanation. He wasn't going to get into the photo now. This was about Kate and the hell she'd put him through.

"Oh," she said, tucking her knees up a little bit snugger under her.

"I was in special ops in Scotland, and Kate Cameron was my superior." He looked down as he rolled the scotch in his glass, the firelight catching on the etched crystal.

"It was my dream job." He smiled faintly at the memory. "I worked my arse off back then, doing anything and everything I could to prove myself, to be better—to stand out from the rest. My hard work paid off, and I rose through the ranks quicker than most. I was one of the best on the force, if not the best for a time." There was no arrogance or pride in his voice, only truth.

"That doesn't surprise me." Quinn smiled lightly.

Alex looked up at her, wondering why it felt like this lass who barely knew him seemed to see him so definitively like she understood who he was.

"Kate was the chief constable which is the highest rank you can hold in the Scottish police force. Somehow, I fell on her radar, and she took notice of me." He paused for a moment taking a sip of his scotch. "And I took notice of her. For such a high rank, she was quite young. Back then, I was in awe of her. Everything about her made her seem unattainable like she was some kind of queen and we were just the people beneath her. She had it all, from her rank, her intelligence, and her beauty, and she was respected by everyone. The woman held all the cards, all the power."

Listening intently, Quinn thought this Kate woman sounded like a unicorn, almost too perfect, but she could see there was anguish in Alex's face when he talked about her. She could almost feel the heaviness. Obviously, things didn't work out with Kate and Alex, and Quinn began to wonder if the anguish she could see was Alex wishing it had. The thought sat like a rock in Quinn's belly. Here in this cabin, it was just her and Alex, but in the real world, it was also Kate and the woman in the picture—and kids.

Quinn knew she had no right to be bothered by any of it. She wasn't anything to Alex, just some woman he was stuck with over Christmas, but she couldn't deny the hollow forming in her chest. Quickly, she downed her scotch, trying to stomp out the feelings whirring in her. As Alex refilled her glass, he carried on telling her his story.

"When Kate started to single me out, I eagerly fell under her spell." He shook his head like he still couldn't believe it had happened. "She was several years older than me. I could claim to being naive, but I wasnae. I knew what I was getting into with her. She was my boss. I knew I was playing with fire. The truth was her attention was like a drug. The more I got, the more I wanted."

White hot jealousy fluttered in Quinn's chest. Despite feeling things she had no right to feel, she wanted him to tell her everything. There was no doubt in her mind that what he was telling her about Kate was something that profoundly affected his life. Quinn sensed that he needed to talk about it, and for whatever reason, she felt like she needed to hear it.

"I look back now and wonder how I could have been so caught up. She lavished praise on me, and I ate it up like a starved dog. I began to crave her praise. I wanted to do anything and everything to please her."

Quinn understood what he was saying. It was a toxic feeling she knew all too well. "I get it," she said. "I know exactly what you are talking about. Well, maybe not exactly, but I understand that desperate desire to please someone just to feel their love. It used to be that way with my mom. There was nothing better in the world than when my mom showered me with her love because of something I'd done for her. It was all about her. I was so desperate for her love that I would have done anything."

"I'm sorry, lass. 'Tis not right what ye went through."

"It's not right what you went through either by the sound of it."

"Aye, but I was an adult and made stupid decisions. Ye were a child just wanting yer mother's love. 'Tis wrong, lass."

Quinn had to hold back tears that threatened to fall at how forcefully he defended her like he truly cared. Like she mattered to him.

"Thank you," she said tentatively. "I'm... It's okay," she began to explain but didn't want to change the subject away from Alex. It wasn't her intent to bring the focus to her own life. "I'm good now. I've put those demons to rest. That was a long time ago. I only brought it up because I feel like I can relate to what you were saying about wanting to please Kate." Her voice went a little softer. "I assume you loved her."

Alex shook his head. "It wasnae love. It was never love. Just lust and a bloody sick obsession." He scraped a hand over his five o'clock shadow. "We had an affair for close to six months. If I'm being honest, at first, it felt fun and exciting. It's like I couldnae see past the rush of it all. I even had myself convinced that we had something real as if it wasn't built on a stack of secrecy. It was doomed from the start though. She was my boss. She was everyone's boss. Nothing good was ever going to come of it. But I had no idea how far off the rails things would go."

Alex stood up and added another log to the fireplace and stood watching as flames licked at it. "After a few months, she somehow convinced me to do her dirty work." He shook his head as if still not believing it had happened. "She wanted me to report back to her on details of the other members in my squadron. She wanted to ken about the wee'est transgressions. She wanted to ken if her name was so much as uttered behind her back. Anything and everything, I was to find out and report back to her. I didnae like it, but I felt I was beholden to her somehow. I wanted to make her happy, to bask in the praise she'd give me and in the reward of it all, the power of it, so I did her dirty bidding," he said bitterly. "I was becoming a person I didn't recognize. I hated it, but I felt stuck in it."

Quinn couldn't imagine this strong man compromising his values for anyone. From what she knew of him, Alex was a man of honour and integrity.

Running a hand through his hair, he sat back down in his chair and blew out a breath as if readying himself for his next words. "Eventually, she wanted me to make formal complaints against certain members of the team with nothing to back it." He shook his head as if he still couldn't handle the thought.

"That's so not you. You wouldn't do that," Quinn snapped with conviction.

Alex's stormy blue eyes landed on her as if he was looking at an angel, and she had to swallow back emotion, sure no one had ever looked at her that way before.

"Ye're right lass. 'Tis not me at all. I couldnae do it. I wouldnae. I didnae realize it at the time, but Kate had targeted specific members because she'd slept with them too. She was worried they would talk and her job would be in jeopardy. She wanted them gone. Off the force."

Quinn sucked in a breath. "Holy shit."

"Aye. I was close with these guys, and the trust we shared went beyond the job. We had each other's backs no matter what. As much as I wanted to please her, I couldn't turn against my team." Alex paused. There was a crease between his brows and his look was distant. If he gripped his whisky glass any tighter, it might shatter. As if noticing tension building in him, he ran a hand through his hair and took a quick sip of his whisky.

"When I didnae do what she wanted though, he continued, things got strained between us. At first, I couldnae understand it." He stared into his nearly empty glass reliving the memories. "Christ, I was so naive." His voice was a bitter whisper. "I had thought we had a good thing going. I thought that things would blow over and we'd get back to normal, but Kate began lashing out at me when I saw her. I realized pretty quickly that whatever fun we'd had, it was definitively over. It became obvious that we needed to break up. I needed some space from her, but it was almost impossible as she was my boss."

"God, that's crazy. I can't imagine. At least you knew you had to get out. So many people get stuck in situations like that, always hoping that things will get better."

"There was no doubt in my mind. Things wouldnae be getting better. In fact, things got way worse." Alex looked edgy just remembering the hell Kate Cameron had put him through.

Quinn shot back the remainder of her scotch and picked up the bottle to refill. Alex lips tugged up in the corners. She'd brought him back to the here and now. As she leaned over to top up his glass, it occurred to him just how much it meant to him to be able to tell her everything and to have her listen without judgment. It was more than he could ask for really.

"Thank ye," he said, picking up his glass.

"So things got worse," she said, encouraging him to continue.

"Honestly, Quinn, the woman went aff her heid, utterly mental. She ended up going to my parents."

"She went to your parents? Why?" she asked dumbfounded.

A bitter laugh escaped him. "She told them that I had got her pregnant and had dumped her."

"Holy shit!"

"Aye," he said soberly detesting the memory of it.

"Was she pregnant?" Quinn asked gently.

"Naw." He scoffed. "Thank Christ."

"Did your parents believe her?" Quinn's eyes were wide.

"At the time, they didnae ken if she was pregnant or no', but they could see her desperation. And they also sensed that things werenae as they seemed. They ken something was amiss. It was awful though. I hate that they had to deal with her at all. I hate that she involved them."

"I don't blame you," Quinn said, taking it all in. "Thank God you have some pretty great parents."

"Aye." Alex said lightly. "I am fortunate. My parents were amazing through it all. They never stopped supporting me, but it was hard on them." There was a long pause before he added, "And then things only got worse."

"Oh my God, how could it possibly get worse?" Quinn was astounded.

"To start, she got me sacked."

"Nooo," Quinn breathed.

"Aye. Her story got more elaborate, no' only did she claim she was pregnant, but also that I had sexually assaulted her." After all these years, the words were like battery acid in his mouth. It still singed his soul that she made up something so vile about him, and worse, at the time, people believed it.

Quinn sat staring at him, and in an instant, a flicker of fear nearly choked him, did she question whether or not it was true? But then he saw the vehemence in her big brown eyes as she bit out wildly, "I'd like to kick that bitch in the shins!"

Alex snorted a laugh. "I'd huv paid money to witness that." *Christ*, it meant the world to him that this little lass sitting across from him would defend him so fiercely.

30
Hell and Hope

Quinn smiled lightly pleased she'd made him chuckle. This Kate woman sounded like a psychopath. How could the nasty woman accuse him of rape? Even when she thought Alex was a jerk cop, she'd witnessed the way he dealt with the situation when those guys had catcalled her. It was obvious to her even then that Alex was a protector, not a predator. The man had saved her more than once. There was no way he'd harm a woman. She knew that to her core.

"I was told if I left quietly she wouldnae press charges and the matter would be closed," he said. "Part of me was relieved to get the hell out of there while I could, but it was a painfully bitter pill to swallow. I loved my job, and I was damn good at it. No' to mention it was infuriating to be accused of such bullshit and to be so bloody helpless to fight against it."

"And that's why you came here," Quinn stated as the puzzle pieces started to come together.

"Naw," he said, and Quinn eyed him, wondering how much more there could be.

"I warned ye it was a long story."

"I've got nowhere else to be." She smiled softly, leaning back in the chair and pulling up a tartan throw blanket around her. "So what happened after you were fired?" she asked, still astounded by everything he'd gone through.

"I fell into a depression. Drank too much. Avoided people. It was a dark time in my life." Firelight glinted off his stormy blue eyes.

Listening to Alex's story, Quinn was beginning to understand why he seemed to keep a wall up. A small glimmer of hope caught in her chest when she realized that he'd let his guard down with her tonight. He was letting her in. She still wondered about how much the woman in the photo played into his reluctance for anything physical with her, but everything he was telling her about Kate made her understand why he kept himself so guarded. Everyone had their stories—their history that made them who they were—and Alex was no different.

"What was the changing point?" she asked softly.

Clearing his throat, he looked down into his scotch glass as he mindlessly swirled its contents.

"One night, I awoke to someone trying to beat the shite out of me with a heavy chain."

"*What?*" Quinn was aghast. The very thought made her blood curdle.

"Kate hired someone to murder me, but she wanted to make sure I suffered first," Alex bit the words out.

"Oh my God, Alex." Quinn felt her eyes sting with tears. She couldn't stand to think of anyone wanting to hurt him never mind kill him. It was insane. Without any thought, she got off her chair, scooted onto his lap, and wrapped her arms around him. The need to be close to him nearly overwhelmed her. She needed to feel him and know he was very much alive and well. It horrified her to think what he'd been through.

"I'm so, so glad you are okay. I can't even fathom what that must have been like," she said as a tear escaped down her cheek.

"Och, lass, 'tis okay," he said, gently wiping her tear with his thumb as his other arm wrapped around her.

The feel of her warm embrace took hold of his senses, and a lump formed in his throat. An emotion he didn't know he possessed hit him square in the chest as he realized that this feisty, quirky, sexy, strong woman genuinely cared about him.

Alex had no idea how much he needed a good solid hug until that moment. Aside from the crackle of the fire, the world seemed to fall away around them as they found solace in each other's embrace. Alex would have expected, based on his recent history with Quinn, that his cock would spring to life with her lush behind nestled in his lap. Even though those thoughts skirted at the edge of his mind, he found that just holding her and her holding him brought a sense of relief, like the burden he'd carried for so long was finally lifted. For the first time in a long time, Alex felt a rightness that he couldn't explain.

Quinn finally pulled back from their embrace and looked at Alex with concern etched in her wet caring eyes. "What happened?" Afraid to know, but needing to at the same time.

Tucked up comfortably on his lap, Alex absently stroked Quinn's back through the hoody she wore. "Well, ye know all too well what happens when someone wakes me from my sleep."

"I sure do." She snickered, recalling the first night in Alex's bed and how quickly she was whipped under his strong body with her wrists tightly pinned above her and his gun dug under her jaw. Her eyes went wide as fear rippled through her. Alex seemed to realize what she was thinking, and he quickly answered her silent question.

"I didnae kill him, lass. Dinnae fash."

"I wouldn't have blamed you if you had," she said seriously.

"He was a fool and didnae get very far. I knew even then that Kate was behind the attack."

"My God, I can't imagine." Quinn's arm was loosely resting around his neck. Her hand was on his strong shoulder.

"He was arrested, and in his plea bargain, he gave up the whole nasty plot that Kate had cooked up. It was supposed to look like a drug deal gone bad." He scoffed. "It could huv been believable as I was in a dark place and had withdrawn from my life."

"You were taking drugs?" she asked gently looking at him worriedly.

"Naw, I'm a cop. I'd seen enough broken lives from drugs that even in my darkest hour I wouldnae go there. It's nasty stuff."

"The whole thing sounds like a twisted movie plot," Quinn said, settling in closer to him.

"Aye, it felt like one. To be honest, her trying to huv me killed was probably the best thing that could've happened. Turned out, it wasnae the first time she'd tried to huv someone killed."

"No!" Quinn could hardly believe it.

"Aye, before movin' to Scotland, she hired someone to murder her ex-husband, but she got off because, at the time, they had no witnesses and apparently not enough evidence. When this came out though, witnesses came forward, and they ended up with a shit tonne of new evidence. She was retried for her ex-husband's murder as well as new charges of attempted murder and a whole host of other charges.

"Other guys on the squad came forward too with their stories about how she'd blackmailed them. This woman was a piece of work. She had covered her tracks right up until the thug who tried to kill me. I'm almost grateful for the prick as he was her undoing. Ironic really that she'd gotten away with so much—fooling some of the smartest people I've ever met—but then some low life is the one who finally takes her down."

"The ultimate revenge." Quinn grimaced.

"Aye. Everything came out. It was nuts, and she couldn't hide from the truth. She not only admitted to everything, but she bragged about it like she was some kind of mastermind."

Quinn was shaking her head. "Insane."

"Totally. It was expected that she'd get life in prison with all the charges against her, but the morning of sentencing, they found her hanging in her jail cell." His look was distant.

Quinn's fingers found the nape of his neck, and she stroked him tenderly as she tried to comprehend all he was telling her.

"Typical Kate. She always found a way out when she was backed in a corner."

Concerned big brown eyes looked into his. "How on earth have you dealt with all that?" she asked gently.

With a sad smile, Alex shook his head. "Kate's death gave me some closure. Not that I wanted her dead per se, but somehow, it gave things a definitive end." He adjusted Quinn in his lap. "The department re-instated me to full status and issued a public statement apologizing for their error. I was completely exonerated of any wrongdoing."

"Wow. Well, that's good at least."

"Aye, it was good," he said. "The problem was, at that point, my head just wasn't in it anymore. I lost my drive. Instead of loving the job I'd been trained for, it felt like a constant reminder of the hell I'd been through. I considered leaving policing altogether."

"I can't blame you."

"An exchange came up for Canada, and I dinnae ken. It just felt like something I needed to do. A chance to start over I suppose. I didn't even ken where the hell Calen was, but I was happy to just get out of Scotland and get away from all the memories that were still too fresh." He sighed. "Do ye ken the worst part of it all?"

Quinn shook her head. "What?"

"I fell for it—for the lies. Fell for her. She had me completely fooled. I should huv known. How could I not huv known that she was a pathological liar, a master manipulator, a fucking psychopath? I still don't understand how I didn't see it," he berated himself.

Quinn could see that it ate at him, and she could only imagine how horrible it would be to be caught in someone's lies and deceit.

"You said yourself, she blackmailed and manipulated many people, intelligent people. The fact that she was even able to get the job as your boss goes to show that this woman was exactly as you say—a master manipulator. She even managed to get away with murdering her husband! Thank God, the truth all came out. It sounds to me like everyone was fooled by her at one point or another. You're only human, Alex. How could you have known?"

Alex absently squeezed the gentle curve of Quinn's hip in his lap. "She did dupe a lot of people, but I just can't understand how I didn't see it sooner. Looking back I did notice things, but I brushed them under the rug. I never would huv thought she was completely mental. I felt on top of my game, invincible until she came along. I was young, successful, and loved my career, and in an instant, my life fell to shite. That woman is my one regret," he said resentfully.

Quinn could hear the indignation in his voice, but she didn't agree with regrets. For a guy who liked to be in control, she could see how frustrating it all must have been, but she saw things a bit differently.

"I get that, but if it weren't for all that happened," she said softly, "would you have come to Canada? I know it sounds cliche, saying things happen for a reason and in this case maybe a bit extreme, but still, maybe there is at least a silver lining to it all."

Alex tensed. "I think ye might be missing the point. I loved my life as it was. I didnae want it to change."

"You aren't happy here?" She cut to the chase.

Alex's hand that was stroking her back now held the arm of the chair. "I was in special ops in Scotland. I had it made," he said as if she hadn't heard how great his life had been.

Quinn untucked herself from Alex's lap and was about to stand when his strong arm caught around her waist pulling her back down onto him. "Dinnae leave." His voice was strained.

That voice nearly broke her. She could almost feel his internal struggle. She softened and lifted a hand to his stubbled jaw. The man held onto so much pain. She could see it now in his stormy blue eyes, and it pierced her heart.

Alex's thoughts were as deep as a Scottish glen, and he held Quinn to him as if she were a healing balm for his tumultuous soul. Without another word spoken between them, the evening's conversation hanging heavily, they soon drifted off to sleep.

Alex awoke a time later. The logs were burnt through, and the remaining glowing embers did little to warm the room. Quinn still lay peacefully in his lap, her head resting against his chest. Alex liked her in his arms. Something about it just felt good. Stroking her soft hair, she stirred.

"Mm," she sighed sleepily. "Sorry, I must have fallen asleep." She yawned and for the second time that evening attempted to get off his lap, but before she could, Alex's arm scooped her up. He stood up holding her close.

"Ooh," she squealed in surprise. Alex chuckled as he carried her to the bedroom. Laying her on the bed, he pulled off his t-shirt and sweatpants before getting in beside her. The coolness of the room had penetrated the bedding, and he felt Quinn shiver before he pulled her tight to him and they both fell back into a peaceful sleep.

31
Christmas Morning With All the Trimmings

The smell of bacon wrestled Quinn from her sleep. As she opened her eyes, her stomach growled hungrily. *Oh heck yes*, she thought. "Mmm," she groaned, stretching. Memories from the night before trickled into her mind. It was a crazy conversation, but she felt like she and Alex had grown closer.

It got a little tense though before they'd fallen asleep. She understood regret, but at the same time, she'd learned how pointless regrets were. All anyone truly had was the here and now, so why live in the past? Was Alex's past stopping him from really living in his present?

Quinn had learned in her own life that you could either let your past rule you or you could let it change you for the better. Not that it was always easy, but she refused to get bogged down in the negatives. She would always find the silver linings.

Biting her lower lip, she realized they never got to talking about the picture from his sporran. Where did his wife and kids fit into the mix? Could they have been before all the stuff with that Kate woman? They had to have been. Quinn was befuddled, but she wasn't going to push Alex—especially not today.

It was Christmas morning, and they both deserved to have an awesome day with no more heavy talk. A spark of childlike giddiness made her smile, and she hopped out of bed and headed down the hall.

As she approached the kitchen, she stopped in her tracks and took in the mouth-watering sight of Sergeant Alex Mackenzie. His sweat pants hung low on his waist, and he was shirtless. The chiselled plain of his abs dipped below his sweats, and he turned back to the stovetop giving her a view of his stupidly broad muscular back and shoulders. *Wowza, Merry Christmas Quinn*, she thought slyly.

Yesterday had been so intense and real that she'd almost forgotten about the sizzling attraction she felt for him. Almost. When she was on his lap, despite the seriousness of the conversation, she was far too aware of everywhere their bodies touched. The feel of his hand absently stroking her back. His strong chest supported her as she leaned into him. His spearmint, woodsy scent. It was hard trying to deny her every visceral reaction to the man. He'd made it clear that nothing physical would be happening between them, so there was no point in indulging her fantasies.

Alex glanced up at her when he realized she was there, and his grin turned her legs into warm Christmas pudding. The man certainly didn't make it easy on her.

"Good morning, Happy Christmas, lass. Did ye sleep well?" Alex asked as he turned back to the pan on the stove.

"Merry Christmas." Quinn said brightly leaning against the kitchen wall. "I did. I didn't even notice that you'd gotten up this morning."

"Ye looked like ye were in a peaceful slumber when I left ye," Alex said, transferring perfectly golden pancakes onto a plate. The thought of Alex looking at her while she'd slept did funny things to her belly.

"I've made us a wee Christmas breakfast," he said, adding a batch of fried bacon to an already piled-high platter and bringing it and the pancake plate to the table.

"Wow," Quinn breathed, looking at the breakfast feast before her. The table was beautifully set with two place settings. Plates, bowls, and platters filled with bacon, eggs, toast, pancakes, sausages, blueberries, strawberries, Christmas oranges, and a box of chocolates filled the little wooden table. In the middle of it all was a red tapered candle giving off a warm glow.

Quinn had never awoken to a Christmas breakfast. In fact, no one had ever made her a feast like the one before her.

"This is amazing," she said blown away. "I can't believe you made all of this."

Alex watched her delight, and it made him feel ridiculously good. Wanting to surprise her, he got up early and got started on breakfast. Christmas morning breakfast in Scotland with his family had always been special and a rather grand event. Alex wanted to create a special Christmas morning for Quinn. Even though it wasn't a Scottish breakfast with his family, he was feeling some of that warm Christmas goodness, and he could tell Quinn was feeling it too. God, watching her light up with joy over things was addicting. He couldn't wait to surprise her with the other plans he had in store for the day.

"I dinnae cook as good as my mam, but it should do," he quipped, pulling out a chair for her to sit.

"Thank you," she said as she sat down. "I suspect your mom would be impressed with all of this." Bear lumbered over to where Quinn sat and laid his head in her lap.

Alex chuckled. "Aye, I think ye might be right. I've let her believe that I have nae idea around the kitchen so that I can sit back and enjoy her cooking."

Alex scooped some kibble for Bear into his bowl and then snagged a piece of bacon from the platter to add to his pup's breakfast. In an instant, Bear was there, and Alex gave him the go-ahead to scarf it down. He picked up his white t-shirt from his chair, and when he noticed Quinn's none-too-discreet perusal, he took his time letting the shirt slide down over his chest and abs. He would forgo the shirt altogether for her, but he could hear his mam now, reminding him to mind his manners at the table.

"This is just incredible, Alex," she breathed. Her eyes scanning the table. "It looks so beautiful."

"Tastes even better, I hope. Please, help yourself."

Alex eyed the lass, wondering what she would go for first. Seeing Quinn reaching for a Chocolate thin square, he smiled. His mom always started Christmas breakfast with a chocolate thin square. And for as long as he could remember, they always bought the same chocolates for Christmas morning.

"Mmmm. Oh my, this chocolate is so good," she groaned. And Alex had to swallow the instant kick of desire he felt seeing the pure pleasure play out on her beautiful face.

Clearing his throat he said, "My mam sent them from home. 'Tis Scottish chocolate made right in the village where my family is from. Isnae Christmas without it."

"Well, I'm still not convinced with the scotch, but the chocolate... Gawd." She sighed, savouring the second bite.

Alex found it hard to tear his gaze from her. Her auburn locks were mussed. She still wore his sweat pants and hoody, but God help him, he found her painfully alluring. Those big dark brown eyes and her full lips. The way she sat with one knee up on the chair. *How did she look so feminine in his oversized clothes?*

32
She Liked It Verra Much

WITH BREAKFAST DONE AND leftovers put away, they washed the dishes together. As Quinn dried the last pan, she asked, "Did you want to finish up *A Christmas Carol*?"

Alex looked at her from under his dark brows with a sly expression on his handsome face. Quinn's pulse quickened, and she wondered why he was looking at her that way.

"What?" she asked not meaning for it to come out breathily.

"I huv a wee surprise fer ye," he said with a low tempting tone in his voice.

Fireworks shot off low in her belly. Did he mean a gift? No. Was he teasing her? Or… An image of him kissing her under the mistletoe skittered through her mind, and she chided herself. He didn't even have mistletoe, and even if he did, he'd made himself very clear upon where they stood with each other. No sex, which she was sure also meant no kissing.

"What kind of surprise?" she asked, her curiosity already killing her.

The expression on Alex's face told her that he was enjoying her piqued interest. "I think it's one ye'll like verra much," he said.

His burr was like a trigger on all her feminine parts. *Jeez Louise.*

"Ye huv to do as I say though, lass. No questions asked."

She eyed him dubiously.

"Do ye trust me?" he asked from under an arched brow.

"Of course," she answered easily and she noted he looked pleased with her answer.

"So will ye do as I say?" he asked apparently wanting her to commit fully to whatever he had planned.

She looked at him, uncertainly biting her lower lip, but she was way too curious to say no. "Fine," she conceded.

Alex grinned, clearly he had her figured out. She was as curious as a cat and he knew it. "Good. There is a robe hanging on the back of the door in the bathroom."

Quinn had seen the thick navy robe there. *But what on earth...* She waited to hear more.

"I want ye to go get it and put it on."

Shaking her head confused, she clarified, "You want me to put on your robe?"

"Aye, take off everything else and just put on the robe." Quinn threw him a wide-eyed look wondering if she'd heard him right.

"Dinnae worry, lass. I promise it's nothing nefarious." He said with a wink.

Quinn stared at him, as if she might be able to figure out what in the heck was happening. When he said nothing more. She nodded apprehensively, "Okay, then."

"Good, little lass." He grinned and her eyes shot to his in warning. She heard his deep rumble of a chuckle, as she turned and made her way to the bathroom.

Quinn took off Alex's hoody and sweatpants and folded them up, laying them on the counter. She wasn't wearing her bra and panties. She'd barely worn them at all as they were the only ones she had, and she was always in big bulky clothes there didn't seem to be a need for underclothes. Taking Alex's robe off the hook, she slid her arms in and wrapped it around her. She couldn't help the reaction that went through her at the feel and smell of his robe wrapped around her naked body. *Nothing nefarious*, he'd promised. Despite the wink, she was sure he meant it. *Too bad*, she thought.

Well obviously, he wasn't planning on sex, but what the heck was he planning? She felt confused. Hmm, maybe a massage. The very thought of his strong hands touching her made her knees weak. If it was a massage, would she even be able to relax for it? With nervous excitement coursing through her, she opened the door and stepped out walking back to the kitchen.

Alex stood at the back door, still in sweats and a T, but now he was wearing his winter boots and a toque too. *What the heck? Not a massage then*, Quinn felt a little stab of disappointment. As she stepped towards Alex, he gave her a half smile and gestured for her to put on her boots.

"You want me to go outside in a bathrobe in the dead of winter?" she complained.

"Do we huv a problem here, Ms. West?" He gave her a menacing look from under his dark brow.

Quinn's eyes flew to his, remembering those words the day he pulled her over, but this time, electricity danced across her skin as she looked up at his stormy blue eyes twinkling with mischief.

Growling, she stuffed her bare feet into her hiking boots. Alex handed her the toque, and without a word, she unceremoniously yanked it on over her hair.

"Good, little lass." There was a twinkle in his roguish eyes.

There were those three little words again. If she didn't feel so aroused, she'd kick him. "Alex, why am I in a bathrobe and a toque?"

"Ye said ye trusted me," he said simply.

Suddenly, it dawned on her. "Oh God, tell me we're not going for a polar dip!" The very thought made her shiver involuntarily.

Alex threw back his head and laughed. "No' exactly."

What kind of answer was that? Quinn eyed him incredulously. Then without another word, he looked at her with a sexy grin that made her heart beat a little faster, took her hand in his, and opened the back door leading her out. The cold winter air hit with a blast.

Quinn felt fairly certain that she was crazy to follow Alex out into twenty-below weather in nothing but a bathrobe, but as they walked around the side of the cabin, she was distracted by the music playing.

"Beach Boys?" she asked completely dumbfounded.

He chuckled. "Aye." The snow crunched beneath their boots as he continued to lead her around the back of the log cabin and then she saw her surprise.

She squealed. "You have a hot tub?" The ice-cold air snaked up her bathrobe as she stood, staring at steaming hot blue water.

"Aye. Surprise!"

She laughed, wrapping her arms tighter around herself to ward off the cold that was already biting into her.

"Go on, lass." He nodded towards the bubbling hot water. "I'll turn around. Let me know once you're in."

Quinn didn't need to be told twice. Noticing a hook on the wall by the hot tub, she whipped off the robe and practically threw it at the hook. She scrambled to get her boots off before she carefully stepped up the two freezing wood steps to get in. As she sank into the hot glorious water, it almost hurt, but, at the same time, the heat felt like heaven. The water seeped up over her shoulders, and she sighed blissfully as it enveloped her.

"Ye in, lass?" Alex called over his shoulder. When he'd been out clearing snow the day before, he had the idea to surprise the lass with a wee dip in the hot tub. Thinking it through though, he realized that she didn't have a swimsuit, and neither did he. Living out here alone, he never needed one.

Realizing they would be naked together in his hot tub, he questioned whether or not it would be a wise move. But they'd managed to cuddle at night in his bed without it going further, so he was sure they could handle the hot tub. Besides, it was a four-person tub. It was not like he couldn't keep a bit of space between them.

That was what he thought yesterday, but now standing with his back turned and waiting on Quinn, he began to question his sanity. It was too late to turn back. God, just knowing she was taking off that robe behind him sent a wave of desire through him. Every nerve ending in his body begged him to turn around and watch her, but he stayed perfectly still willing his cock to behave.

"Your turn," she called back. He turned and walked a couple of steps towards the tub and Quinn watched him without even thinking that she shouldn't. He took off his boots and pulled down his t-shirt and sweatpants in what seemed like one quick move. She caught the briefest glimpse of him in all his naked glory before he too was in the tub. *Wow*, how could she have forgotten that manhood? *Holy heck.*

"Ah, Christ, that's good." He breathed letting the hot water warm him through.

"It's sooo good. I had no idea you had this greatness in your yard."

He looked up at her with a satisfied grin. "I knew ye'd like it. I thought about it yesterday, but then the day got away from us. I thought I'd surprise ye with it this morning."

"Way better than a polar dip," she quipped.

His chuckle was deep. "Ah, ye cannae say that 'til ye try it."

"I think I'm happy to stick with a hot tub." Quinn felt giddy. The hot tub was up against the back of the cabin, but the view in front of them was breathtaking. Thick snow decorated the layers of tall fir trees. The cabin was cozy and lovely, but Quinn hadn't been outside since the other evening and the fresh mountain air made her feel alive.

"This is incredible, Alex." She breathed still in awe. Then she smiled hearing the Beach Boys "Wouldn't It Be Nice" start to play. "The music is beyond perfect."

"I knew ye'd like that too," he said dryly.

She laughed. "Christmas tradition?"

"Nope. Just seemed the right kinda mood." Alex leaned back, stacking his muscular arms along the sides of the tub and giving Quinn a sexy view.

"Tropical summer vibes in the winter. So good," she quipped, trying not to stare at the man's perfectly sculpted biceps. The music made her smile inside since the Beach Boys' music was the complete opposite of what you'd expect to listen to on a cold crisp Christmas day. Yet, it really did seem perfect. *Hot Cop has a sense of humour*, she thought, smiling inside.

"How is it we are only now going in this hot tub?" she asked gently swishing her fingers through the water.

"Ah, good question. I honestly just hadn't thought of it, and then yesterday, I needed to get the pH right. Worked out well though, no? Nice little Christmas gift fer us both."

"It's the best." She sighed contentedly.

He nodded. "Oh, I almost forgot. One more surprise." Reaching over the side of the tub, he pulled up a bottle of champagne.

"What? Nooo! You've been holding out on me, Sergeant Mackenzie."

He laughed. "I saved it. Gotta have champagne on Christmas Day."

"Ahh, so that's a Christmas tradition."

"Aye." He grinned, popping it open, pouring them each a glass, and then reaching across the hot tub handing her one. Taking it from him, Quinn clinked his glass before sitting back, taking a sip, and looking back out at the winter wonderland that surrounded them. Movement in the trees, caught her eye. She thought she was seeing things, but then a large deer walked into the clearing.

"Oh my God, Alex, look!" she whispered excitedly. The deer paused, listening, and then bounded off the way it came.

"There is a lot of wildlife out here. It's pretty amazing."

"You really do live in the most heavenly place." She sighed happily, taking a sip of her champagne. The cool bubbles went down easily.

"I love this song," she crooned, turning around to him. "Kokomo" had come on. Quinn felt a little jolt tickle down her skin as she noticed the way Alex was watching her. There was something in his gaze that hadn't been there before.

Desire. She'd seen it a couple times before, but it always seemed short-lived. She held eyes with him, and when he didn't look away, she felt her breath go shallow.

Long ago, she'd decided to always live for the moment, come what may. As nervous as she felt now, she intended to stay true to herself. Decision made, she glided low through the steamy water towards Alex, and he watched her with unbidden hunger in his stormy piercing eyes, giving her the courage she needed. Her heart was racing, and she feared his rejection. But she'd regret it if she didn't run with what she was feeling.

Still neck deep in the water she now stood right in front of him. He casually took a sip of his champagne. His glittering blue eyes never left hers. It was like time stood still. Electricity sparked between them.

"Hi," she said coyly, looking at him from under her brow and hoping to God he would bite. She desperately needed him to meet her halfway.

Catching the brief trepidation that flashed in his eyes, disappointment stabbed at her, and she was about to move away when he spoke.

"Stay, lass." His deep voice dripped with hunger. Then he reached up and cupped his wet hands around her face, looking into her eyes with stormy desperation and need, and when those eyes dropped to her lips, Quinn felt heat sear low in her belly. His breath turned ragged, and he paused as if grappling one last time with the decision. When his mouth finally claimed hers, she whimpered.

It was as if time stood still for Quinn. The feel of his lips on hers was electric. Her body reacted, and desire rushed through her leaving her body needy and wanting. Alex opened his mouth against hers, letting his tongue sweep her lips as he tasted her, savoured her, and then devoured her.

A moan escaped her, and Alex groaned in response slanting his mouth over hers as if taking everything he ever wanted from her. His hands moved down her back in the steamy hot water and grasped her behind. With a low growl, he hauled her up against him.

Quinn felt momentarily shocked at the contact of their bodies. Skin on skin. She felt his erection strong and thick pressed between them and desire spread through her body like wildfire. His kiss was so passionate, so raw. Quinn had wanted him to kiss her so many times, but this was beyond anything she'd imagined.

With the hunger in his kiss and the way his hard sculpted body ground against hers in the hot water, Quinn felt achy and needy—desire possessing her. She couldn't get enough of his mouth on hers and his hands touching her—holding her like her body was his for the taking. She pressed into his every touch, wanting to be consumed by him.

33
Flood Gates. Ms. West. Sergeant Mackenzie.

WITH GREAT EFFORT, ALEX tore his mouth from hers. *Jesus.* He hadn't recalled snogging ever being quite so intoxicating. Quinn's big lust-filled eyes looked up at him longingly. Her lips were puffy from their mouth play. *God,* she was heaven. And Christ, it was fucking bliss to give into this need that had consumed him since he'd met the lass. It had built in him like a volcano, molten lava unable to stay contained. Wanting more of the temptress in his arms, he dropped his mouth to hers again. His need to fuck her was going to make his head explode.

"Mm, Ms. West, I'm gonna need ye back in the cottage. Now," Alex ground out between kisses.

Quinn pulled back, throwing him a flirty smile. "So demanding, Sergeant Mackenzie."

"Aye, Ms. West. I've another Christmas present for ye inside by the fire." Powerless to his need for her, he kissed her between words.

Giggling against his lips and holding his face to hers, she whined, "But it's cold between here and there. And I'm rather comfy right where I am." She rubbed her body against his to make her point.

Christ. Alex was tempted to take her right there and then. It had been a very long time since he'd had sex with a woman. And God, how he wanted to have sex with Quinn West, but he realized as he looked into her beautiful face, that it was so much more than that.

"Dinnae fash. I'll keep ye warm, lass." His voice dripped with promise.

"Fine," she pouted, and he was sorely tempted to kiss that pout from her face, but he had other plans.

Letting go of him, she sank back into the water up to her chin and watched him unabashed as he exited the hot tub. Looking at his body, she anticipated what was to come. With his legs so thick and powerful, his muscled back, and his tight ass... *Jeepers*. Hard to believe he was the jerk cop who'd pulled her over less than a week ago. *Hot Cop*, she thought.

Fully naked and looking like a god, he quickly shoved his winter boots on and stood at the edge of the hot tub, gesturing for her to come to him. An irresistible sight if she ever saw one. She stayed low in the water and moved to the side of the tub where he stood.

"Ready?" he asked "Put your arms around my neck, lass. I'll carry ye in."

She looked at him with her brown eyes glittering. Standing up on the seat in the hot tub, she felt the rushing bite of cold mountain air on her body and practically leapt into Alex's arms. He easily caught her and held her firmly to his strong naked torso as he deftly carried her to the back door and into the cottage.

Setting her down on her feet, he dropped a quick kiss on her lips. "Go warm by the fire. I'm just going to grab the champagne."

Alex stepped in the back door and saw Quinn wrapped in a blanket and sitting in one of the comfy chairs in front of the fireplace. She looked up at him, pinning him with her big brown eyes and he felt desire course through him anew. Christ she could bring him to his knees with that look.

When he'd gone back out, he considered that this might be the stupidest decision, but he no longer gave a shite. Over the past couple days, Quinn West had filled his every sense—poured over him and dripped into every crevice of his being like hot custard drizzled over fucking Christmas cake. His restraint was out the window, and at this point, good fucking riddance. It was high time to sink his cock into the warm sweetness of Ms. Quinn West.

"Come here, little lass." His voice was husky and deep.

Quinn stood with the tartan blanket wrapped around her and walked towards him. He didn't think he'd ever seen a more perfect sight. When she stood before him, she opened the blanket, letting him feast his eyes on her naked body.

"There's room for two in here." She looked at him from under her lashes.

"God, Quinn, ye are beautiful," Alex breathed, lifting his hands to run them over her curvy hips.

Goosebumps arose on her skin as he methodically ran his hands slowly and gently over her every curve. His eyes appreciatively followed his hands as he took in the shape and feel of her body.

Any thoughts of being immune to this woman were long gone. She felt too perfect in his hands. Alex's need for her went far beyond anything he'd known. He'd desired women before, but this was different. He was completely under her spell, and if he was going to pay some kind of price, so be it. He needed to sink into her, to watch her as she took him in, to taste her as he pleasured her fully.

"Christ, woman, ye are perfect." Alex's breath was ragged.

"Glad you finally noticed, Sergeant Mackenzie." She threw him a provocative grin.

He growled as he grabbed her ample behind and hauled her up against him, letting her feel the proof of just what she did to him, and he felt satisfied when he heard her breath hitch against his neck.

Running the tip of his nose along her jaw, he whispered, "Aye, lass, I noticed."

His mouth found hers, and their tongues collided, clawing for more. Alex was aware of her lush breasts crushed against him, and he couldn't resist their temptation any longer. Even though her mouth was heaven, he broke their kiss and set her back down on her feet. Noting the longing in her eyes, he threw her a wicked look from under his brow right before he dropped down to his knees. Those luxurious breasts were at just the right height for him to taste.

"My God," he groaned as he took in the sight of her.

She giggled breathily, and he grinned up at her before snatching one of those perfectly pink nipples into his mouth. She cried out in ecstasy. Her hands clung to his shoulders and neck.

Alex savoured her delectable breasts, unable to get enough. He reached his hand up between her silky thighs, finding her core wet and wanting. His cock throbbed, and he groaned as he slid a finger and then two into her. The need to slide his cock into her slick heat overwhelmed him.

Standing, he hiked her up in his arms and carried her to the great room, laying her down on the area rug in front of the fireplace. Lowering his body down onto hers, his skin sizzled, aching for more. Kissing her full lips, his pulsing cock nudged at her wet slit, teasing as he allowed the length of him to slide slowly from bottom to top and back again. Christ, how had he refrained from sex for so long? The feel of her, the smell of her—all of it was making his body thrum.

"Fill me up, Sergeant Mackenzie," she begged him breathlessly.

A self-assured sexy smile spread across his face. "As ye wish, Ms. West." Slowly, he pushed himself into her letting her feel every inch of him. The sensation of her wet tight sheath wrapping around his hungry cock was almost too much to take. He had to focus on not coming too soon.

"Oh, God," she whimpered as he filled her up only to slide back out and in again. Quinn lifted her hips, taking him in deeper.

The fire crackled warmly in the fireplace beside them. He slowly pulled out, watching her beautiful face as he did. God, how he needed this—needed her. He slammed back into her full hilt, and she moaned as her back arched up taking him in. Alex was riveted by the ecstasy on her face as he filled her up again and again.

Needing to taste her and feel her even more, he hiked up to his knees and lifted her body easily up against his. He caught her groan of pleasure with his mouth as he helped her to ride his thick cock. The feel of her naked body pressed against him, matching his every thrust was almost his undoing. He couldn't hold back much longer.

The pleasure was building in him like a rocket ready to launch. It had been a long time since he'd been with a woman, but right now, he felt like he was in another dimension with Quinn. Maybe he shouldn't have been surprised that making love to her would be so incredible, but with each move of their bodies, the connection and strength of their lovemaking felt shocking to him. Sex had never felt like this. All he wanted to do was give her pleasure, to please her, and the more he did, the more his own pleasure grew.

Quinn felt like she was in some erotic dream. Her body begged for more and more of him. It was greedy and hungry. He was an incredible lover, passionate and intense, but he knew how to expertly stoke her every desire. She was on top of him with their bodies pressed together. She felt her pleasure building with every move. She was on the edge of heaven. His blue eyes were heavy with intense carnal desire. God, she loved the way he watched her like she was the most desirable woman in the world.

"Ach, lass, I canna hold back with ye riding me like that," he growled as he swiftly lay her back onto the rug beneath them. His body was suddenly back on top of hers—his cock still deep in her. She was momentarily surprised, but then he slid in and out of her, grinding slowly, methodically. And she melted into bliss.

"You feel so good in me, Alex," she whispered, feeling her core tingle and ache as her orgasm began to bud.

"Aye, lass, I want to feel yer pleasure wrapped around me. Milking me." He expertly pumped her body as a heaviness grew low in her belly. The walls of her core tingled. Quinn was weak with pleasure and looked into Alex's glittering blue eyes. When he threw her a knowing cocky half grin and a wink, she completely shattered. Into a million pieces. Juicy electric pleasure-filled pieces. Her sex throbbed heavily around his cock.

Alex was mesmerized as she threw her head back, and her body arched in bliss. The feel of her orgasm pulsating around him threw him over the edge. He growled as his cock released like a shooting fountain. Wave after wave of bliss rocked him until he was spent and finally collapsed down over Quinn, breathing heavily.

Catching his breath, he lifted onto his elbows and looked down at the woman who'd just given him hands-down the most intense orgasm of his life. Her beautiful face was flushed, but she looked sated. Reaching a hand up, she touched his stubbled jaw, and he leaned his lips into her hand, kissing it.

And then it happened. Alex was sidelined by the dark heavy cloak that suddenly closed around his mind like thick black smoke darkening a blue sky, choking out the sun.

34
Walls and Shattered Piñatas

QUINN COULDN'T IMAGINE A more perfect moment, the way Alex looked at her now with such tender affection her heart felt full. This was the best Christmas ever.

After a moment, Alex rolled to the side and onto his back and threw an arm over his head. Quinn nuzzled into the crook of his other arm and stroked his chest.

"That was an unexpected Christmas present, Sergeant Mackenzie," she teased.

"Aye," his breath was a heavy sigh.

Quinn didn't miss the change in him. She suddenly sat up and looked down at the man who'd just made crazy amazing love to her. Her heart hitched because the tenderness she saw in his face mere moments ago was gone, and instead, very clearly on his too-handsome face, all she saw was regret.

Bitter tears pricked her eyes, and a lump wedged in her throat. How the heck could he regret what just happened? She couldn't understand. It had been the most incredible lovemaking she'd ever experienced. Didn't he feel it too?

Scrambling up, she grabbed a blanket from the chair and wrapped it around herself. She needed to get some space from Alex, who still lay tense and gloriously naked on the floor. It hurt how good he still looked despite the fact he was a total ass.

Quinn tucked herself onto the far end of the couch away from him. He stared up at the ceiling. His only movement was a slight tick in his jaw. Then he rolled over, lumbered up, and strode to the bathroom without a glance back at her.

Quinn's heart felt heavy, and she wrapped the blanket a little tighter around her as she looked out the window. She desperately wished she could be anywhere but here in his cabin—where he clearly didn't want her.

The bathroom door opened a moment later, and he stepped back out dressed in sweatpants and a black police t-shirt. Catching sight of him, Quinn's heart flip-flopped, and she felt a burst of anger that she would still react to him even now... Even when he didn't want her.

Stalking towards her, he dropped the hoodie and sweatpants she'd been wearing in the morning beside her. And it felt like a not-so-subtle hint that he didn't want to see her body or know she was naked under his blanket on his couch. That he wanted to pretend that they hadn't just had the most incredible sex. Quinn snatched the clothes, throwing them on as quickly as she could as Alex moved to sit in one of the chairs. His forearms rested on his knees, and he rubbed his thumbs in the corner sockets of his eyes as if he could rub away what just happened between them.

With a heavy sigh and without even looking back, as if she wasn't physically sitting there behind him with her heart shattering, he spoke.

"I'm sorry, lass. I dinnae want to complicate things." His voice was hollow and distant.

She scoffed at his halfhearted apology. "Yes, I know. God forbid you let yourself feel something for me."

"Dinnae say that." He lifted his head to look at her, and she could see the weariness in his stormy blue eyes.

"Why not? It's true isn't it?" she challenged him, feeling raw.

Alex rubbed a tired hand over his jaw, leaned back in the chair, and said nothing.

"I'm not her, Alex," Quinn said quietly, afraid that his walls were already too high to break through.

"Do ye no' think I ken that? Ye're nothing like her, thank Christ. Kate has nothing to do with this."

"No?" she questioned. "Perhaps your mystery woman in the photograph then." She shot him an accusing look, daring him to finally lay his cards on the table.

Alex sighed heavily. "Trust me. She has nothing to do with this either."

"Oh, I'm to trust you now?" she snapped, frustrated by the whole situation. "You are all warm and fuzzy one minute and then cold hard ass cop the next. What am I supposed to think? I'm starting to feel like a hostage here."

His piercing eyes snapped to hers, and for a moment, she regretted her words. "I would never keep ye here against yer will." His voice was cold steel. "I cannae help the situation we find ourselves in."

"I'm well aware." She stiffened refusing to look at him. The silence drew out between them, and Quinn stared out at the thick snow outside. Only a few short hours ago, it brought feelings of Christmas coziness, and now, it just looked bleak to her.

She tried to understand what in the heck happened, but deep down, she knew. She knew it was Kate Cameron. Kate Cameron haunted Alex. Thinking about all the things that made him so amazing didn't matter, because, in the end, he was still shackled by his past. Walls that were erected at the drop of a dime. Any time Quinn felt like Alex was opening his heart to her, feeling something for her, it was as if his heart would suddenly snap closed like an oyster trying to protect itself. And he would lock her out.

She was locked out now, and it smarted. Her own heart felt battered and numb while her body cruelly felt the lingering vestiges of their lovemaking.

Alex's mind battered him. He'd lived by the oath of being immune to women for so long that he didn't know what to do or think about his current predicament. Perhaps Quinn was right about Kate. He thought that woman was long behind him. Talking to Quinn the night before made him realize even more, that everything with Kate and what had happened all those years ago was truly over. Long over. He'd moved on with his life. Hadn't he?

Being immune to women, not letting them in, not letting them close had become second nature to him. He didn't think twice about it, but now, a lass had done the impossible. She'd slipped past his walls. Quinn West had bloody well obliterated his walls like a kid with a stick, smacking into a fucking reindeer piñata. Alex's proverbial candy was strewn everywhere, and he had no idea how to get it back in the box. She'd had cracked him wide open, and it scared the shite out of him.

It was his conversation with Quinn last night that had shown Alex how far in the past Kate and all the hell she'd put him through was. The old reactions and feelings he'd had when he allowed himself to stew had all but fizzled out. Kate

Cameron was a non-issue in his life. She was long gone like the misery she'd caused.

Alex had awoken in the morning with that newfound knowledge, and he genuinely felt as if the grip she'd had on him had been released. He felt lighter than he had in years. Those feelings were short-lived because now he felt almost dizzy with anxiety. Fear. And he didn't do fear. He wanted to roar. His carefully constructed life felt tipped off its axis, and he didn't have a clue how to fix it. It terrified him more than anything ever had.

"Talk to me, Alex. Help me understand." Quinn's voice cut through his fractured thoughts.

She appeared so fragile sitting with her arms wrapped around her knees. Her face barely poked out from the oversized hood of his sweatshirt. Part of him wanted to scoop her up into his arms and kiss away the sadness that was etched on her beautiful face.

Instead, he said nothing. He didn't know what to say, what to think. He was spiralling, freaking out, and the only thing he could think to help it was to have her gone. As if reading his mind, a shadow seemed to cross over her features before they set in a hard line.

"I wish I'd never met you." Her words could have shattered him, but he already felt shattered. Lost. Fucked right up.

As she stood, they both heard a sound in the distance, and it quickly grew louder. Quinn's big eyes looked at him questioningly, but before he could say anything, a loud thumping on the front door made her jump.

"The ranger," Alex said, feeling numbness seep through him. If it was the ranger, the road back to town was likely open. Thank God. Quinn West could leave. Leave his cabin. Leave his life. And maybe, he could put his world back to rights and breathe again.

Quinn didn't say a word, but he could see in her eyes what he felt. The final nail in the coffin had just been hammered in.

35
Broken Hearted Silver Linings

Quinn sat alone on the bed in her room at the inn. For someone who'd always coveted time with herself, the loneliness that had taken up residence in her soul was a bitter pill to swallow. Snow fell outside, and she watched it absently. It had been just over twenty-four hours since the ranger had shown up at Alex's and brought her back to the inn.

As soon as she had service again, her phone dinged with messages, but that first night, she didn't have the heart to look at them. Eventually, she'd messaged back to Belle and Megan, wishing them a Merry Christmas, explaining that with the snow storm she hadn't had service for a few days. Fortunately, neither one of them questioned it. Quinn wasn't ready to talk about any of what happened with Alex and she didn't know if she ever would be.

Christmas night felt like a blurry nightmare. It all happened so fast. She didn't know what she expected really, but the abrupt ending to it all felt wrong. The ranger had come to check in on them and let them know the road had opened up. And just like that, whatever fairy tale she thought she'd been living in hit a definitive brick wall and shattered. The sudden need to get the heck out of there propelled her to ask the ranger if he could take her back to the inn. He was hesitant, but Quinn couldn't stay in Alex's cabin for another minute. She practically ran to get in the ranger's truck when he'd reluctantly agreed to drive her. Alex didn't say a word of protest, and the sting of his silence felt barbed.

Christmas day at the inn was jovial and lively, loud and boisterous—a jarring contrast with the peaceful time alone with Alex in his cabin. The restaurant was full of people celebrating and feasting. Quinn felt like she was in some kind of a vortex on the outside looking in. She went to her room and sobbed until she finally fell asleep. When she awoke, the reality of being alone in the bed hit first, and then the memory that whatever had happened between her and Alex was over. The fairy tale had come to an end. A dull ache sat heavy in her chest.

She couldn't help but torture herself with memories of every touch, every look. The fun they'd had. The deep conversations and the light ones. It had felt like a dream, and now, it was done. Over. As if it never happened in the first place.

She tried to tell herself she was being dramatic, but her heart knew what her heart knew. The reality was that she'd fallen hard for Alex. There were boyfriends in the past, men she'd fancied herself in love with, but the connection she'd felt with Alex went far beyond what she'd ever known. She'd always believed having a boyfriend came with the automatic pass to being in love. Like a gift that came with a gift tag, a boyfriend came with love. With that belief entrenched, she assumed that she was in love with her past relationships. Lo and behold, it turned out she had no idea what falling in love was. Now, on reflection, it turned out she'd never once in her life been in love. Until now.

God, if this truly was love, it was awful. How in heaven's name could she feel so connected to someone, so crazy about someone, and that person not reciprocate? There were moments when Quinn thought Alex felt it—that amazing unexplainable thing between them. That magic thing. When he was making love to her, she felt as if their very souls had become one. She laughed bitterly at her naivety. What a fool she was. He'd not felt the same things she did because if he did, she would not be here alone with her heart thrown out like used Christmas wrapping.

She wished she could stop ruminating, but it had become a shamefully addictive pastime. How was it in the sweet gentle moments they'd spent cuddling, talking, sharing, she'd felt so in tune with him? She'd shared so much about her life with him, and he seemed to get her in a way that only her best friends did. Alex seemed to understand her on a deeper level. Or so she thought. It was painfully confusing, and the more she thought, the less she understood how things had gone so awry.

In between crying, she wrote, and in between writing, she walked around the town trying to feel some sense of the appreciation she'd felt when she'd first arrived here. She wanted to feel normal, but she didn't. If only she could go back in time and reverse all that had happened. Instead, she just felt a hollowness in her that she couldn't seem to shake.

On her second walk of the day, she hoped to feel human again but was unable to escape the heaviness in her heart. As she passed by the old brick library, she heard a siren, and her pulse kicked into high gear. Heart thundering, she stood waiting for his truck to come around the corner, waiting for him to come to her. She tucked her hair behind her ear and licked her lips, wondering what he'd say, what she'd say. When an ambulance turned the corner and sped past, Quinn's shoulders slumped, and she chided herself for the momentary excitement she'd felt. What was she thinking? Alex would throw on a siren and come for her in some grand gesture. *Stupid*. It was a new low when she considered what minor law she could break so he'd come give her a hard time. Mean Hot Cop that she'd grown so effing crazy for. She rolled her eyes at her ridiculousness.

After all the time spent thinking and analyzing every detail of every moment they'd spent together, Quinn came to a surprising realization. There was no doubt in her mind that Alex had a wall around his heart, but what startled her was she'd been guarding her heart too. She didn't let people in either.

Her best friends, yes, because they knew her heart from the beginning it seemed, but other than her best friends, Quinn hadn't connected deeply with anyone as an adult. Maybe she was more like Alex than she realized. It was both heartening and disheartening that Alex had tenderly found his way into her soul. She'd trusted him—with everything. She'd given herself wholeheartedly. Something she'd never done before. Now she knew why. Betrayal. It hurt. Badly. He was probably right to keep up his guard.

Good for him, she thought numbly. He wasn't going through the hell she was. He'd protected himself. *Bravo, Alex*, she thought bitterly.

Quinn had been through so much in her life. She was convinced she could handle anything that came her way. Yet here she was, pining for a man she'd known for a week. She would have bet her last dollar that he was her soul mate. A few days back, she'd have called it magic. Now she'd call it madness.

Ironically, the pain in her heart somehow translated into some serious creative spells with her book. A few times, she'd sat down and ideas flowed in bursts. Everything else around her felt like shit, but her writing was keeping her sane. Nothing felt like a silver lining at the moment, but if she had to choose something, her writing would be it.

36
Brotherly Love

"Ye need to fix it."

"Have ye listened to a fuckin' word I've said," Alex snapped exasperated.

Alex and Lachlan sat at Alex's wooden kitchen table with a half-drunk bottle of scotch between them as they argued.

"Aye, ye dumb arse." Lachlan thumped his hand on the table. "Go grovel and beg fer that woman's forgiveness. Then we can all get on a plane back to Scotland and make it home in time fer New Year's fuckin' Eve."

Alex couldn't believe what he was hearing. Of all people, his brother knew better than anyone the hell he'd been through. How could he be so flippant about this? Did he not understand the lass had exploded his world, and he had no idea how to put it back together?

"I cannae. My life was good. No, it was bloody near perfect," he amended, "before she came along, and now everything feels all off-kilter," he argued, feeling foul as he gulped back the contents of his glass.

"Jesus Mother of Christ. Yer a complete fuckin' numpty! I hauled my arse across the giant fuckin' pond because I huv never known ye to be so oot of yer mind."

Alex gave his brother a black look, sitting back in his chair. "I didnae ask ye to come, did I?"

"Naw, but evidently, ye need somebody to talk some fuckin' sense inta ya. Ye miserable sod."

Alex sat pensively, still a little surprised at his brother's appearance. On Christmas morning, Lachlan's wife, Violet, had apparently surprised Lachlan with a ticket to come to Canada. His sister-in-law knew that Alex was supposed to be in Scotland over Christmas, and when his plans cancelled, according to Lachlan, she'd insisted that it was "high time" the brothers saw each other. *Whatever that meant.*

Lachlan also admitted that they were both worried about Alex, which annoyed him immensely. He did not want anyone worrying over him. He was just fine, damn it. And currently, his brother was doing very little to help his mood anyway.

"Ye need me to spell it out fer ye?" Lachlan rubbed his forehead looking desperate for some sleep.

"No' really," Alex snapped.

Lachlan groaned, laying his head down on the wooden kitchen table in resignation.

"Listen, I was shocked as shite to get a call from ye this afternoon to come get ye at the airport. Then ye sit at my table, drink my whisky, and try and make it sound like I'm going daft. I'm not." Alex said pointedly.

Lachlan lifted his head and peered at his brother through jet-lagged eyes across the table. "Ye huvnae come up fer air talking about this Quinn West lassie since ye picked me up, so dinnae tell me that *I'm* the one makin' ye sound daft. Ye're doin' that well enough yerself. And perhaps, I'll keep the eighteen-year-old quarter cask bottle of Cailleach in my case, fer myself. To hell with ye."

"In yer case? Now? And yer only just mentioning it? Christ, mon." Alex ignored everything Lachlan said except about the fine whisky.

Lachlan stared at his brother like he was their crazy uncle Rory, who always spouted bizarre conspiracy theories at Christmas dinner.

"If ye haud yer weesht fer a minute and listen, I may go get it."

"By all means, say wha' ye huv to say, then let's drink the good stuff. 'Tis Christmas after all," Alex quipped lightly.

"I cannae believe yer so bloody dense," Lachlan said. "This cold Canadian air must be numbing yer brain cells."

Alex shot him a scowl. "Fuck off."

Lachlan's lips tipped into a lopsided grin, and he leaned in over the table. "Let me let ye in on a wee secret."

Alex arched a dark brow as he sat back, folding his muscled arms across his chest.

"Ye, dear brother," Lachlan said slowly as if ensuring Alex was listening, "are in love, like the real fuckin' deal. Hook, line, and sinker. Brawly smitten." Then Lachlan leaned back in his chair, and a pleased smile spread from ear to ear, like the cartoon Grinch, all satisfied with himself after he'd hatched his plan to keep Christmas from coming.

Alex stared at his brother's twinkling blue eyes. "Christ Lachlan, ye huv lost yer bloody mind. Next, ye'll be trying to convince me ye witnessed Santa squeezing his fat fucking arse down the chimney on Christmas Eve."

Lachlan sighed in resignation, then smacked his hands down on the table and pushed back his chair, its feet scraping across the floor. "Ye daft sod. I'm knackered. I'm going to bed." He nodded in the direction of the settee. "Now get out of my bedroom and leave me in peace."

Alex lay in his bed feeling spent, although a nervous energy still buzzed through him. The last thing he'd ever have expected was for one of his siblings to show up here in Canada the day after Christmas. Especially not Lachlan given that he was married and had his boys and wife at home.

If Drew had shown up on his doorstep, Alex would have been less surprised since Drew was known for doing the unexpected. Even if his baby sister Orlagh had shown up, it would have been less of a shock since she'd always talked about wanting to get out of Scotland.

It wouldn't surprise him if one day she made her way to this side of the pond. His thoughts turned to Helena, the sister they'd lost. Christmas time was always tinged with a combination of happy and sad. God, how he missed her. He knew that they all did.

Seeing Lachlan felt really good though. He'd missed having his family around. He loved the numpty despite his delirious blethering tonight. The man was jet lagged and too damn in love with his own wife. He was seeing the world with some kind of rosy glasses. Alex scoffed out loud. *In love. How ridiculous. Christ.*

37
Four Letter Word

"Mornin'," Lachlan said as Alex strode into the kitchen and filled a glass of water from the tap.

"Mornin', ye sleep all right?" he asked between gulps.

"Well, it's not the most comfy of settees, but to be honest, I slept like the dead." He was sitting up and stretching his head from side to side. "My neck is kinked up like a bloody cinnamon twist."

"Maybe ye should go shove yer head in the snow?" Alex suggested brightly.

"Fuck off," Lachlan replied, and Alex's lips quirked in a smile. It was nice to have his brother around.

"How long are ye intending to stay?" he asked, refilling his water glass.

Lachlan cocked his head. "As soon as ye pull yer head out of yer arse, I can think about headin' home."

Alex bit back a laugh. "I cannae begin to imagine wha' ye mean," he said sardonically.

Lachlan strode into the kitchen. "Where's the coffee?"

"I'll make it. Go sit," Alex muttered.

Lachlan brokered no argument. He pulled out the chair at the table and plopped down. A few minutes later, Alex brought two mugs of coffee to the table and sat down across from his brother. They sipped in companionable silence.

"So?" Lachlan eyed at Alex expectantly.

"So what?" Alex said, leaning back in his chair, feeling exhausted. Even his bones felt zapped of energy. He sipped his strong black coffee—mud, as Quinn had referred to the taste—silently willing it to take the edge off. He knew better, though. It was a miserable sort of tired plaguing him. He hadn't slept well. Again. It wasn't so much that he felt sleepy; it was more an epic dismal mood he couldn't manage to shake. If anything, it seemed worse by the hour.

"Did ye think about what I said?"

"What?" Alex looked dumbfounded.

"Love," Lachlan responded as if it was obvious.

Alex glared at his brother, his head beginning to throb. "Ye cannae be serious."

"Christ, mon, listen, ye used to be a fun guy to be around, and I know ye went through yer shite. More than anyone should ever huv to go through," he added. "No word of a lie, Alex, I huv been here for, ooh..." Lachlan looked down at his watch. "What's it? About sixteen hours now? An' in the first five, ye didnae come up fer air. Have ye no' listened to yerself and the way ye talk about her? Ye havnae blethered about anything else," his brother said, daring Alex to argue with him.

Alex looked stupefied. "It was a fucked-up week. One ironic run-in after another with the lass," he said as if that explained it.

"Tha' is no' what I gathered from everything ye blethered about yesterday." Lachlan threw him a challenging brow.

"Aye, well, it was bloody confusing," Alex muttered rubbing his temples.

"Confusing how?"

"I dinnae ken why it's confusing, only that it is."

Lachlan rolled his eyes swiping his hands down his face as if trying to keep a grip on his patience. Crossing his arms over his chest, he said, "I'll wait." Then he looked at Alex expectantly, as if waiting on one of his children to explain themselves.

Gulping back the last of his coffee, Alex plonked his mug on the table and sighed in resignation. "I dinnae even ken what to say." He shook his head and raked a hand through his hair. "Part of it felt like the best time I think I've ever had in my life. Like our conversations and just the day-to-day with her—it was unbelievable." He paused.

"And the sex," Lachlan provided as if helping Alex sort out his thoughts, but Alex shot him *a shut-your-face-or-I'll-shut-it-for-you* look. Lachlan put up his hands in a truce. "I'm only sayin' tha' part sounded like it was good too."

Alex sighed. "Aye, tha' part was... Christ, I dinnae huv words fer it."

Lachlan looked like he wanted to say more but thought better of it. Instead, he stood, taking Alex's mug and his own to the counter, refilling them, and bringing them back to the table.

"Thank ye," Alex said. "I dinnae ken about love." He rubbed Bear's neck, his trusty pup resting his head on Alex's lap. "I mean, what the fuck is love anyway? It isnae a real thing, and if it is, I suspect 'tis fuckin dangerous. I'd rather stay the hell away from it."

Alex stood and Bear plodded off to lay in front of the the fireplace. He strode to the kitchen, took a red bowl from an open shelf and a box of cereal from the cupboard and filled up the bowl to almost overflowing.

"Violet and I are in love. Madly in love." Lachlan grinned in obvious defence of his brother's denial of love's existence.

"That's different," Alex muttered, not turning around as he grabbed a carton of milk from the fridge. "Cereal?" he absently asked, and Lachlan shook his head.

"I think I'm too bloody jet-lagged to eat."

"Suit yerself," Alex said plonking back down at the table.

Lachlan rubbed his forehead as Alex spooned a hearty helping of cereal into his mouth. Lachlan looked like shite, but he suspected it was more than just the jet lag. He knew his brother better than anyone, and he knew that it drove him crazy that Alex wasn't giving him the answers he wanted to hear. But Christ, *love*. The mon was obviously not thinking clearly.

"Yer no' thinking clearly," Lachlan muttered as if he'd jumped into Alex's head. Although, he believed it to be the other way around. Alex held his spoon midway to his mouth. Lachlan did have an uncanny ability to read Alex's thoughts, and it didn't seem to matter that they hadn't seen each other in over two years.

"Yer, the one with the jet lag," Alex quipped back, taking the spoonful of cereal into his mouth.

"Remember how ye were when we were kids?" Lachlan asked, suddenly changing gears.

Alex eyed him suspiciously. "What do ye mean?"

"Out of all of us siblings, ye've always faced danger head-on. In fact, ye've revelled in it ever since we were kids. Ye used to scare the shite outta mam."

Alex chuckled. "Aye," he said between spoonfuls of cereal. He had fond memories of growing up. He'd gotten up to some crazy antics. His poor mam. "Ye remember at Bluff's

Head when everyone dared me to jump 'cause they didnae think I'd do it?"

"Ye crazy bastard. Nobody forgot that one. The Coast Guard had to hunt ye down."

Alex laughed. "It was a bit touch and go there, but I managed to stay afloat long enough to be rescued." They'd definitely gotten into some crazy stuff as kids, but without a doubt, Alex was the trailblazer.

"Christ, our poor mam. If our boys ever pulled a stunt like that, Violet would go mental." Lachlan shook his head before looking back at Alex. "Anyways, ye numpty, the point is ye ha' never been a coward."

Alex sobered eyeing his brother. "No, 'tis not who I am."

"Then why the fuck are ye so afraid of this wee lass?"

Alex dropped his spoon in his empty bowl and sat silently contemplating. "Because I cannae lose her," he said almost too quiet to hear.

"What?" Lachlan's blue eyes lit with a glint of hope. "I believe ye told me yesterday, ye already huv. She's gone, no?"

"Aye. What I mean is, if I—" Alex stumbled on his words. "Well, if I admit...that I... Well, that... If I admit that I have feelings." Alex looked at Lachlan as if his own words stunned him. "Jesus." He breathed. "If I admit that I have feelings, then I dinnae think I could handle losing her."

Lachlan sat back in his chair, looking like he was about to fucking slow clap. "Then ye sure as hell better go get her."

Alex felt like a reindeer caught in headlights. "Ye're right."

"Well, Jesus Christ, wonders never cease. I dinnae think ye huv ever said that."

Alex suddenly broke out into a grin. "Aye, well, there's a first time for everything, but dinnae expect to hear it again."

"Ach, there's the brother I ken and love. I can tell by the look in yer eye, the lass doesnae stand a chance."

"Aye," Alex agreed. When he wanted something, he would stop at nothing to get it.

"I'm excited to meet the wee lass who's brought my brother to his knees," Lachlan teased with a mischievous twinkle in his eye.

Alex shot Lachlan a warning glare as he stood from the table. His brother raised a challenging brow, goading Alex to deny it. He knew damn well his brother was testing him, and the truth was Lachlan was right. His little lass had Alex on his knees, and Christ, if he didn't want to be there. He'd happily beg on his knees to worship his goddess.

"I suggest ye hurry yer arse up then, Lachlan. We're leaving within the hour," he said unable to keep the grin from his face.

38
Seeing Double

Quinn thanked the barista for her Gingerbread latte. The tasty drinks had pretty much become breakfast lunch and dinner. In an otherwise gloomy mood, these lattes were a highlight. The little local cafe made them so sinfully delicious. Walking out of the café, she made her way back to the inn to do some writing.

The sunny glorious day and the mountain backdrop did little to warm her aching heart, but she still appreciated it. It was hard to believe the crazy snow and cold of the storm were just a couple of short days ago. God. It was like the whole thing had been a dream. The storm. Being stranded alone with Alex. She sighed, taking a sip of her sweet creamy coffee. The warmth of the sunshine on her face felt heavenly despite the sadness she felt inside.

As she rounded the corner and the inn came into view, her heart thundered. There was a police truck parked out front. She took some deep breaths and tried to calm herself. Even if it was him, which it wasn't necessarily, he could be there for any number of reasons. She walked a little faster, needing to get closer to see.

Then she froze in her tracks when Alex walked out the front doors of the inn dressed in his black uniform. God, he looked good, and she couldn't help the flutter low in her belly at the sight of him and all those muscles. The flutter was short-lived though when he got in his truck and sped off, lights and siren blaring.

She could have cried. Had he come to see her? Maybe not. Either way, he was gone now. The familiar cloak of melancholy settled over her again. Even her delicious latte was no longer cutting it, and she dumped it in the garbage just outside the inn.

As she walked into the lobby, she thought her eyes were surely playing tricks on her, and then she began to question her sanity. There, in one of the velvet wingback chairs, sat Alex. His handsome profile to her. She stared sure she was losing her mind. The man before her in a thick navy sweater and dark jeans was Alex, but then she thought back to the unmistakable Hot Cop who'd just driven off. She'd recognize that deliciousness anywhere. That was him. She was sure of it, but then how could he be here? Uneasiness washed over her as she stood staring at him.

As if sensing her, he tilted his head, looking her way with warm eyes. Her brain was stumped. It was Alex, but not Alex?

"Quinn?"

She stood stone still, staring. What the hell? "Alex?" she asked, wondering if she needed to get medical treatment.

"Lachlan." He shot her a handsome lopsided grin as he stood. "Alex's brother."

Alex's brother? His brother was a twin? Her brain was still processing as relief seeped over her. At least she wasn't losing it—thank God—but what the heck?

"Lachlan," she said, looking at him for confirmation or explanation.

"Aye." He smiled warmly, standing up.

"I knew Alex had two brothers, but he never mentioned that you and him were twins." She studied his features fascinated, stupefied by how much he looked like Alex. Upon closer inspection, she recognized he was more slight than Alex, although still heavily muscled, and there was something different about their eyes. Oh my God. Quinn's mind flew back to the photo in Alex's sporran. Was it Lachlan in that photo? With his wife and boys?

"Ach, lass, sorry if I gave ye a start."

She nodded still uncertain as to what was going on. "Right, well uh, nice to meet you," she said about to go past him to her room.

"Please, dinnae go. Are ye busy? Could we maybe go to the restaurant here? Have a wee bit o' lunch?" He looked sweetly convincing. *Jeez*, it did not help that he looked just like Alex. The more she studied him, the more she could see the subtle difference not just in their eyes, but their smiles too. Both were ridiculously good-looking though.

"Does your wife have long blond hair?" she suddenly asked.

He looked dumbfounded. "Violet? Aye, she does. Why do ye ask?"

"I saw a picture with you and her, although I didn't know it at the time." She couldn't believe Alex hadn't just been straight with her. Why would he let her think it was him in the photo? And then it occurred to her. It was a wall that he could use to keep her at bay. It stung. Just one more barrier he'd try to use to keep her away.

"Come on, lass. Let's go have a blether," Lachlan said gently.

"Excuse me? A what?" Quinn said, wondering what the heck he meant, but there was a kindness in his eyes that made her think he meant no harm.

Lachlan chuckled. "A blether, a chat, lass. In the pub." He gestured towards the inn's restaurant.

"Oh right." She wasn't sure it was the best idea given the state of her heart. God, before everything went wrong with Alex, Quinn would have jumped at the chance to get to know his family.

Everything felt so different now though. She wasn't sure what to think, but there was no way her curiosity would allow her to decline Lachlan's invite.

They sat by the window with a view of the festive street and people bustling by. Oddly enough, this was only the second time Quinn had been in the inn's restaurant. The first time was with her girls, and that felt like a lifetime ago now. The very last thing she expected was to be here with Alex's twin brother.

"It's truly so lovely to meet ye, Quinn," Lachlan said with a disarming smile.

Hmm, he definitely came across as nicer than his brother. She smiled awkwardly, not knowing what to say to him, and she was oddly grateful when the server showed up at their table.

"Hi, my name is Brittney." Quinn didn't miss Brittney's once-over of Lachlan, not that she could blame the girl. She almost laughed. "I'll be your server. What can I get you to start?" Her eyes landed squarely on Lachlan.

"Scotch?" he offered, looking at Quinn expectantly as if he hadn't even noticed Brittney batting her lashes.

Quinn surprised herself with a nod in the affirmative. She could use a stiff drink.

"Two Taliskers, please. Neat."

"Uh, I don't think we have that."

"Och, right. Well, how 'boot an Oban then?"

Brittany shook her head no.

Realizing it may be a lost cause Lachlan finally said, "Well whatever single malt ye huv would be lovely, lass."

Brittany blushed, naturally charmed by the handsome Scot. Quinn tried not to smile. The Mackenzie twins were seriously good-looking. Although one seemed a little more charming than the other...

"For sure." She smiled brightly at him. "I'll see what I can find for you." Lachlan watched as Brittany turned and headed for the bar, and Quinn could see the doubt in his eyes.

"Well, as long as we get some kind o' whisky at the very least," he muttered, turning back to Quinn.

She smiled lightly at him, wondering if all Scots took their scotch so seriously or if it was just the Mackenzie clan.

"Alex was here earlier, too, but he got a work call and left in a hurry," he said. "I assume it was something important."

Quinn just nodded. She didn't know what to think.

"Alex had come to see ye," he explained.

Quinn looked up at him. "Why?" she asked bluntly not even noticing the uncomfortable expression on Lachlan's face. After the way things ended with them, she was surprised he wanted to see her at all. God, for all she knew, she'd left something at his place, and he was just getting his brother to deliver it.

"Well, I suspect 'tis better if he talks to ye about that himself," Lachlan said gently, right as Brittany flounced up to the table, bringing them their drinks. "Jamison's Irish Whisky." She grinned, clearly pleased with herself for managing to find him a whisky.

Lachlan gave her a gracious smile. After confirming they didn't need anything else, she walked away. Lachlan took a sip and said, "'Tis no' a single malt. No' even scotch." He shook his head, sniffing at it. "But will huv to do I suppose."

That made Quinn smile, and she recalled thinking that Alex was Irish when he had given her that stupid ticket the day they met. It seemed so long ago now.

"I didn't realize Alex was expecting any of his family to visit over the holidays," she said, taking a sip of her whisky vaguely aware that she'd somehow grown accustomed to the taste and could almost say she liked it.

"He wasnae. My wife Violet surprised me on Christmas day with a ticket to come over here. I had no idea. It's been a long time, though, and I think she is hopin' I'd bring him back home."

"For good?" Quinn asked, feeling a pit form in her stomach. The thought of Alex leaving Canada was a heavy one. They weren't together, but if he wasn't here...it would mean the door would be closed forever. It seemed so final. And yet, wasn't the door already slammed shut?

"Naw, just for a visit. I dinnae think he's ready to come home for good. I'm not sure he ever will be."

"Oh right." Quinn felt oddly relieved. The restaurant was fairly quiet as it was mid-afternoon, and silence stretched between them. She fiddled with her white paper napkin on the dark wood table.

Lachlan studied her. "Ye huv a similar look in yer eyes as my brother did last night."

Quinn almost scoffed. "The look of exhaustion?"

"I meant the look of sadness," he said gently, and Quinn's glance flicked up at him. "Lass, I cannae speak fer Alex, but believe me when I say he cares fer ye."

"He has an odd way of showing it," she muttered, anxiously tearing off little shreds of a napkin.

Lachlan sat across the table from her, sipping his whisky, looking relaxed. He was so like Alex but also completely different. Lachlan seemed kind and gentle. She had to admit he was also very easy on the eyes. All those lovely traits, but it was cold, moody Alex that her heart ached for. The truth was she'd glimpsed a big heart somewhere under Alex's gruff facade. Lachlan and Alex may be identical, but they were very different. Not once did she find Lachlan to be lethally sexy like his brother, and he certainly didn't make her pant with need the way Alex did every time he set his stormy blue eyes on her. She squeezed her eyes closed trying to push out those thoughts.

Christmas music filled the otherwise quiet atmosphere of the inn restaurant. For the first time, Quinn realized that Christmas music might forever be ruined because of her heartbreak over Alex. Normally, she loved hearing Michael Bublé croon about jingle bells and white Christmas', but currently, she'd prefer utter stone-cold silence paired with her heartache over the cheery blare of festive music.

When she opened her eyes, Lachlan's lips were quirked in an almost smile, and he had a knowing expression on his face. "I hope my numpty brother has no' wrecked yer Christmas. He can be a stubborn arse, I ken."

Quinn saw the twinkle of mischief in Lachlan's eyes, and she almost smiled. "He can be an arse all right."

Lachlan chuckled.

"It's like he's determined to keep a wall up—keep people out. Or at least keep me out," she said, taking another sip of her whisky and feeling its heat roll down her throat.

"I dinnae think it is ye. I think it is all women," Lachlan said sadly. "He went through some very hard times in his life, and I think he was trying to protect himself somehow. I believe my brother has sworn off women like they're the plague."

"Great," Quinn scoffed.

"That is until ye came along," he clarified.

Quinn eyed Lachlan, gauging whether or not she believed him. "I'm pretty sure he's put me in the plague category and sworn me off too," she said, quietly fiddling at the shreds of napkin on the table.

"Never," he quipped confidently.

Quinn shook her head, not convinced.

"I dinnae ken what to say, lass. 'Tis no' my place to speak fer my brother. I will say this, though; Alex has always been fearless in his life. Nothing shakes the man."

Quinn snorted. "I've noticed."

"Aye, well I think ye may have cracked that a wee bit," Lachlan said, rolling the whisky in his glass.

"You think he's afraid of me?" Quinn scoffed. She couldn't fathom lethal Cold Mean Cop Alex being afraid of anything.

"I think he's in uncharted waters," Lachlan amended.

Quinn didn't know what to make of that. She wanted to ask more, but she also suspected Lachlan was not prepared to say too much on his brothers behalf. Quinn sighed heavily, leaning back from the table. "Honestly, Lachlan, I understand, in a way, why Alex has built impenetrable walls."

"Not impenetrable, lass," Lachlan interrupted her.

Quinn regarded him, not allowing herself to think on those words. "It kills me to think what Alex endured. The fact that Alex has found peace in his life and moved on is more than I think most people could do." She paused. "But it also kills me to think about what he will miss out on because he still keeps himself so guarded."

Lachlan eyed her like he wanted to say something, but held back.

"Maybe I'm not the one for Alex, but if he keeps himself and his heart locked in a fortress..." She shook her head feeling tears sting her eyes, but she swallowed them away. "He has so much to give. I saw it, he's... he's..."

Lachlan reached across the table, putting his hands reassuringly on hers as he looked at her helplessly like he didn't know what to do. "He's a damn stubborn arse is what he is."

Quinn laughed despite herself.

He patted her hands. "Ye're right lass. We all huv seen it, and we all huv tried to talk to him to tell him. It was like he couldn't hear what we were saying. But ye got through to him, Quinn."

Quinn shook her head sadly. "I don't think so, Lachlan." She was well aware that Alex was the most incredible man she'd ever met, but none of that mattered if he would throw up his walls any time he allowed himself to feel.

Quinn looked up at Lachlan's kind eyes, so like Alex's but a deeper shade of blue. Not the stormy blue piercing eyes of Sergeant Mackenzie. The ones that could reach right into her soul. The ones that didn't even bother to look at her as she slipped out his front door for the last time. She pulled her hand out from under Lachlan's and tucked her hair behind her ears.

"I didn't get through to him," she said pointedly. "Believe me, Lachlan, Alex's walls are up and fortified. I may have cracked a window, but he abruptly closed it and pulled down the shade," she snapped and gulped back the rest of her whisky.

Lachlan had a gentle smile on his face as he listened.

"Honestly, even if he did leave the window open, it's not enough," she said, feeling fired up now. She wasn't going to settle for little scraps from Alex.

"I understand, lass, and ye are right. He's either invested or he's not."

"Exactly," she quipped.

"I hope ye will give him another chance though," he said quietly, giving her an imploring look that she suspected was very effective at getting what he wanted.

"Ha! It's not like he's given any indication he even wants one," Quinn bit out not taking the bait.

Lachlan looked at her as if he wanted to say something but seemed reluctant.

"Here's the thing, Quinn. I huvnae even been here for a full day yet, and I huv seen the walls. I know what ye are talkin' about, but I've also seen the brother I've always known."

"Well, I'm glad for that. Truly, I am." She shifted in her seat.

"Since I've arrived, I've also seen a side of Alex I've never seen before. I dinnae ken everything that happened between ye, but I do ken my brother is different. Something *has* changed, Quinn."

Quinn didn't know what to make of what Lachlan was saying. She knew Alex hadn't seen his family since moving to Canada. Of course, he would be different. Or did Lachlan mean something more?

"Let's leave it at that, lass. I dinnae want to speak fer him, but I hope that ye will hear him out."

"It's not like he's here asking to be heard," she muttered.

Lachlan chuckled. "Aye, well, he may be a bit tied up at the moment. He came here to see ye, Quinn, but work pulled him away."

Quinn sniffed as if she still wasn't convinced. "Hmph."

"Right then, how about some scran?" he said, picking up the menu. "I'm starved."

"Scran?" she asked reluctantly.

"Grub," he said without even looking up.

"Food," she clarified as Lachlan studied his menu. Her mouth quirked in a smile, and she picked up her own menu.

They ordered a charcuterie board and spent the afternoon chatting or "blethering" as Lachlan had called it. Quinn found she quite enjoyed herself, and it somehow took her mind off her sadness despite the fact much of the conversation centred around Alex. Talking with Lachlan was like getting an unbidden view into Alex's life.

Lachlan told Quinn about his wife and boys and spoke about them with such love and adoration that Quinn couldn't help but feel a twinge of envy. They sounded like such a loving family. Lachlan also talked about growing up with Alex. Quinn found herself so immersed that she'd all but forgotten her heartache.

The sky began to darken outside the window. Lachlan looked down at his phone. No word from Alex.

"Haven't heard from him?" Quinn assumed so from Lachlan's expression.

"No, he must still be tied up with work. Ach, Quinn, I'm so sorry, lass, but I'm going to huv to get on my way. I'm thoroughly enjoying our chat, but I confess the jet lag has caught up to me."

"No, no, that's fine. I can drive you. I have my car just out front." Quinn was happy to offer Lachlan a ride back to Alex's. She did feel a bit nervous about being back at his place. Even if it was only to drop Lachlan.

"I dinnae want to put ye out. I can take a cab it's fine," he said through a stifled yawn.

Quinn smiled. "I learned the hard way that cabs and Ubers don't go up Alex's way. I'll take you. It's the least I can do."

The drive was just over half an hour, but Quinn was glad for the distraction. She wasn't in a rush to get back to her stewing heartache. Lachlan drifted to sleep as they drove, but Quinn didn't mind. It was still better than being alone at the inn right now. Alone with her thoughts. It had been nice getting to know Lachlan and learning more about Alex. Really nice, but also really shitty. Just a painful reminder of all the lovely that was not hers.

Quinn gave Lachlan a nudge when they got to Alex's cabin. He awoke with a start.

"Sorry, I didn't mean to scare you. We're here." She nodded towards the cabin. It was a relief in a way not to see Alex's truck parked outside, but still, it was hard to see his place again. A surreal feeling settled over her as memories from only a couple of days ago flooded her. That time had come and gone. It was over now.

"Thank ye, Quinn," Lachlan said getting out. "It was truly such a pleasure spending the afternoon with ye. I hope to see ye again soon, but if for some reason we do not cross paths, I wish ye all the best, lass. Truly, I do." His expression was warm.

Quinn nodded, trying not to feel sad for all that she knew could have been, but likely wouldn't. "It was a really great afternoon. Thank you, Lachlan."

39
Oh Mean Cop

As Lachlan disappeared into his brother's cabin, Quinn looped around the driveway and headed back down the mountain road. She couldn't help the tear that slid down her cheek. It had been lovely meeting Lachlan, but it drove home all that she was missing out on with Alex. Alex's family sounded wonderful, and if they were anything like Lachlan, she was sure they were all amazing. God, she wondered if Alex knew just how lucky he was to have such a family. To have people who loved him so much and had his back. To have a sibling who would travel across the world just to check in. It was something Quinn had never known in her life.

She drove along the darkened winding roads back to the inn deep in thought. Flashing lights in her rearview mirror caught her off guard, and then the whoop of the siren caused her heart to stutter. Her first thought was Alex. Would she ever not hear a siren and think of him? She growled in frustration. She'd been speeding. Again. Apparently, she hadn't learned her lesson.

With the glaring headlights and flashing blue and red police lights in the darkness behind her, she could just make out the silhouette of the officer stalking towards her car, and her heart thudded in her rib cage. The knock on her window startling her from her spiralling thoughts.

Through the window, she saw his black uniform and his black gun in its holster around his trim waist. She rolled her window down. "I need ye to step oot of the vehicle." His voice commanded her before she could say a word.

Mean Cop. "Alex, I'm not getting out. If you want to give me a ticket, then just do it, and get it over with," she said angrily with her heart fluttering in defiance.

"It's Sergeant Mackenzie, and I told ye to step oot," he said in a deadly serious voice.

Quinn's cheeks burned as her pulse kicked up wildly. What the heck? How dare he talk to her like that? Oh, she would tell him exactly where he could go! She huffed angrily, getting out of her car and slamming the door behind her, not caring how loudly the sound echoed in the quiet of the night. But then when she was standing toe to toe with him, her traitorous heart thundered in her chest. *Frick*. She'd spent the afternoon with his gorgeous twin, but it was nothing compared to the gorgeousness of the man before her. Mean Hot Cop was bite-your-lip-as-heat-licked-between-your-thighs sexy. Dark stubble lined his strong jaw.

He was chiselled rugged sexiness, and she loathed herself for wanting to jump his bones. Fortunately, she was too angry to get completely sidetracked by his hotness.

"I'm out, okay. Now what, Alex...Sergeant Mackenzie?" She couldn't keep the scorn from her voice. She was ready to blast the man, but when she looked up at his too-handsome face under the shadow of his police cap, she was almost brought to her knees. Alex Mackenzie's stormy blue eyes were shining on her....*lovingly?*

He stepped closer to her and cupped the side of her face gently with one strong hand. "Christ, I missed ye," he murmured before bringing his lips down on hers and claiming her in a feral-searing kiss.

Quinn whimpered and felt like her knees might buckle. There was so much passion in his kiss. How could he make her melt just like that? His kiss lit her on fire and drowned her at the same time. The headiness of him taking her, sweeping his tongue into her mouth, needing her. But a voice in the back of her mind emerged through the greedy hunger she felt for him. *No, Quinn*, she thought. *No.* It'll just end in more heartache. As hard as it was, she forced herself to pull away from him.

"Alex, I can't do this." Her breath was heavy as she turned away from him.

Quinn's words were an ice-cold shower on Alex. He stepped back from her, realizing it was going to take more than kisses to win her over. But when she turned back to him, he saw the hurt in her eyes, the hurt he'd put there... A fiercely protective feeling came over him. He needed to fix this. Fix his mistakes. And he silently vowed, then and there, that he'd never be the cause of her hurt ever again.

"Oh my God, what happened?" Her expression suddenly changed when she noticed his bandaged hand.

"It's nothing, lass." He tried to brush it off.

"Tell me," she said firmly.

Alex didn't want to talk about his hand, but he supposed it was a good thing that she cared to know at all. She said she didn't want his kiss, but she'd kissed him back too, at least for a moment. He'd felt it. He desperately wanted her forgiveness. He never wanted anything so badly, but at the moment, the lass was fixated on his bandaged hand.

A car drove past them, reminding Alex that they stood on the side of a dark mountain road. "Come, let's sit in my truck and talk." There was trepidation in her beautiful brown eyes, and it looked like she might argue, but much to his relief, she nodded.

He opened the front door, offering her his good hand to help her in, and he felt stupidly pleased when she let him help her up. He'd take the small win. Striding around to the driver's side, he got in beside her. She sat with her hands folded tightly in her lap. Her big eyes looked at him expectantly. God, it was so good to see her but it tore at him—the apprehension that emanated from her. There were dark shadows under her eyes, and her pretty face had subtle puffiness to it. He knew all too well the telltale signs of too many shed tears, and his gut twisted. How could he have hurt her?

"Are you okay?" she asked, nodding toward his bandaged hand, breaking his thoughts.

"Aye. 'Tis fine," he said, lifting it and feeling a slight throb.

"Well?" she probed.

Alex sighed, knowing she wanted details. He wanted to talk about the two of them and not his stupid injury that should have never happened.

"If you're not going to talk to me, then I'm just going to go," she said wearily, reaching for the door handle.

"Stay." His voice was hoarse. She looked back at him and whatever she saw in his eyes convinced her because she nodded and settled again in the passenger seat.

"I got a call today. A drug bust that went awry."

Quinn's eyes widened. "In Calen?"

"No, in Cache." Cache was a city just shy of an hour west of Calen.

"How come they called you all the way out there?"

"I have tactical training, and they needed backup," he answered nonchalantly. "It was a shite show when I got there."

Quinn shook her head as if trying to comprehend what Alex was saying. "I know you're a cop, but I still find this weirdly disconcerting," she muttered.

"Aye, well, I dinnae often get called out of Calen." He looked out the front windshield into the darkness. "To be honest, it felt good to do the work I've been trained fer. Like moving a muscle that hasnae been used in a while. Bear loved it too."

"Oh my God, where is Bear?" she asked, suddenly concerned.

"Ach, not to worry, lass. I dropped him back at the cottage with Lachlan. Bear was snoring in front of the fireplace when I left him."

A small smile tugged her lip and she nodded, in obvious relief. Alex liked that she'd grown fond of his pup. Hopefully, she was fond of the owner too.

"I'm almost afraid to ask, but tell me about this "shite show."

Alex's lips twitched in a half grin. "We got inside this old warehouse, and two bams came at me with knives." He opened and closed his fingers on his injured hand as he spoke.

"What?" Quinn gasped.

"Bams—Two guys," Alex corrected, looking up into her concerned big brown eyes.

"Not that part," Quinn snapped, exasperated. "They came at you with knives?" She couldn't keep the dismay from her voice.

"It's okay, lass. I wasnae in danger," he reassured her, feeling a puff of hope form in his chest at her concern.

She looked at him like he'd grown two heads. "What the heck does a dangerous day look like to you?" she bit out, aghast.

"Perhaps there was a wee bit of danger," Alex conceded with his lips tugged into a smirk. "Anyway, while I fought off the one bam, the other one managed to slice my hand." He held up his bandaged hand, still unimpressed that the guy had managed to cut him.

"Oh my God, Alex." Quinn looked at him with so much concern in her eyes that it nearly choked him up. But it also fortified his hope. She cared.

"'Tis fine. Only a nick." He cleared his throat trying to keep emotion from creeping in.

She gave him a sideways look. "I don't think they wrap up nicks like that," she said, nodding towards the hand that was bandaged like an oversized mitt with an opening on the end for his fingertips.

"Aye. Well, at the time, I barely noticed I'd even been cut."

She shook her head and looked like she was trying to imagine the scenario. "What happened when you did notice?"

"I got pissed off, took their knives away, and zip-tied them. Then went to help with the rest."

She bit her full lip worriedly, and it did that thing to him that it always did. God help him.

"The rest? How many guys were there?"

"Twenty-four, but it was me and the rest of the SWAT team taking them down. We had the place secured within seven minutes," he stated as if it were the time it took to cook a pizza and not take down thirty-one men with weapons.

"Holy shit!" Quinn stared at him wide eyed.

Alex chuckled at her reaction. "Aye, not a bad time. Fortunately, no one was seriously injured, and we got all the bastards. That's all that matters."

"Wow," Quinn said with a stunned expression, but those sexy brown eyes gave her away. Not that she was going to say it, but Alex could see she was impressed too, and that pleased him immensely.

"Bear was the hero of the day. He took down a few guys. He was made for this stuff, I swear. I'm going to have to pick him up a steak." Alex said fondly.

Everything Alex was telling her sounded more like a gangster movie than real life. She supposed she'd thought of Alex as a sort of peacekeeper/ticket-giver. She knew he'd been involved with more dangerous work back in Scotland, but she didn't realize that he was doing that kind of work here in Canada too.

She was quiet for a moment as she tried to process everything he'd told her. It was crazy to think that while she sat having a lovely visit with his brother, Alex was taking down bad guys like some kind of superhero. The thought made her shiver and more with arousal than anything else. Crap. She should keep her attraction to him in check. This was the same guy who'd broken her heart a mere two days ago.

"Your workday sounds completely intense and honestly insane." She eyed him dubiously, "And I have a feeling you like it that way."

Alex's lips lifted in the corners and his stormy blue eyes lit with a twinkle. "'Tis not my usual, but I confess, I do enjoy the rush of it all. 'Tis very satisfying arresting bloody bams who've grown so arrogant they think they're untouchable. That moment when they realize the game is up." He looked at her from under his dark brow, and a little shiver rippled up Quinn's spine. Try as she might. She couldn't help it. Her nether regions were hanging on his every word. Lethal Alex was hard to resist.

She shook her head, not wanting her thoughts to go there. "Is your hand going to be okay?" she asked, returning to a safer subject.

"Aye. I had to have thirty or so stitches on the back of my hand, but I'm lucky it didn't sever any nerves. It should be as good as new in a couple of weeks. On the bright side, I get paid sick leave from work."

"Ah, yes, a thirty stitch little nick," she said, her voice honey-sweet with sarcasm.

His mouth lifted in a smirk. "Something like that."

"Right," she muttered. "Does it hurt?" She reached for his injured hand to hold it in both of hers while she tenderly touched his fingers that were free of the bandage wrap. It bothered her that he'd been injured, and she just needed to feel him to make sure he was truly okay.

"It's a bit sore, but no' so bad." His voice grew gruff.

"Look at me, lass," he said gently. When she raised her big brown eyes to meet his, Alex felt the breath rush out of him. Christ, his feelings for her were overwhelming, but he refused to hide again like a coward. "Quinn, I'm so, so sorry, lass. I was a complete arse."

Quinn didn't say a word. Instead, she eyed him patiently waiting for him to elaborate. He knew he had to explain himself, but it was hard to find the words.

"Making love to ye, lass... God, I've never known anything like it." He looked up at her, needing to know she understood.

"Neither have I," she admitted quietly, toying with her hands in her lap.

Alex smiled lightly. He was glad she'd felt it too. "Honestly, Quinn, it scared me. I didn't know what to think. I hadn't expected it. I hadn't expected ye."

Her big brown eyes studied him intently. "What happened between us, God." He breathed, raking a hand through his hair. "I didnae ken it could be that way. It was like a rush of freedom and bliss I dinnae think I've ever felt before. It was exhilarating, but at the same time," Alex sobered, "at the same time, I felt terrified," he admitted.

"Of what?" she asked, her eyes curious but soft. He could happily die drowning in the depths of those eyes. He wanted to lean in and kiss her, show her the need that burned within him. But he knew he owed her more.

"I think I was scared of letting ye in and letting go of the life I'd made." He looked out to the dark mountain road through the windshield as he tried to put words to what he'd felt. "I dinnae ken. Since coming to Canada, I've lived a life of discipline and structure. I've made myself and my life impenetrable, but then ye came along. It's like ye cracked into my carefully crafted world, the moment I laid eyes on ye."

"I did?" she said with a small voice that made him want to pull her into his arms.

"Aye. Ye penetrated my impenetrable walls and opened up a part of me I didn't even ken existed." He shook his head. "I dinnae ken why it scared me, but it did. After I made love to ye," his voice grew husky, "it's like it came to a head. I didnae ken what was happening only that everything felt different and it's like I wanted to hide away like a coward."

Alex stared out the window regretting how clueless he'd been.

"You penetrated my world too." Her shaky voice cut through his thoughts. Alex's eyes landed on hers.

"And can I just say how ironic it is that the man who runs head first into danger would call himself a coward?"

He smirked, loving that she was teasing him despite everything.

"Thank you for opening up to me." Quinn said softly. "I didn't understand what had happened between us. It had all felt so good and then it came to a crashing halt. It was so confusing."

"God, lass I'm sorry. I ken I should huv talked to ye, but at the time, I felt almost paralyzed. I thought if ye were gone, I could somehow right myself." He shook his head still not understanding it himself.

"And did you? Right yourself?" Quinn asked soberingly.

"Naw, I didnae, not in the way I thought I would. For years, I huv kept a wall up and made sure not to let any lass in. I didnae want to put my faith in any woman again. Even my coworkers joked that I was immune to women. It had begun to feel true. I wasnae affected by lasses. I had no interest. Until ye came along." He eyed her, but she just listened without saying a word. It unnerved him since Quinn was usually so talkative, but he carried on, needing to get it all off his chest. "Ye were right Quinn, about Kate. I always thought she was my past, but the truth was, she was still affecting my life." He shook his head, realizing the absurdity of it as he spoke the words out loud.

"The past is the past, and I've come to peace with mine. But I suppose what she put me through had a lasting effect. I didnae want to be played the fool ever again. I didnae want my life to be in another's hands. Even though logically I knew no one would ever do to me what she did, I still viewed having a woman in my life as a complication. I refused to let anyone in. I didnae want to feel things again for a woman or to huv any involvement for that matter. My life felt good the way it was. It felt safe, and I was in control of it."

"And now?" he could hear the uncertainty in her soft voice.

"Now? Now, the only thing I fear is losing ye," he said matter-of-factly.

Quinn's eyes widened as she sucked in a breath.

"With ye, Quinn, it is not about feeling things *again*. It's more like I didnae ken these feelings could exist at all. It's like I've broken free from a prison I'd made for myself. And it's all because of ye."

Her eyes were misty with unshed tears. Alex didn't want to make her cry, but he did want to get it all out. He owed her that. "The time we spent together was," he stopped to think how to put it into words, "extraordinary. Otherworldly. I dinnae ken the last time I felt so happy and more myself. Ye reminded me who I am, Quinn West." Now she looked as though she was actively trying to hold back the tears, but Alex wasn't finished yet.

"I acted cowardly on Christmas Day." His voice was gruff. "And from the bottom of my heart, I am sorry fer it."

"It wasn't cowardly, Alex." She took in a shaky breath. "It hurt and in the moment I was angry and confused, but at the same time, I understood. I knew why you put the walls up." She put her hand in his and for the first time, he felt the hint of relief trickle over him.

"It's not okay, though. The truth is I didnae want to put up walls with ye. Not ever. What I love most about ye is that I can be myself." He squeezed her small hand in his.

40
Truth and Taunting

Quinn sucked in a breath. He said "love." She shouldn't get ahead of herself, but there was that word. Did he love her? His hand squeezed hers.

"Could ye forgive me fer the way I behaved?"

"Forgiven." The word slipped out and she meant it whole heartedly.

Quinn never expected Alex to open up to her this way and she still wasn't sure what it meant for the two of them, but it felt pretty damn good that the walls were down—and by the sounds of it not just down, but gone. At least with her. The fact that he could speak with her what was on his mind so openly and honestly was a testament to that.

Alex let out a breath as if he'd been holding it. "Ach, thank God, I'm truly sorry, Quinn. I will never shut ye out again. Ye have my word lass." His eyes were intense on hers as he squeezed her hand in his.

Quinn's heart was bursting. His words meant the world to her. She believed him. Somewhere deep inside, she knew she could trust what he was saying. God, all she wanted to do was sit in his arms and kiss his handsome face, but his police truck made that a bit awkward. The console was a plethora of electronics.

Alex seemed to sense the direction of her thoughts, and right on cue, someone came over his radio. "Mackenzie, are you headed back to the station?"

Alex pressed a button and answered. "Aye, I'll be there at 1900 hours."

"Ten-four."

He leaned back in his seat and looked at her. "I huv to get the truck back to the station. Will ye come back and stay at my place tonight?" There was a sweet hopeful look in his stormy blue eyes.

She nodded a smile touching her lips.

"Ah shite," he groaned, throwing his head back in his seat.

"What?"

"Lachlan, my brother." He looked at her subdued. "He's at my place."

"Oh right, I met him. We actually had a really great afternoon together."

Alex looked at her from under a raised brow. "Really?"

"Yeah, it was nice. We had such a good chat. He seems like such a genuine guy."

"He's great, but he's married. And I'll kill him if he so much as looked at ye wrong," Alex blurted.

Quinn threw back her head and laughed. She kinda liked possessive, jealous Alex even if it was at his brother's peril.

"Dinnae think I joke, little lass."

Quinn settled in a smile, knowing full well, that Alex would never do anything to harm Lachlan, but loving all the same that he was protective over her.

"I'm well aware he's a married man, to Violet. The blond-haired woman from the photo in your sporran." Quinn regarded him, silently daring him to deny it.

"Ah, shite. Right, the picture." He winced as he leaned back in his seat.

"Yes. The picture," she chirped her eyes boring into him.

He looked incredibly uncomfortable, and Quinn felt vindicated. *Good, let him wallow in guilt*. He'd intentionally let her believe that it was him in that picture, and she waited to hear how he would explain himself.

"Ach, lass, when ye assumed the photo was of me and my family, my wife, and babies or whatever ye thought—" Alex stopped mid-sentence looking contrite. With a heavy sigh, he dared to look into Quinn's expectant eyes. "I'm sorry, lass. It feels so daft now that I wasn't just straight with ye. I should huv been honest."

"Yes, you should have," she said emphatically, but then she almost laughed seeing big strong sexy Alex looking like a guilty puppy. She bit her lip as she observed him and realized she didn't enjoy watching his guilt. "I understand why you didn't tell me the truth."

"Ye do?" he arched a disbelieving brow.

"I think you knew I wouldn't get involved with a married man. I practically handed you a brick to build your wall. An easy way to keep me out." She eyed him to see if she was on the right track.

"Aye, I suppose. It did feel like a little extra fortification, but it was silly really as I'd already said I wasnae married," Alex countered.

"True," she agreed. "But you still left me feeling apprehensive. It's the only picture I'd seen in your cabin, and it was hidden away. A mystery. And my God, from what I could see, it was you with your loving wife and children. I believed you when you told me you weren't married, but then I assumed you had to be divorced. I couldn't understand how you could have just abandoned your children."

"I'd never ever do that," Alex interjected.

"I know," Quinn said. "I was baffled, and you were so tight-lipped about it. I wondered if they'd all died!" she blurted.

"Christ!" Alex's lips tugged like he was about to laugh, and Quinn saw the mirth in his eyes.

"Don't you dare laugh." She shot him a glare.

"I'm sorry, lass."

She could see the great effort it took him not to laugh, and she couldn't help but find him all the more appealing. Curse him.

"Ach, Quinn, I confess, I suppose I knew ye were thinking that it was me in the photo with Violet and the boys, but I didnae consider that you'd try to rationalize their whereabouts. I didnae think much about it at all except that suppose I thought it would be easier if you assumed I had too many skeletons in my closet." He looked repentant.

"I knew there were skeletons, but I have skeletons in my closet too. Everyone does."

Alex nodded resting his good hand over the steering wheel.

"When you opened up about Kate, I would have thought you'd come clean about the picture too."

"Aye, I suppose it would have made sense. That night I told you about Kate, it changed things for me. I hadn't ever spoken about everything that had happened to anyone. People knew, of course, but I never talked about it."

Quinn's heart squeezed. How had he carried that all these years without talking about it? "I'm glad you were able to talk about it with me," she said, gently putting her hand on his arm.

He looked down at her hand stroking his arm and then his eyes drew back up to hers with that stormy blue that seemed to set her soul on fire.

"I never want to keep anything from ye, lass. Talking to ye freed me somehow. I'm sorry fer the picture and fer being such a coward. Truly I am. Can we start over? No more walls. No more secrets or half-truths."

The moment he'd implored her with those eyes, she was lost. She nodded, feeling the soft sting of unshed tears.

"Ach, Quinn, I have never liked dishonesty. I believe in being truthful contrary to what I may have shown you. I want there to be truth between us. Always."

"I want that too." She smiled as a tear escaped and slid down her cheek.

Alex reached up and gently wiped it away, but the moment his finger touched her bare cheek, she felt a sizzle jump through her. The air between them changed. Invisible electricity snapped heightening their awareness. Quinn shifted in the leather seat of his truck not missing the hunger in his gaze as it dropped to her lips, but as quick as she saw it, he seemed to blink it away.

"I'm going to huv to get the truck back to the station soon," he said reluctantly, and Quinn understood the silent message. If he kissed her, she'd be in his lap quicker than a kid ripping open presents Christmas morning.

"So back to yer date with my brother today?" Alex eyed her from under a dark menacing brow.

Quinn giggled, seeming to find pleasure in his jealousy. "I admit, I did enjoy his company," she said to toy with him.

"Not too much, I hope." In truth, Alex was so pleased to know that Lachlan and Quinn had hit it off. It struck Alex that he wanted Quinn to meet the rest of his family too. He cared deeply for his family, and now, he realized he also cared deeply for the woman sitting beside him.

"He's certainly not as handsome as you," she teased.

"We're identical twins, lass," Alex deadpanned.

She laughed. "Maybe so, but there are differences." She threw him a flirtatious look that stoked his fires.

"Do tell," he murmured intrigued.

"First off, your smile is similar but different. His is crooked and almost boyish, but yours? Yours is rugged and very manly," she said as her eyes dropped to his lips.

"Aye?" He could barely think straight.

"Mm-hmm, and your lips…" Her voice trailed off breathlessly.

"My lips?"

She bit her own lip, and he felt his cock thicken in his uniform. "It's just that they are so kissable." Her voice was breathy, and Alex struggled to contain himself.

"And your eyes..." She leaned in closer to him, over the console of electronics.

"My eyes?" he repeated, barely able to breathe as he leaned in closer to her.

The way she looked at him said it all. Like she was hungry and he was a buffet she wanted to devour. Alex was hanging on by a thread.

She reached up and slowly ran a finger over his stubbled jaw. "Don't get me wrong, your brother is a handsome man, but you, Sergeant Mackenzie." She bit her lip again, inching her face closer to his. So close, he could feel her gentle breath against his mouth. "You are so hot," she said in a breathy whimper like his hotness was scorching her.

"Christ, lass." Alex was entranced. He wanted desperately to kiss that tempting mouth, but he was too damn aware that they were in his police truck.

"When I first saw you step out of this truck, you were so tall and broad and dangerous looking dressed in your uniform."

"Dangerous?" Alex asked fascinated.

"Mm-hmm… I confess, you scared me a little, but it turned me on." She bit her lip shyly.

Alex had to adjust his now very hard cock in his uniform. Jesus. He loved this confessional. "The day I gave you the ticket?" She had the hots for him then?

"Mm-hmm, I think even then I wouldn't have minded if you handcuffed me, bent me over the hood of my car, kicked my legs aside, and did as you pleased," she drawled, eyeing him and seductively licking her lips.

"Christ," he breathed. Alex could hardly believe what he was hearing. He had no idea his little lass had such a dirty mind, and God help him, he fucking loved it. It scorched his soul. Blood was pounding through him now as he looked at her stunned by her admission.

"I know it's wrong, but I was also turned on that first night in your bed when you thought I was an intruder." She looked up at him with big innocent eyes that were in complete contradiction to what she was saying to him. "You were so strong and lethal." Her voice dripped with desire, and Alex was on the edge riveted.

"Ye liked that?" he asked in equal parts astonishment and intrigue.

She nodded coyly.

Alex groaned, his cock almost splitting his pants now.

Her teasing lush lipped grin was almost his undoing. "My point is, your brother is a good-looking guy and super nice, but you?" She shivered. "Mmm."

He was a hair's breadth away from hauling her onto his lap and devouring those full taunting lips when his radio came on again. "Mackenzie, park out front instead of your stall. They want to take the truck in for detailing."

Alex was snapped painfully back to reality. "Copy that," he responded soberingly.

He blew out a breath, trying to calm the blood that was pounding through his veins. As much as he wanted Quinn now, he knew the second he kissed her, he'd need his cock in her, and that certainly wasn't gonna happen on the side of the road in his police truck.

"I'd better get the truck back," he said reluctantly.

She nodded, sitting back in her seat. She tucked a strand of hair behind her ear. It should have been benign, but after everything she'd just said to him, every fucking thing about her, every fucking move she made, had him on fire.

"To be clear, I want to pick up this conversation where we left off." He shot her a look from under his arched dark brow.

With a demure little smile, she opened the door and hopped out of the truck. Alex got out and walked alongside her to her car. The cool night air doing little to calm his desire for her.

"Ye'll head back to my place?" he asked, hating to leave her even for a short time. Even though they'd talked about things and Quinn had said she'd forgiven him and that she understood, he somehow felt like he just needed to keep her close. It was irrational, but he didn't want her to change her mind.

She nodded. "I'm going to zip back to the inn to grab a few things first, but I'll be back at your place within an hour or so."

"Okay sounds good, lass. I'll see you soon."

He wanted to kiss her, but he knew that when he kissed those lips again, he'd not be stopping. Instead, he brought her hand to his lips and kissed it before opening her door for her.

41
What Happens at the Inn, Stays...

Quinn walked into her room at the inn with a smile glued on her face. She already couldn't wait to see Alex again. Their conversation had made her so happy. She felt assured that they really had something, and finally, Alex was embracing it instead of denying it. For now, that was enough. Quinn felt crazy about him. She knew in her heart she was in love with him, but she wasn't going to rush it. Quinn didn't know if Alex was in love with her too, but she did know that he had strong feelings for her. For now, she'd take it for what it was.

Pulling out her bag, she grabbed a few things for overnight. Pulling out her cream flannel pyjamas with the little blue reindeer, she paused and bit her lip, wondering if she should pack them. It was not like she had anything sexy to wear aside from maybe a lacy bra and underwear. Not to mention, Lachlan was at Alex's, so it's not like they'd be having steamy sex anyway. Heck, she didn't even know if she'd be sleeping in Alex's bed for that matter. Practicality won out, and she grabbed her cozy pj's and stuffed them in her bag. Screw it, Alex's place was freezing at night. She'd be glad for her flannels.

After packing a few things, she decided to take a shower and freshen up before heading back to Alex's cabin. After showering, she stood in front of the bathroom mirror, thinking about what she would wear to head over to Alex's as she put on a light bit of makeup. Would she get any alone time with him tonight? She hoped so, but she wouldn't count on it. Not that she minded really. She'd quite enjoyed chatting with Lachlan, and she'd love to see their brotherly dynamic. It still seemed wild to her that Alex had a twin.

She likely wouldn't have much alone time with Alex tonight, but eventually, she would, and the thought alone set off butterflies low in her belly. She couldn't wait for that. It was all she could do not to kiss his face off before she left in her car.

Walking out of the bathroom and to the closet, a knock on the door made her jump. Quickly throwing on an oversized white terry towel bathrobe courtesy of the inn, she peered through the peephole, and her breath caught at the sight of Alex standing with his arms crossed in his black police uniform. Her heart jumped in her chest. She quickly opened the door, wondering what had happened that he was here now. With everything so fresh between them, she couldn't help the trepidation that crept through her.

"Hello, Ms. West." He threw her a wolfish grin that sent a quiver straight down to her girl bits. Stepping into her room, he closed the door behind him, sliding the chain with his black leather-gloved hand. *Holy shit*. Quinn's heart thudded as he looked over his shoulder, his piercing stormy blue eyes landing on her.

He turned and crooked a finger for her to come to him, and she obeyed stepping forward and looking at him wide-eyed. "Good, little lass," he whispered before his arms wrapped around her. His leather-clad hand gripped her ass as he deftly snatched her up and pulled her against him. She let out a little squeal of surprise, and he grinned, bringing his mouth down hard on hers.

Quinn felt shocked and aroused in almost equal measure. She greedily wrapped her legs around his waist, her robe falling open as he kissed her with a ferocious intensity that sucked her breath away. The feel of his tongue colliding with hers made her whimper. He was kissing her thoroughly, and she pressed her body tighter against his not able to get enough of him. When he seemed to adjust her in his arms, she instantly remembered about his bandaged hand.

She pulled back from him breathlessly. "Alex, what about your hand?"

"I dinnae need my hand for what I've in mind lass," he said as his mouth devoured her once again. Carrying her to the couch, he sat her down on it as he dropped to his knees in front of her. Quinn couldn't imagine a more enticing picture. Big strong Sergeant Mackenzie knelt before her in his full police uniform, even his coat and cap. Something about it felt so wickedly naughty. She let her robe drop off her shoulders, and she reached up to cradle his stubbled face in her hands.

Alex slowly ran his black leather-clad hand up her smooth leg, his eyes following the trail of his fingers. Then his eyes, dripping with desire, landed on hers.

"Are ye wet fer me, lass?" His hand stroked her inner thigh achingly close to her core.

She bit her lip and nodded.

"Good little lass, now lay back and let me taste ye." His brogue was thick and heavy.

She nudged back on the couch and let her knees fall open, and Alex leaned into her. His stubble grazed her inner thigh, and then his wet tongue ran slowly along the length of her seam from bottom to top and back down again.

"Christ, ye taste good," he ground out. Then he took off his cap, laying it on the couch beside her before dipping his head again and pushing his tongue past her folds to lick deeper.

Quinn whimpered as she let her bare feet rest against his broad uniform-clad shoulders, and he tasted and pleasured her like his tongue had stumbled upon a hot caramel fountain. Quinn opened her eyes, barely able to take the exquisite scrapes of his stubbled chin and the point of his nose touching her as he fully consumed her with his masterful tongue.

His eyes collided with hers, seizing hold of them and making it impossible to look away. He watched her as he pleasured her, and she watched him back, mesmerized as his tongue slid and tasted her. His mouth was soaked with her desire. He devoured her until she was arching hard against him.

"Come on my tongue Quinn," he commanded flicking it over her nub before sliding it down and into her, tongue fucking her. With a cry, her body shattered and fell into wave after pounding wave of bliss.

Quinn's legs slid off Alex as she lay there with her core throbbing. All she could think about was having him inside her. Filling her up. Her eyes opened as he stood up, and she watched as he took his gun out of its holster and set it carefully on the dresser. Then he removed his belt and holster. He took off his black leather glove and winter bomber coat tossing them on the armchair in the corner.

Jeepers. The sight of his black short-sleeved shirt tight around his strong biceps had Quinn tingling hungrily all over again. She watched as he began to unbutton his shirt, but he winced. His hand, she realized. Not missing a beat, she quickly got up and stood before him taking over the unbuttoning. There was just the sound of their breathing, and she could feel his eyes watching her as she worked. She slid his shirt off his muscular shoulders, pulling it off. She couldn't resist running her hands over the smooth muscles of his chest and his rippled abs. The man was built like a Greek god.

"Will ye help me with my pants too?" His voice was strained with pent-up desire.

She bit her lip and gave him a sultry look before her eyes took in the sight of the thick rod pressed against his pants. Quinn swallowed. Alex was a big man, everywhere. Reaching down, she carefully undid his button and slowly rolled down the zipper over his massive erection. Even her nipples were tingling, wanting all that thickness in her.

Grabbing the black fabric from the sides, she tugged down and his pants loosened. She squatted low, pulling them past his knees as his hand ran through her hair. She helped him step out of the pants, and then he was left standing before her in black boxer briefs. From her squatted position before him, she reached up to remove that final barrier, but his hand gripped her hair at the base of her neck, tugging and forcing her to look up at him.

"I need five minutes to shower," he growled, and she knew he was as hot as she was with need.

"No," she moaned hungrily her hands gliding up his body as she stood.

"I'm all grubby from the day, lass. I'll be quick."

"Sergeant Mackenzie." Her voice dripped with seduction as she looked up at him. Her face reached only as high as his chiselled chest. Leaning her face into him, her nose touched against his chest, and she breathed deeply taking in his essence. It was intoxicating, a combination of mountain air, a hint of cologne, and the sweat of a hard and dangerous day's work. Looking up at him coyly for a brief moment, she dipped her head letting her tongue glide up the quivering ridges of his strong abs. His saltiness on her tongue made her wet all over again.

"I want you just the way you are."

42

Fireworks First, Then New Year's Eve

Alex could hardly breathe, but his heart was pounding hard and his cock throbbed painfully.

"I want to feel you in me right now," she whispered, looking up at him with her big brown eyes imploring him with their innocence in complete contradiction to what she was saying and doing to him.

Alex didn't need convincing. He couldn't take his eyes off hers. Decision made, he lifted her curvy body up and against him on fire with the feel of her skin against his. She moaned as her legs tightened around him, and he felt pre-come seep out of him. He needed in her now. Backing her against the wall, he held her steady as he guided his thick hungry cock into her, and then he thrust. She cried out her pleasure, spurring Alex on. He held her up as he slammed into her over and over with a desperate need, and God, every single thrust sent him hurdling towards heaven.

Jesus, she was a complete fucking fantasy. Alex didn't think he'd ever felt so out of control with desire. Once again, making love to Quinn was bloody mind-blowing. Kissing her lush mouth and not letting their bodies come apart, he carried her to the bed. He lay her on it and continued sliding in and out of her hot wet sheath.

Quinn groaned beneath him. "Don't stop".

Looking into her ecstasy-filled face, it took everything in him not to come.

"Ye are so beautiful," he breathed raggedly, and Quinn opened her hazy eyes right as she bucked beneath him. Feeling her release, Alex pumped one final thrust, and his own exploded out of him. He growled as his body spurted wildly, and his mind was ejected into paradise.

"Jesus Christ," he murmured breathlessly as he rolled onto his back, spent. Quinn lay tucked beside him as the final ebbs of their orgasms faded, leaving them blissfully satiated.

As Alex finally came back down to earth, he realized Quinn was quiet beside him. Normally, she always seemed to have something to say. Was she afraid he'd put his walls up like last time? Not wanting her to worry for a second, he rolled over to face her, and seeing the hint of weariness in her eyes, he reached his hand up and touched her cheek. She turned to face him, and he threw her a barely contained grin.

"Ms. West," he said.

"Sergeant Mackenzie." She responded in kind.

"Have I mentioned how in love I am with ye?"

She sat up suddenly, looking down at him searching his face. "You're in love with me?" He could hear the uncertainty in her voice.

He reached up and stroked her cheek, feeling like he might burst from this love business. "Aye, I am. Well and truly."

Her face lit up as she stared down at him, and Alex was sure he'd never seen anything more perfect in his life.

"I dinnae ken if I ever believed in love. At least, I didnae think it was for me. But then ye came along and fuckin burst my heart open."

Quinn giggled. "You fuckin burst my heart open too."

Alex laughed, and he pulled her on top of him so she straddled him. She leaned down over him, and he put a hand on the back of her head bringing her lips to his. Then she pulled back again eyeing him. "I love you, too, Sergeant Mackenzie."

He grinned. "I love you, Ms. West. Although I think I'd like to make ye a Mrs. Mackenzie."

She laughed as a tear slid down her cheek. "I think I'd be good with that," she whispered.

Alex sat up beneath her. "Would ye actually marry me, lass?" he asked between kisses.

"Mm-hmm," she agreed as she got lost in his mouth on hers.

"How about a wedding in Scotland?" he asked continuing to kiss her.

"Yes." She smiled against his lips.

"A New Year's Eve wedding?" His tongue slid against hers.

She pulled back to look at him. "As in four days from now?"

"Aye." He grinned, leaning back in to kiss her stunned lips.

"Alex, are you serious?" she asked against his mouth.

"Mm-hmm." He was utterly consumed with tasting her.

"Okay," she agreed, opening her mouth to his as he lifted her body and slid her onto his ready cock.

"Good, little lass."

Epilogue
Scotland and Home

Quinn wasn't convinced Alex was serious about marrying her. Never mind the New Year's Eve nuptials until they were on the plane headed for his home. Lachlan flew back with them and drove them to his and Violet's home when they arrived at Glasgow airport. Quinn was stunned to discover that their home was a small castle near the sea. The perfect spot for a wedding.

Quinn was exhausted from the travel and the time change but wired at the same time. She couldn't stop gushing over the quaint stone homes, the stores in the village, the countryside, and the highland cows. And the Lochs. Scotland was capturing her heart almost as much as the man beside her.

On their second evening in Scotland, Quinn had gone up to bed, and Alex had promised to join her soon. "No rush," she said seeing how happy he was to be in the company of both of his brothers. It was the first time the three had been together in over two years. The whisky and laughter between the men were in abundance.

After washing up, Quinn lay in the comfy queen-size bed in Lachlan and Violet's guest room, and she got Belle on a video call on her phone.

"Quinn!" she exclaimed when she answered.

"Hey Belle, give me a sec, I'm going to add Megs too."

"Hey girls," Megs said. "Is everything okay? I snuck into the washroom at work, so I can't talk for long."

"Well, I wanted to see what you ladies are doing next week?" Quinn began.

"Where are you?" Belle squinted looking closer at her phone. "And why are you in bed at four in the afternoon?" she added suspiciously.

"I'm in Scotland, and I was kinda hoping you both might be able to join me." Quinn smiled into the phone as if she'd just invited them to come around for cocktails versus inviting them to travel halfway around the world to see her.

"Scotland!" the two girls exclaimed at the same time. And at the very same moment, Alex strode into the bedroom, rosy-cheeked and a little inebriated.

"Christ, lass, I already missed ye," he said rather clumsily climbing right on top of Quinn nearly knocking her phone on the floor as he covered his mouth hungrily over hers in a tipsy, but definitely not ineffective, kiss.

"What? What the heck is happening?"

"Who is that?

"What's going on?

"Quinn? Quinn!"

Her friends' questions sputtered in rapid-fire succession, and she giggled against Alex's mouth. He seemed to latently realize that there were other voices in the room, and he lifted his lips from Quinn's and turned a confused look to the phone she held beside them in her hand. Quinn wished she could have snapped a screenshot of her two best friends' jaws dropping to the floor and her sexy fiancé looking the most adorable version of confused as he paused on his hands and knees over her, whilst looking awkwardly at them.

"Ach, Hiya, lassies. Sorry 'bout tha'. I dinnae mean to interrupt yer bletherin'. Hope ye can make it to the wedding. I'll leave ye lassies to it then." He grinned into the phone and then turned and planted another quick kiss on Quinn's lips before hoisting himself off the bed and sauntering into the ensuite, tearing off his t-shirt as he went. It was impossible for Quinn not to watch him. God, she adored the sexy man.

Quinn finally looked back to her phone, and it was as if her friends were frozen on the screen.

"What in the hell was that?" Megs finally was able to speak.

"It was Hot Cop!" Belle bit out excitedly, her face still pressed up closely to her phone.

"Oh, my fucking God, Quinn! Are you getting married to Hot Cop?" Megs' face was now also right up against her phone.

"In Scotland?" Belle added in a shrill squeak.

Quinn grinned from ear to ear, leaned in close to her phone too, and nodded. "I am."

Alex watched the woman he loved and happiness penetrated his every cell. Her reaction to his homeland and his family made him feel things he'd never felt before. He was proud to show her around and have her on his arm, and her reactions to every little detail filled him with pride. Despite witnessing his brother's love with his wife, Alex had written off the existence of true love. But Quinn changed everything for him. She opened his eyes and heart. Quinn West—Quinn Mackenzie, made him a better man. He was whole with her by his side.

Alex hadn't been too concerned with the actual wedding. He just wanted the lass to be his wife. He had the feeling Quinn was of the same mind, but the women in his family took great pleasure in the preparations. The best part of that for Alex, was watching his bride-to-be, fitting in with his family, as one of them now. Quinn had come home from a full day of wedding gown shopping with them and as she cuddled into Alex that night, she told him, how she felt for the first time in her life, like she had a family, a real family. Alex wasn't one to get misty-eyed, but his little lass had him wiping a tear or two.

The wedding itself was a few days after New Year's Eve because his sister and sister-in-law, Orlagh and Violet, insisted that they required at least a few days to get it planned. Quinn had hoped that her friends would be able to make it, but unfortunately, with such short notice, the best they could manage was a virtual attendance. Knowing how much the girls meant to Quinn, Alex was already planning for her friends to come to Calen as a surprise for Quinn's thirtieth birthday in a few weeks.

They stayed in Scotland for another week and went on day trips to see various sights, including Cailleach, the Mackenzie clan distillery. Alex hadn't realized that he hadn't told Quinn about it. She muttered something about how it made sense now, the Mackenzie boys' obsession with Scotch.

They finally headed back to Canada and said their goodbyes. It was tough, but they all agreed they'd gather again soon in one country or another.

Alex loved seeing his family and home again, and it was all the better because of the woman by his side. It was like Quinn brought him out of his not-so-peaceful slumber. She made him feel alive, excited for the future, and helped him let go of his past. Alex felt truly happy. And he knew his wife was happy too, eager to get back to "their" cabin and write her novel.

They cuddled up in Alex's bed back in their cabin. It felt more like home than it ever had. Bear lay on the floor beside the bed, content. He pulled his wife in closer, revelling in the feel of her naked lush behind pressed against his ever-hungry cock. He reached his hand up and gripped around her pretty little neck, lifting her jaw up and back into him.

"I hope ye dinnae intend on sleeping tonight. Mrs. Mackenzie," he whispered in her ear.

"And would you punish me if I did? Handcuff me perhaps? *Sergeant Mackenzie.*" Her sultry voice taunted him in the darkness as her hips ground back into him. Aye, it was good to be home.

Sneak Peek
Scotch Series

Scotch & Dreams: releasing in the spring of 2025

1

She had zero recollection of how she got here, how long she'd been here or even where 'here' was. Deep blue eyes were intense on hers. Concerned. Intimate. Caring. They weren't familiar eyes, but in her haze of confusion, those eyes brought her an unexpected yet solid sense of comfort.

"How are ye feelin'?" The man spoke slowly, gently. His bur was deep, rich and as warm as honey on her fractured thoughts.

"I-I don't know. My head hurts," she said in a voice that didn't feel like her own as she touched her swelling forehead. She felt strange, her thinking muddled. It was odd, she was certain she didn't know the man who was kneeling inches from her, but he felt safe somehow. Not lock-your-doors safe, but fall-into-my-arms-and-I-will-catch-you-safe.

Panic was lurking around the outer edges of her mind, ready to choke her, but his touch, his voice, and his presence were helping to pull her from its sticky grip. Strong hands gently, but firmly held her shoulders. Deep blue eyes anchored onto hers and wouldn't let her go. Later she would recall the strange intimacy of it, but at the moment everything felt off, unfamiliar, fleeting.

"What's yer name, lass?" His voice was a salve on her battered mind.

"Violet Munro." The name tumbled out without a preamble. When she tried to retrieve thoughts, they seemed to flit around like uncatchable fireflies. She was certain of her name, but how or why she was certain of it felt like a complete mystery. It was just there. Her name was clear and rose to the surface all by itself. A moment's relief seeped into her.

"Verra good," he smiled at her with the warmth of an embrace. She found him mesmerizing. This stranger. Finding an escape from her jumbled thoughts she let herself fixate on the details of his features. He was a magnet for her mind, visceral, technicolour in her haze of grey confusion.

Studying him brought a desperate focus to the heap of disarray in her brain. His white button-down shirt was crisp with navy pinstripes, and there was a sharpness to his navy blazer. The way the golden skin of his neck looked in contrast to the white of his shirt. His straight nose ended in a slight flare to his nostrils. Blue eyes so deep and rich they tugged at her very soul. And his smile with its slight crookedness, imperfectly perfect. She felt a sudden wild urge to press her lips to his, to see what it would feel like to be kissed by such a contradictory mouth.

Her senses felt heightened in some ways, so aware yet so out of sorts. Bewildered as she felt, one thing was crystal clear: this man was an angel in the ashes. The kind of man every woman's fairy tale heart yearns for. The strong hero who could love her to the furthest reaches of her soul. He was warmth, comfort and sexiness. Violet concluded as she stared into his otherworldly blue eyes, that she had to be dreaming. Her world was as solid as a puff of smoke but for this man.

"Do ye ken where ye are, Violet?" She made the mistake of breaking eye contact to view her surroundings. A beach, the sea's waves washing gently onto the white sandy shore. The air was mild. Long tufts of grass grew at the back side of the sand. She could see a pier all lit up with fairground lights in the distance and a smaller wooden pier directly in front of them. The sun was setting, casting a pinky-purple hue.

Violet looked down beside her and noticed that she was sitting on the long grass. She ran her fingers through the green-gold cool blades. Hot tears pricked her eyes. *I'm on a beach*, she thought to herself. *But I don't have the slightest idea how I got here. Oh fuck.*

The dream man gently wiped away a tear that rolled down her cheek. She leaned her face into the palm of his hand. She desperately sought the comfort he so freely gave. "I-I don't know where I am." She swallowed, trying to hold back the fear that threatened to drown her. "I don't recognize any of it." She looked into his eyes, searching for something, but she didn't know what. She was lost. "How did I get here?"

Quiet tears spilled down her face as grappled with the knowledge that she couldn't recall anything, save for her name. She shivered maybe from cold, maybe from shock, it didn't matter.

"It's going to be okay lass," he murmured as he slipped off his blazer and draped it around her shoulders. Then his strong comforting arms wrapped around her, like they belonged there. She settled against him but was still unable to quell the shivering that wracked her body.

SCOTCH & SHORTBREAD

About the author

August Lindsay grew up in the prairies of western Canada, just a few hours' drive from the Rocky Mountains, the backdrop for her debut novel Scotch & Shortbread. When she's not writing steamy slow burn romance novels, she can usually be found in nature-- hiking, horseback riding and taking the occasional cold plunge! She is equally happy to be curled up in a cozy chair, candles lit, reading or writing. Travelling is high on her list of life priorities, with Scotland being one of her favourite destinations. Her love for Scotland began in 2007 during her first road trip through the Highlands, sparking the inspiration for her Scotch Series. Above all, she treasure's time spent with her friends and family.

www.augustlindsay.com
Instagram: @august.lindsay.author
Facebook: August Lindsay

Milton Keynes UK
Ingram Content Group UK Ltd.
UKHW031444291124
451807UK00005B/366